The
Nutting
Girl

The
Nutting
Girl

∽

Fred DeVecca

coffeetownpress

Seattle, WA

coffeetownpress

Coffeetown Press
PO Box 70515
Seattle, WA 98127

For more information go to: www.coffeetownpress.com
www.freddevecca.com

Cover art by Peter Ruhf (www.peterruhfdesigns.weebly.com)
Cover design by Sabrina Sun

The Nutting Girl
Copyright © 2017 by Fred DeVecca

ISBN: 978-1-60381-575-8 (Trade Paper)
ISBN: 978-1-60381-576-5 (eBook)

Library of Congress Control Number: 2017938975

Printed in the United States of America

To Steve Adams and Christoffer Carstanjen

two Morris friends lost on 9/11/01

Acknowledgments

∾

SHELBURNE FALLS, MASSACHUSETTS, where *The Nutting Girl* is set, is a real town. Every site and business described in this book exists, or did when it was written. Thus, I must first thank everyone and everything in this vibrant and unique village.

Some Shelburne Falls area people and institutions should also be specifically thanked: Bruce Lessels from Zoar Outdoor and Police Chief Steve Walker for technical information on river rescues. Two of my early readers—Patricia Donohue, for urging me to go with this title, and Emily Arsenault, who pointed me in certain plot directions. Kate Pousant Scarborough, whose late-night metaphysical walks and talks with me shaped many conversations that appear here. Ginny Ray for giving me the opportunity to write about and get to know the inner workings of this town and the characters who make it what it is. All the sitters, servers and staff at the Vipassana Meditation Center. The Marlboro Morris Men. Mocha Maya's, where most of this book was written. Peter Ruhf for his spectacular cover art. And two women who came into my life just as I began writing *The Nutting Girl*—Susan

Gesmer, for having such a deep appreciation for universal love and beauty, and Tiffany Pentz for patiently listening to my daily reports on this book's slow progress, and for influencing it in ways that she will never know (mainly because I will never tell her).

Thanks also to Ian Robb for his scholarly opinions on the origins of the songs sung in this novel, and to the nuns of the Poor Clare Monastery in New Orleans for insight into the daily life of a Franciscan monastery and convent.

And lastly, special thanks go out to the three women who shepherded this book to completion—Catherine Treadgold and Jennifer McCord from Coffeetown Press, and my literary agent Janice Pieroni.

Contents

Part One

to be consoled as to console,
to be understood as to understand,
to be loved as to love

Chapter One

∼ᴗ∽

Just Like Chicken

I WAS WAITING. I'm good at that. Detectives spend a lot of time waiting.

And watching. I'm good at that too.

There were two hundred fifty of us crammed into barely heated cabins for the weekend, but it was still morning and the others were sleeping, or doing whatever one does at an event like this.

Me, I was waiting. Alone. In the pavilion where the "Men's Sharing Circle" would occur in half an hour. I was early, as usual.

I was not thrilled about being part of the Men's Sharing Circle, whatever the hell it would prove to be, but it was Michael's wedding and he seemed to want all the guys from the team to be there. So, dammit, I was there.

As I paced and shuffled, a young woman opened the door, and with professional grace, assisted a brittle and elderly man into a green Adirondack chair.

She, not being a man and thus not invited to the circle, scooted off without saying a word. There was a Women's Sharing Circle going on simultaneously elsewhere. Perhaps she was scooting off to that, or maybe she was just hired help.

My new companion was a skinny old dude wearing a blue Yankees cap. He just sat there, eyes closed. He must have been ninety, and I at first feared he might actually cease breathing right there on my watch. I hate it when people die on my watch. It's happened before.

I was tired and the old fellow did not look like fun company. My eyes started to glaze over. I heard a voice. It was Yankees-cap Guy.

"Where the hell am I?"

"You're at Michael's wedding. Waiting for the Men's Sharing Circle."

"The what?"

"The Men's Sharing Circle."

"What the hell is that?"

"I have no idea."

After a few minutes of silence, he spoke again. "Are you the priest?"

"No. Our friend Alex is doing the ceremony. There is no priest."

"No. I mean you. Aren't you that priest?"

"No. You've got me confused."

"No, dammit. You're that priest."

"I was once a monk. That's probably what you're thinking of. I was never a priest."

"What's the difference?"

"It's pretty complicated." I did not want to get into it with this old fellow. Not here. Not now.

"Complicated?" he said. "I can handle complicated. I'm not a child. My mind still works."

"I'm not sure mine does," I replied. "And I'm not sure I can handle complicated. I prefer simplicity these days."

His eyes penetrated mine from under the visor of that Yankees cap.

"You might surprise yourself," he said. "Give it a try."

I hesitated. He could tell I was faltering.

"Okay," he said finally, "skip it, you damn coward. Have it your way. No point in trying to stretch yourself or take a risk, is there, you wimp."

Trying to keep calm, I uttered the explanation I had pretty much memorized over the years for occasions like this when it became easier to respond than to obfuscate.

"A priest is ordained. He can say mass, give sacraments. A monk dedicates his life to God by withdrawing from the world into a separate community."

"Okay. Yeah. That sounds more like you. Withdraw. Separate. Run away. Hide. Yep. Now I get it." He stared at me some more, and then he said, "No. Okay. Wait a minute. You're the cop. I never met you, but you were in the papers. A long time ago."

"I was once a cop. Then I was a detective. A private detective."

"What happened on Lavender Street? Something happened there, right? I remember hearing about that too."

"There is no Lavender Street."

"Not now. There was, once. Wasn't there? Not here. Somewhere. I don't remember. I just remember folks talking about it a long time ago. Stuff only us old guys remember."

"I'm not an old guy."

He laughed. "That's a matter of opinion."

He went on, "Well, have it your way if you want. If you don't want to go there, you don't want to go there. I don't give a damn."

I did not respond, and in my silence, the old guy apparently changed his mind about allowing me to not go there.

"So, what happened, anyway? You were a monk and now you're not. You were a cop and now you're not. You were a detective and now you're not. And something happened on Lavender Street a long time ago."

"As I said, it's complicated and I don't want to talk about it. And there is no Lavender Street."

"Okay, whatever." He chuckled. He closed his eyes again,

then opened them and said, "We're men. And here we are at the Men's Sharing Circle. What do you want to share with Michael? He'll be my grandson in a little while, you know."

"You're Angela's grandfather? No, I didn't know that."

We introduced ourselves. Rather, he introduced himself. He already seemed to know me. His name was Harvey.

Then I answered his question. "I don't know. I don't think I have any brilliant words for Michael. I see him all the time anyway. If I think of any wisdom, I can tell him some other time. How about you?"

He thought this over, and then replied, "I'd tell him that there are light parts to marriage and dark parts, just like a chicken."

I laughed. "Light meat, dark meat. That's pretty good."

"Do you like chicken?" he asked me.

"I love chicken. I love all birds."

"Me too. I've been married for seventy years. I'm ninety-four years old. That's the key to a good marriage. Understanding that it's like a chicken."

"You're a smart old dude, aren't you?"

"Yep."

"Got any words of wisdom to share with me? I could use some."

"Well, what the hell are you anyway? You were once a cop but not anymore. You were once a detective but you're not anymore. You were once a priest—"

"Monk."

"Whatever. Doesn't sound like you're anything now."

"I'm not. I'm retired."

"Retired from what?"

"Retired from being a monk, a cop, a detective, pretty much everything."

"Sounds like retired from living to me."

All I could do was look at him. He continued, "Everybody's something, even if they're retired."

"Not me."

"Well, fuck that. You're too young to retire anyway. If they'd let me, I'd still be out there running that damn backhoe."

"And I'd still be a monk … if they'd let me."

Those were the words that came out of my mouth. I immediately regretted them because I knew they were not true. I did not want to be a monk. I was plagued with too many doubts. What I wanted to be was someone who knew what he wanted to be.

I did not correct my words. I let them hang there for Harvey, a man who had complete certainty about what he wanted to be. I wished I were more like him. That's why untrue words passed my lips.

"Well, screw 'em," he said. "Screw the bastards, all of them. Be a damn detective. Be a damn monk. Be whatever the hell you want. Screw 'em. Screw 'em all."

I held up my fingers in the peace sign, and Harvey said "Peace and love, man." I could not tell if he was speaking ironically. In any case, we both laughed.

"Okay, now I know what you are," he said. "You're a damn hippie. I always hated hippies. But at least you're something."

"Hippies believe in love," I replied. "You don't disagree with that, do you?"

He chuckled. "If you put it that way, I guess not."

"Love is what it's all about," I said un-ironically. "That's the very core of my belief."

Harvey laughed at my words. "You talk funny. Kind of like a priest."

Did he wink at me? Maybe he did.

"But basically, you're right," he went on. Then he added, "Screw Lavender Street too. Whatever the hell happened there."

About then, the rest of the guys started to dribble in, a few at a time. I started chatting with them and Harvey's eyes closed again. Once again he dozed off.

The Men's Sharing Circle proved to be even less inspiring than its name implied. We all did our sharing, and Harvey did indeed pass on his chicken wisdom to Michael, and in an hour it was blessedly over and we all moved on.

Michael and Angela got married. Coincidentally or not, chicken was served at the dinner.

And that was that.

But I couldn't stop thinking about Harvey. The sonofabitch had been married, to the same woman, for seventy years, had four kids, seven grandkids, and was here with untold dozens, maybe hundreds, of loving family members.

And me? Well, I lived alone with a large dog in a small house.

Who was I to talk of love to the likes of Harvey? What did I know of love?

Nothing. Despite my empty words, I was afraid. I was afraid, not only of love, but of life, or at least a few important parts of life. And Lavender Street? I hadn't thought about that for thirty years and never wanted to again. That's why I was retired. Retired from pretty much everything. Retired from feeling. Retired from life. That's why I was nothing.

I was scared of feeling. Scared of life. I was scared to death.

I was *chicken*.

Chapter Two

࿐

Screw 'Em All

Sunday morning, after an early breakfast, the gathering began un-gathering. Those who had the farthest to travel left first. Michael and Angela were foisting half-consumed bottles of wine, with improvised corks, onto the departing guests with admonitions to not drink them on the drive home.

Home for me was only about four miles away, and I hitched a ride back to town with Charlie, who admirably restrained himself from sipping the merlot and left me on my front porch.

"Enjoy the day," he instructed. "Looks like a nice one."

"I enjoy every day. Every day's a nice one."

"You always say stuff like that," he replied as I was getting out of the car, clutching my bag, "and yet, when I look at you, you look like crap. You look lost."

I slammed the door and said, "I'm not lost," but the door had been shut and he didn't hear and I didn't really care.

The house seemed even smaller and emptier than usual, with no dog to jump up on me in greeting. Marlowe was still in the kennel, where I couldn't pick him up until tomorrow. I saw no reason to stay in alone. It was a quick, five-minute walk into the center of town, and that's where the people were. Despite a weekend full of people, I uncharacteristically yearned for more and went in search of some.

It was a Sunday in April, but winter's chill was still in the air. It was the time of year that could not make up its mind what it wanted to be. The calendar said spring but the cold hung around like a lover who has already left you in her heart. A metallic *chideep-chideep* echoed around my ears out on my lawn—a barn swallow. I took out my "smartphone" and recorded a few seconds of it. My phone may be smart, but me—not so much. It has infinite capabilities, but all I can make the damn thing do is be a tape recorder, almost exclusively for bird songs, and once or twice maybe, a phone.

I like birds and love to listen to their songs, and I like to keep them available for me to listen to late at night. They help me sleep.

I was in the center of the village of Shelburne Falls. It has a Bridge of Flowers, which is kind of self-explanatory—a bridge filled with flowers. And there's a lovely spot where the Deerfield River flows over a dam, creating whirlpools and waterfalls that swirl over rocks—the Glacial Potholes. And its main street is classic small-town, circa 1950s—Bridge Street. It's a delightful place to stroll.

People were out on this day. I'm quiet and shy, but everybody knows me here and for me, walking through Shelburne Falls is like schmoozing at a cocktail party—if I went to cocktail parties. Everyone stops to chat, whether I want them to or not. And that's what I was doing—strolling and schmoozing, sauntering as if I were sipping on a martini, talking with whomever corralled me about movies, the weather, music, the Red Sox's chances, existential angst, ironic detachment, the nature of God … all that light, superficial stuff.

The usual suspects were around, but there were others too. There are always a few tourists, but today I saw strangers of a more exotic stripe than I was used to—ten of them maybe, men and women, all in a group, dressed mostly in black, many with tablets, some furiously jotting down notes on yellow-lined pads. Their leader was a bright-eyed, scraggly bearded hipster wearing a black-wool watch cap stretched down over his ears.

This young fellow was clearly someone special, someone important. He had long, blond Dutch-boy hair falling out under his hat and tied in a ponytail in the back. Very tall—at least six feet seven—almost alarmingly skinny, with a not-quite-successful attempt at a beard on his innocent, cherubic face. He was looking at everything, seeing everything, stopping and staring, often seemingly at nothing, but you had to believe he was seeing something where others saw nothing.

He would take out his cellphone and snap a picture of each curiosity he encountered—a twisted limb on a tree or an oddly shaped stone. He spoke to no one, except he would whisper occasionally into the ear of the tiny figure at his side—a slight and fragile female wearing sunglasses, a thin scarlet scarf wrapped around her head like a veil, and floppy gray sweatshirt and pants. He had to bend down dramatically to reach her level, but he did it over and over while I observed.

This odd group was wandering with a sense of purpose. Their bright-eyed leader would take them to a site, which they would size up for fifteen minutes or so. A sharp, lanky man would put some kind of optic device to his eye and look at things from various angles. When he finally spoke, everyone would take notes.

I could not help but follow them around. It's the detective in me—though I'm retired, that instinct never dies. I began chatting idly with a few of their members, the ones floating in the periphery away from the core group. They were friendly enough, but responded vaguely, if at all, to my more specific questions. I, however, had little to ask of them. Basically I only wanted to watch.

I tagged along until I grew weary of them, which happened

after they led me back to the wooden deck overlooking the falls. I was about ready to leave.

Spray hit my face, as it was hitting theirs. There is an old stone staircase there, leading down from the platform to the swirling waters of the river as it pours down over the rocks. The town had fenced and sealed it years ago after being sued multiple times by stupid people, swimmers who went down there and jumped into the river and injured themselves.

The tall hipster and his diminutive companion were standing by the locked gate to the staircase. The tiny person's eyes went blank, then lit up. She started dancing. There was no music, but she was dancing. It seemed like something else though, something more. She was moving all parts of her body as if none of them were connected, or if they were, it was in some kind of non-physical, almost spiritual way. And she had this smile on her face, like she was somewhere else entirely. I gotta admit, it was entrancing. It was devilish. It was angelic. I couldn't tear my eyes away.

She was done dancing. She stopped, looked around, and then she hitched her foot onto one of the cross-spokes and hoisted herself onto the top rung of the gate, where she precariously balanced herself, first on both feet, then on one. She laughed, pulled off her scarf, and let her long, blood-red curls fly horizontally in the wind. She was queen of the world, if only for a few moments.

The hipster wanted to grab her. You could see it in his body language. But even touching her would be dangerous and could push her off into the swirls below.

She laughed. Her voice was high and harsh and filled with both wickedness and elation.

The guy decided he had no choice. He grabbed her by the one leg still planted on the fence and picked her up like she was a slippery bad child. She squirmed and lashed about and yelled at the guy as she struggled to elude his grasp, but he held on to her with more strength than one would guess he possessed.

He lowered her back to earth. She wriggled like a hooked trout for a few seconds then twisted back at him, stopped, and grew suddenly centered and silent once more. I thought I saw a smile in there too.

"Fuck you. Fuck you all," she said calmly as she turned and scrambled away—away from the water, away from harm, and away from the scraggly hipster who ran after her. She picked up the pace as she rounded the turn back onto Bridge Street. He was close behind in hot pursuit.

The rest of their entourage watched but made no moves. This was clearly between the two of them.

That was enough for me. I didn't wait to see what happened next. Instead I made a point of detouring down the narrow lane in front of the bowling alley so I wouldn't run into them again. There was trouble brewing here, and I did not need trouble.

I knew who this guy was. I may not get out much, but I do know a little about film. This was Nick Mooney, quite possibly the finest young director alive—a genius, but notorious for going over budget, bedding down his female stars, and leaving havoc in his wake.

I still had some monk and some detective left in me, so the urges to save and investigate bubbled up, but I didn't need whatever it was they were tempting me with.

Screw them. Screw 'em all.

Fuck them. Fuck 'em all.

Though home would be empty, bereft of big dogs and humans alike, I went there. Once inside, I closed the door.

Chapter Three

∾

Good Chicken

SOMETIMES A RANDOM event like hearing the mutterings of a possibly addled reactionary old fart can change one's life. In any case, those words—screw 'em, detective, monk, and chicken—resonated in my skull after that weekend had passed.

Lavender Street, though? I try never to think about Lavender Street.

I became intent on following Harvey's advice. I would do whatever the hell I wanted to do. Little did I know that life was conspiring to make me a detective again, and in a manner of speaking, a monk too. I would not, however, be chicken.

But I was eating one, a crispy yet pleasantly greasy fried one, along with mashed potatoes and gravy and some green beans, at the bar of the West End Pub the following night when it became clear that it was not my fate to avoid Nick Mooney forever.

He sat down next to me, looked at my plate, and told Josh, who was tending bar, "I'll have what this guy is having."

"Good choice," I told him.

Josh asked him what he wanted to drink and Mooney looked at my root beer and said, "I'll have what this guy is having."

When he got his drink, we clicked glasses. Mooney was still wearing the same black-wool watch cap pulled down over his ears. Maybe he always wore the damn thing.

"You don't have to drink what I'm having. Have a real drink," I told him.

"I don't drink."

"Neither do I."

"I know." He sipped his root beer.

"Frank Raven," I said by way of introduction.

"I know," he replied. "Nick Mooney."

"I know," I replied.

"And how exactly do you know me?" he asked.

"I run a movie theater. It's my job to know what the hottest young director in the country looks like."

"That's pretty good. A lot of people know my work, but few know my face."

"What the hell are you doing in a town like this, Mooney?"

"What else? I'm making a film. And I'm thinking of making it here. I'm scouting locations. "

"Good. That'll be cool. Have fun."

"I expect we will. But first, I need your help. I want to hire you. I need a good detective."

"You seem to know everything there is to know about me. You should know I'm retired."

"Retirement's not always forever. My Uncle Lyle was retired and now he works for me."

I looked into his almost too-bright eyes. "Did you ever catch your girlfriend, Mooney?"

"She's not my girlfriend. And no, I didn't. That's why I need your help."

"I saw you guys there yesterday. Quite a show," I said.

"Yeah. That's what we do. We put on shows. I saw you too."

"You don't miss much."

"Neither do you."

"Who is she?" I asked.

"You're kidding, right? You know who I am, but you don't know who she is?"

"I'm not kidding."

"She's just the biggest star in the world. You ever hear of Juliana Velvet Norcross—VelCro? I thought this movie stuff was your job."

Though not exactly plugged into popular culture, even I had heard of VelCro. I had never seen her in a movie, and in fact I wasn't sure I'd ever seen a picture of her. But she certainly was famous and I had heard of her.

"That was her?"

"What world do you live in, Raven? Yes, that was her."

"I live in my own world, Mooney. I'm still catching up on Madonna. Have you heard her new album? "

"What's an album?"

He laughed under his breath at his little joke. So did I.

Juliana Velvet Norcross was her full given name, but she was, in the nomenclature of the day, universally known as VelCro. "Train wreck" did not do her justice. She was an apocalyptic disaster of staggering proportions, with arrests for white powder and brown powder, driving under the influence, and resisting arrest. She was known for flavored vodka, rehab stints, fiery affairs with people of both genders, drunken tirades, nude internet photos, notorious late-night incidents, and hospitalizations for "exhaustion." She was one of those celebrities who always placed high on "Who Is Most Likely to Be Dead in a Year?" polls.

And she was universally acclaimed the finest and most brilliant young actor of her generation.

She had talent to burn and she was doing her best to do exactly that.

And she had just turned twenty-one. Now she was gone. And Mooney wanted me to find her.

"It was like she vanished into thin air, Raven. I saw her, then I didn't. She was only half a block away and then she was nowhere. I went all around town, into alleys, into every shop and restaurant, every nook and cranny. No VelCro anywhere."

"The cops are good at this stuff, Mooney. Why me?"

"Nobody's supposed to know we're here. At this point, this is all top secret. The press would go fucking crazy if word got out. This girl is dynamite and everyone wants a piece of her."

He sipped his root beer. "And we need somebody who knows the area, knows the rhythms here and the places no one else knows. We do our research when we come into a town, Raven. We bring some of our own, sure, but we go local as much as we can. We find the best carpenters, the best electricians, the best caterers, the best places to stay, the best everything. You're the best detective. We want you."

I sipped my root beer. "Your research is out of date, Mooney. I was the best detective ten years ago. I'm retired now."

"No, Raven, our research is current. Nobody does this better than we do. We're the fucking FBI, the CIA, the NSA. We're SMERSH and SPECTRE and UNCLE and the Mossad all rolled into one, and we've talked to anyone who knows anything about this area. Our intelligence tells us no one knows this burg better than you do. You are the man. You are *our* man."

"If you guys are so damn good, why don't you just find her yourself?"

"No. We don't do anything ourselves. Except make movies. What we're good at is finding the best local people to do things we can't do. And we can't find VelCro."

"I am good at finding things," I admitted.

"We know."

"Yeah. That's what I do. Or rather, what I used to do. I don't do anything now."

He stared into my eyes and asked, "Why, Raven? Why don't you do anything?" He spoke to me like he really wanted to know. Few people do that—say what they really mean.

Should I give him an honest answer—this guy I didn't know? *Yeah, what the hell.* Better him than someone who did know me well. Safer that way. Less risk of it coming back to haunt me.

"Mooney, all I ever wanted to do all my life was to find things. And I was good at it. Better than anybody. And that's what I did. But once I did it, there was nowhere else to go, nothing else to prove. When you're the best, you can't go anywhere but down." I sipped my root beer. "And that's what I've done. Go down."

Mooney looked at me and said, "Yeah, all the way down."

He sipped his root beer and slurped it a little. "What are you afraid of, Raven?"

"I'm not afraid." I knew I was lying.

"Yes, you are. We've studied you, Raven. *I've* studied you and I think I understand you, maybe better than you understand yourself. Every time you do something, you get shot down. You were a lonely, sensitive kid, and you sought refuge in a monastery. They threw you out. Then you were a cop. There you literally got shot down. You died, Raven. You died then and you've never come back to life. That was two strikes. Then you became a detective, and here you got a hit—not exactly a home run, but a good solid triple. You were good at it. But by then, the fear was thick and it paralyzed you. You couldn't stand to succeed. It was too different for you, not what you were used to, and new things terrified you. So you quit that too. Actually you didn't even quit that, you just let it fizzle out slowly, like a battery running out of juice. You faded out, and that's the most cowardly thing there is. You run a movie theater now, but you're going nowhere with that. You keep it as quiet and simple and under the radar as possible. It's just a placeholder for you. Something to make the time pass slightly less miserably than it would otherwise. You're scared to death, Raven. You're the biggest fucking chicken I've ever seen."

I did not respond.

"I was a chicken once too," he went on. "My first film sucked and I was scared to make another one. But I did. I pulled myself up and next time I made a good one. Some say it was a great one. They all forgot that first one. I know how to come back from the dead, Raven. You don't."

My root beer was almost gone.

Mooney continued, "But don't worry, Raven. I'm here to save your ass. I'm here to bring you back to life. I'll give you a reason to live. Stick with me, pal, and I'll change your life forever."

His speech was done. So was my root beer.

He finished up with, "First step: eat your fried chicken and then find me the girl."

It was good chicken.

Chapter Four

∿

Looney Tunes

SHELBURNE FALLS IS tiny. It is hard to disappear here, especially if you are the most famous person in the world.

I half expected to see paparazzi around. VelCro had been seen briefly, minus her veil, and perhaps word had leaked out that she'd been spotted in town. But no, things were normal, which is to say boring and quiet. Anyone seeing a skinny kid in frumpy gray sweats would not make the connection with Hollywood starlets, despite her flowing red mane. Not here. It would be too much cognitive dissonance. This is not a place VelCro would frequent.

Mooney had been standing near the Foxtown Diner when he lost sight of her and by that time she had been in front of Mocha Maya's Coffee Shop. That's about half a block away. He'd checked Mocha Maya's and no one there had seen her. And he'd checked every other building anywhere near Bridge Street—nothing, not a trace.

First I stood in front of the Foxtown, which I had done hundreds of times, just to get a sense of the place. I tried to imagine how it might feel if I were there for the first time, to see what new eyes would see.

The sun shone down upon me and it was warm on my skin. But I saw nothing of note.

Then I walked to Mocha Maya's and did the same thing. Same sun. Same skin. Same nothing.

Where would you go? Where could you go?

Next to Mocha Maya's is Town Hall, and upstairs from that is the theater—a funky, century-old movie hall I'd been running for more than fifteen years. The police station is on the first floor, along with town offices, so the door to the building would have been open yesterday when VelCro did her vanishing act.

She disappeared on Sunday, so no town workers were around then, and Mooney had checked with the police, in a generic manner, so as to not reveal the identity of the person he was seeking. The police had seen no one, but then their office door is frequently closed, so they wouldn't necessarily notice anyone entering the building.

That's where I went next—Town Hall. Chief Loomis was in the police office, but as usual his door was mostly shut, just open a crack. I didn't bother him. The door leading upstairs to the theater was locked, as it should be. It's always locked when there's no show going on. There were no shows this weekend since I had been camped out at the wedding.

But the elevator would not have been locked yesterday. It's supposed to be locked when there are no shows, but it's one of those things no one really does. No one ever really locks it because the town workers occasionally need access to get to some of the files stored up there—one of those small things I would know but no one else would.

Indeed, the elevator was not locked. I rode it up to the theater and was greeted by the familiar, friendly, oily smell of freshly popped popcorn.

Generally it is spookily dark and quiet when I enter. Today it was dark, but not quiet, because there was a movie playing up on the big screen. For an audience of one.

VelCro was curled up comfortably in the front row. Towering

over her were gigantic, colorful, moving images of Bugs Bunny
and Elmer Fudd. She was watching our *Best of Looney Tunes*
DVD, munching popcorn, and occasionally guffawing—lost
in her own little world.

I watched the wascally wabbit fwustrate the lisping hunter
up there on the screen for a minute and then turned on the
house lights, which flooded the place instantly.

"You need a new popcorn machine," she shouted, not
looking up.

"That one's fine," I replied.

"No it's not. I broke it."

She continued to laugh at Bugs and Elmer. "This is too
funny! I can't believe I've never seen these before."

I went to the projection booth and turned it off.

"Oh, man …" she complained. "Come on."

I went back down to the front row. On the seat next to her,
I could see a half-empty fifth of lime vodka—a dull, sickening
green color—and a similarly filled gallon of orange juice. One
of our large cups was in her hand. Next to the OJ and vodka
was a baggie with a half-inch of white powder.

I gave her a look—one of *those* looks that said I'm not messing
around—and she voluntarily handed me the cup, spilling a few
drops. It was almost empty. Her seat had that medicinal reek
of vodka. You're not supposed to be able to smell vodka, but
all alcohol has an odor. I should know. The smell of pot filled
the air too.

"You having a fun party?" I asked.

"It's a fucking blast! But it would be better with more people.
Wanna party, Mister Theater Man?" She held out the vodka
bottle to me.

I replied, "No, I don't party."

"Well, I sure do," she said, and took a chug from the bottle.
"And fuck you anyway. I'm having fun."

We stood there and looked at each other.

"Don't swear," I said. "And you're going to fix that popcorn
machine."

"Oh, fuck you. I'll buy you a new popcorn machine. I'll buy you ten new popcorn machines. Then I can break some more. I'll buy you a hundred of them. I don't care."

"No, I like that one. You'll fix it. And don't swear."

She just laughed at me.

I gave her another one of those looks. I could tell this gal was pretty smart because she clearly understood my looks. Somewhat sheepishly and reluctantly, she shuffled back to the lobby where the popcorn machine lived. She stood at attention in front of the red popcorn machine with faded yellow words stenciled on it that no one could read. I had long since forgotten what they said.

"What did you do to it?"

"That little arm thing stopped working. It's the thing that stirs the kernels while they pop."

"Shit," I said, "that's happened before. It's a pain in the ass."

She opened the Plexiglas doors to the machine and stuck her head in it.

"Be careful," I told her. "It's still hot."

"I know. I burned myself on it before. Do you have a screwdriver?"

There was one in the back. I found it and handed it to her. She was fiddling away inside the popper.

"You gotta reach around to the back of the kettle," I told her, pointing. "And you gotta tilt the screwdriver up a little."

"I can fucking see that."

"Don't swear at me," I told her. "It's very unbecoming behavior in a nice young woman like you."

"You swear."

"Well, I'm not a young woman. And I'm not nice. Don't swear."

"Yeah, whatever. Oh, shit ... this little jigger is totally busted."

I grabbed her by the shoulders and gave her a tug, pulling her out from the guts of the machine.

When she was out, and looking at me, I said, "I mean it. Don't swear."

Her eyes met mine and I could tell she got it. Then she held her palm out to me, showing me the popcorn stirring arm that rested there.

"See, it broke off here at the base. It's no good."

"They're hard to find," I said. "I used to be able to order parts, but this machine is too old now. Nobody handles them anymore."

She started walking around the lobby, and then in the refreshment room, she looked at the assorted crap lying around.

"What's this?" she asked, holding up an ancient metal table fan from back in the days before we had air conditioning put in. "Does this still work?"

I looked at it. "No. That hasn't worked in years."

"Do you have any pliers?"

I found some and handed them to her. She started prying the old-fashioned iron grill off the fan's face. When she had the grill off, she twisted at one of its cross-spokes until it broke away from the frame. She eyed it, then used the pliers again, this time to break it down to the length she wanted it to be.

"This'll work," she said.

She stuck her head back into the machine, and in deft movements of her delicate, tiny hands and fingers, operated with surgical precision for a good ten minutes.

"Try pushing the kettle over on its hinge," I suggested.

She didn't reply but kept at it even more intently than before.

"Here," I said, pointing at the glass in the back of the contraption. "You gotta line up those three holes."

Her voice echoed out from inside the glass box. "I know what I'm doing. Do you want me to do this or not?"

"I'm just trying to help," I pleaded.

"Just let me fucking do it, okay? Oops, I'm sorry." She pulled her head out and looked at me. "I really am sorry, Mister Theater Man."

"That's all right. You gotta find that tiny connecting piece— that little bridge thing."

She stuck her head back in and said from inside, "I *know* … Jeez …."

Three minutes of intensive care later, she emerged, saying, "Voilà. It is done."

"You gotta tighten it securely," I told her, "or it'll just fall off again."

"Check it yourself."

I did. It was hard getting my head and hands into the works back there. It was a job for a smaller person, like her.

"Looks okay," I reported.

"Let's check it out," she said. She poured a cup of popcorn and some oil into the drum and turned the machine on. It churned away happily, the improvised new arm stirring the kernels smoothly and superbly. Soon we had a perfect batch of fresh popcorn, which I scooped into a bag.

She stuck her hand into the bag and sampled a mouthful.

"Oh, that's real good. That's the best batch yet …. So, I want to see the rest of those cartoons. Those were funny."

"Yeah, but first we gotta do this," I said.

I made her pick up the bottle of vodka and the bag of powder and flush them down the toilet. She put up only token resistance.

We went back up to the theater and I turned out the house lights and cranked up the projector again. We both sat down to munch popcorn and watch the show.

I asked if she wanted to drink some of the remaining orange juice, but she preferred a Diet Coke instead, and I went back to the refreshment room and got one for each of us.

She howled at the Roadrunner and Wile E. Coyote stuff.

I howled too. Those things are hilarious.

After they ended, she helped me clean up a bit. Not much cleaning was needed. We went down via the elevator and back onto Bridge Street.

"That was fun," she said. "But you lied to me, Mister Theater Man."

"I did?"

"Yeah. You told me you weren't nice. That was a lie. You are."

Chapter Five

❧

Too Much Red?

VELCRO RETURNED HERSELF to Mooney's care. He couldn't believe she had given him the slip so easily.

It was simple—it took her a fraction of a second to duck into Town Hall as he chased her. She did it in a flash. Once inside the building, she saw an elevator and took it wherever it went, which was up just one floor—there were only two floors in that building. Much to her delight, she found herself in a theater. She was a movie star. She felt at home in a theater and decided to stay a while.

But first, she re-veiled herself and went across the street to the Keystone Market. She bought the OJ, walked over to Good Spirits for vodka, and settled in for her own private film festival. We had stacks of DVDs in the projection booth, and the new digital projector was simple to operate for any young person raised on ubiquitous electronics. Popcorn was relatively nutritious and she figured she could hide out there until the next movie played, which wasn't until the following weekend. Or she got bored, whichever came first.

She had no plans for what to do after she got bored. It wasn't her style to think that far ahead.

And that's when I found her.

Mooney and VelCro left town. I had no idea if Shelburne Falls had passed Mooney's test to serve as the location for his next picture.

Life went on, as it tends to do, and the next morning found me up at dawn going for my constitutional into town to buy my morning paper.

The street leading from my house to the center of town is known as the "Hill of Tears." In the town's center, you'll find the shops, the people, and the excitement. The name "Hill of Tears" comes from its heartbreaking, tear-inducing role in the town's annual 10k road race. The path climbs dramatically from flat land to a thousand-foot peak, and then, near my house, it runs like a sliding board down to the village and skids back to level ground near the river. This was my route into town and back each day—easy going in, excruciating coming back.

Near the bottom of the hill stood a ramshackle and rambling brown house with yellow trim and a bit of peeling paint, despite being kept up pretty carefully. It was located at the entrance to the village proper, on a dead-end side street branching off the Hill of Tears, not far from the railroad trestle. Set back from the road, it usually gave no sign of life as I strolled by each day. There were no cars in the driveway and no lights on. Thus, the slightly haunted appearance.

At this point in my walk, the sounds of the village began to emerge—the rumble of traffic and the muffled roar of the river. When a train passed by, the earsplitting clamor of cars was so close and strong that the ground shivered like a death rattle, and its whistle was piercing. It always whistled—long and loud—and reverberated over the hills that held the village like a mother's kind arms.

Somehow, out of these noises, I would detect at each passing the sharp tweeting of a bird emanating from the home. It was a sweet song arising from the industrial cacophony. If I paused for a second, sometimes all the competing sounds would cease and nothing would be heard but the tweeting of the bird.

This morning, bright and crisp, it happened again. It was just after dawn. The sounds of the village halted, the bird sang a merry *fweep-fweep*, and I stopped to listen. I took out my smartphone and recorded a full minute of chirping. Almost magically, just after I stopped recording, the town reawakened and the competing noises began anew. I finished my trip, bought my *Shelburne Falls Independent*—yes, we have our own newspaper—and huffed back up the hill to my home. It was part of my morning constitutional to record birds whenever I could.

The next morning, with a red sun rising over the river, I again walked down the Hill of Tears. This time a totally different scene was taking place in front of the usually still house.

A tiny, slim redheaded woman of roughly my age and her teenage doppelganger were frantically running around the place, the girl flopping a large blue towel around. A town fire truck was parked in the driveway, and two intrepid firemen— one brandishing a fish net on a long pole—purposefully worked the perimeter. All were gazing upward. A black cat, along with a gray one, stalked the scene hungrily. All the doors and windows to the house were open.

Above it all, deliciously free but not at all sure what to do with its freedom, darted a small, evanescent, deep-red, plumed parakeet. The bird did not seem inclined to travel far. It flew around the house and circled the maples in the yard, just high enough to stay out of reach of anyone, including the net. Attempts to approach it were futile. It would fly away again. It landed temporarily on the railing of the front porch, but took off each time a human approached. The girl tried in vain to shoo it into the house with the towel.

"Here, Penelope," called the woman, pursing her lips with a kissing sound.

The girl admonished her, "Mom, that's no good. She won't listen."

I walked over. "Can I help?"

The woman had the bemused look of someone who had already been through a lot at this early hour when many had not yet even awakened. "Thank you. We're just trying to get Penelope. There she goes …."

She dashed off on a brief parakeet quest and quickly returned. "She got out while Sarah was feeding her. She's never done that before."

"Can you show me her cage?"

She took me inside to a home where the daily routine had clearly been interrupted mid-getting ready for school/work. A half-drunk cup of tea sat on the table next to a partially consumed English muffin and a soggy bowl of shredded wheat. The morning's *Independent* was folded and open to the local news page. There was a notebook and a math textbook. The place smelled of warmth and goodness and love.

There was an unused dining room next to the kitchen, and just beyond that, a living room with mismatched furniture, shelves crammed with books, and a partially reupholstered, overstuffed chair. In a far corner was a birdcage sitting on a homemade platform, spilled birdseed on the floor nearby. The window just above the cage was open, the cool morning breeze wafting in.

The woman turned, standing only inches away. She looked up at me. This close, I could see the lines in her face and the gray streaks in her red hair. She was lovely. She smiled as if this was just one more crazy, funny event in her crazy, funny life.

"Darn bird. Sarah does love her though."

The birdcage door was still open. "Do you have any string?" I asked.

She rummaged through a few drawers before emerging with a nearly empty spool of twine. Taking one of the pens out of my pocket, I used it to prop open the door to the cage and tied one end of the twine to the pen. Then I picked up some of the feed from the floor and spread it on the bottom of the cage.

I went outside, asked the others to stop their quest for a few minutes, and returned inside with the woman. The girl, Sarah, followed. That stillness was there again.

In the silence, I held up one end of the string. On my phone, I found the recording of the bird from yesterday, cranked up the volume to eleven, and played back the full minute of song.

Nothing.

I played it again.

Then Penelope swept in through the open window with a flourish of crimson, through the door to her cage, and began to munch happily on the seed. I pulled the string, knocking over my pen. The door slammed shut and Penelope was safe at home.

Sarah clapped her hands. The woman maintained that same bemused bearing, but I could detect relief too.

I explained, "They respond to their own voice. Or even to the voices of other birds. They love their songs. She's not adapted to the wild. She belongs here. Most beings end up where they belong. Once they adapt to being somewhere, they stay. "

The firemen left. The two humans cooed at the birdcage, one on either side—three shades of red lined up beautifully. The older one saw me and smiled.

"Too much red for you?"

"No such thing. I like red. I like birds and I like red. And that's about it. Dogs too, I guess. Maybe movies. But that's a pleasing shade of red."

"She's an unusual mutation."

Sarah said, "Not me! Penelope."

The woman went on, "Yes. The bird, not the girl. Some have red crowns or red breasts. Even red rumps. Almost none are all red like her."

Sarah said, "At least my butt and boobs aren't red."

Her mom glared at her, but soon I saw a smile in there. I like smiles. I need them. This one warmed me up.

We all sat at the table. Sarah finished her soggy shredded wheat and left for school.

I had a cup of tea with the woman. Her name was Clara. She thanked me and I walked back up the Hill of Tears to my home, where I read my own copy of the *Independent* and had another cup of tea. Usually I drink coffee. This time I had tea.

Chapter Six

The Nutting Girl

MOONEY AND VELCRO were beginning to disappear into my memory banks. I started to run into Clara in front of her house every so often. Truth be told, I was taking more walks into town in hopes this would occur. I tried to milk these encounters, to steal as much of the lovely lady's time as I could, but she wasn't around much. On the few occasions when I saw her, she was in the middle of something. Most people have more obligations than I do.

I learned a few minor facts about her life and Sarah's. She told me little about Penelope the Parrot, however. These encounters were gradually becoming the highlight of my day, brief and seldom though they were. I was reluctant to make them happen *too* often, mainly because it felt so damn good to be connecting even in this quick and superficial way with a female. I was afraid that if they were any longer or more regular, they would not fit comfortably in my solitary life.

The more dependable bright spot of my week came on Tuesdays, my one un-solitary night. This Tuesday evening found me, as it had for the past thirty-five years, back at the theater for the weekly practice of the Shelburne Falls Morris Men.

Morris dancing is a form of ritual dance to celebrate the change of seasons. It originated in agrarian England hundreds of years ago and is mentioned in Shakespeare's plays as an ancient activity. During the 1960s "folk revival," teams sprouted up in America, and here in New England especially. Many towns have their own troupe. We don't get paid for it. We dance at local fairs and town events, but mostly in the woods and streets, just for fun and usually for ourselves alone. It's invigorating and athletic. Singing and camaraderie and drinking beer are a big part of the culture. I like all of it, except for the beer part, but even that's fine as long as I'm not the one drinking. How often in our society do men get a chance to dance together?

We practiced our dancing on the cleared-off stage. We were in two lines, three men in each line, with five other guys standing off to the side watching and kibitzing and chiming in with observations and the occasional joke. Danny stood in front of us, playing his accordion. The bells on our legs accentuated every beat. Stanley was leading us in drills. Each line surged up to the other, did a hop, and back-stepped to its original position. The half-gyp. We did it over and over and over. The intent was to travel as one, stay in line, jump high, and look good while doing it. The new, younger guys were performing the move with gusto and leaping up toward the stars. We old dudes had less lift in our weary legs, but the young guys spurred us on, and we tried to match them step for step, jump for jump.

I was succeeding. I was, right? Sam, our youngest lad at fifteen, stood across from me, and damn it, even though I had forty years on him, I could jump as high as he could. I knew I could.

"Lines!" shouted Stanley.

You were allowed to look to either side while you danced, at least at practice, and see how good the lines were. They were supposed to be straight. Ours sucked. Some guys were way out front, others behind, like pistons misfiring.

I sat a few out, hands on knees, bent over, puffing, while the music and the rest of the team continued. Then Danny stopped playing and Stanley said, "There were some good parts to that."

Michael added, "And a lot of suckitude too."

We worked on whole gyp and then rounds. Stanley and Michael did a two-man jig that the new guys had not seen before. "The Nutting Girl," a very old classic.

This particular dance ends with all the guys singing a verse together:

> With my fal-la-lal to my ral-tal-lal
> Whack-fol-the-dear-ol-day
> And what few nuts that poor girl had
> She threw them all away.

There are more lyrics to this song, but we only sing the last chorus in the dance. It's a traditional English tune about a fair maiden gathering nuts in Kent. She meets a young plowboy who enchants her with his singing and "lays her down." Soon she can "feel the world go round and round." Not long after, she forgets entirely about her nuts and "throws them all away."

The night wore on. Blessedly, since I was now exhausted, it was 8:30 and time to go to the pub. I locked up the theater, and the guys, still dressed in all-white costumes, went outside and crossed the bridge to the West End Pub.

EVEN A LONER, at times, needs his tribe around him. These guys were my tribe, and we watched one another's backs. This stuff is important.

At the pub, we pushed several tables together and all sat down, the rushing of the river behind us loud and clear through the windows. Robbie was talking about having to repair the roof on his yurt, which was damaged in last week's storm. Brian asked where one obtained yurt-repair parts. Stanley suggested the Yurt Mart. I said I preferred Yurts-R-Us. We all laughed.

Then the singing started. Some sea chanties at first, then a few tearjerkers about dead dogs and dead babies. I led us all in "Sorrows Away." The harmonies shook the rafters. As Danny began leading us in singing "Ale, Ale, Glorious Ale," two figures entered the room—Mooney and VelCro.

They sat at the table next to ours. Mooney was in his brooding hipster black watch cap and matching black shirt and jeans. VelCro had on her usual diaphanous scarf-as-veil and sunglasses, but otherwise she wore a different costume—a long, flowing, flowered and colorful peasant skirt and matching frilly top. On her feet were hiking boots and blue-and-green-striped knee socks.

Her garb did little to hide her stunning beauty, with wisps of red hair curling out from the edges of her veil. Still, her body carriage and demeanor did not support the image of stylish, upscale starlet. Instead, it helped her fade into the Shelburne Falls goatherd-as-heartbreaker aesthetic. No one would ever discern a Hollywood vixen through those duds and in that tiny, frail, unsure-looking child.

They were both sipping from glasses containing clear, fizzy liquid, with lime on the rim. VelCro had a bowl of nuts in front of her. She'd slowly picked one up, gaze into it as if it revealed the world, and then put it into her mouth.

That's when I saw it: she was the Nutting Girl made flesh. She didn't seem like the type to go throwing her nuts away for some jovial, singing plowboy, but she had the look of someone who could, in an instant, toss everything in the world away and be gone. Just as she had a few weeks before when she disappeared into my theater.

The way Mooney kept her close told me he saw it too. He leaned in toward her when he spoke and touched her on the shoulder. Once, he brushed a wisp of red hair from her eye.

The singing continued. Mooney even gamely joined in on the choruses.

Slowly, the rest of Mooney's people arrived. It was the entourage I had seen him with that first day in town, all ten of them, dressed in mandatory West Coast black. They set up camp by pulling a few tables together beside Mooney and VelCro. Now we had a crowd crunched together like sardines there in the tiny back room of the West End.

There were two contrasting tables squashed together—the Morris guys in whites and the film crew in blacks. A bond of sorts was forming between the "black table" and the "white table," a bond forged by song. I was sure they had never before heard the songs we were singing, but the choruses were easy to pick up.

Michael sang "South Australia," which is better known to the public at large, and they joined in on this too, even getting a little rowdy and demonstrative on the "heave away, haul aways," brandishing beers in the air, spilling more than a few suds.

"Didn't do this stuff in the monastery, did you?" said Stanley.

"Well, actually … yes, we did. Where do you think I learned to sing?"

"Wasn't that like all Gregorian chants or something?"

"No, we sang lots of stuff."

"Songs about ale and pirates?"

"Not so much. We did sing about dead babies though. And dead dogs."

It went on till quite late, the two tables communicating wordlessly. Well, wordlessly unless you count the words in the songs. We never spoke to them and they never spoke to us. Instead we sang. Some things transcend speech. Like music. Like song. That's something I learned in the monastery too.

I never approached Mooney's table—I was having too much fun—and neither he nor VelCro approached me.

Well after midnight, as the party wound down, I was

navigating my way back from the men's room, located inconveniently through the kitchen and down the stairs. At the top of the stairs, away from the rest of the group, stood Mooney like God making sure no riffraff snuck into heaven.

"This is a fun town. We like it here. We're coming back. We're going to shoot the film here."

"Good. Make us look cool."

"We'll do that. You want another job?"

"I'm retired, Mooney."

"You made yourself un-retired before. I need you to do it again."

"What for? The girl's not missing."

"I want her to stay that way. I want you to keep an eye on her when we shoot."

"She must have bodyguards, right?"

He nodded. "Sure, up the wazoo. And assistants, and companions, and aides, and friends, and boyfriends, and girlfriends, and hangers-on, and assorted people who I don't know what-the-hell they do. But she doesn't have anyone like you."

"You mean a washed-up alcoholic, depressed and desperately lonely former detective and monk?"

"Yeah, exactly. A washed-up alcoholic, depressed, desperately lonely former detective and monk who knows every person and place and corner in this burg, who knows if something looks off-kilter, or sees something that shouldn't be there, or feels vibes that just aren't right. And who's already proved to me he knows what he's doing. Someone very much like you." He paused. "I pay very well too."

I didn't ask how much.

"Don't you want to know how much?"

"When I work, I don't really do it for the money. I generally do it as a favor for people I like. If they pay me … great. If not, well, I survive."

"Don't you like me?"

"I hardly know you, Mooney."

"I like to be liked. What can I do to make you like me?"

I remained silent.

"I'm covering your bar tab tonight. I got it. For you and your whole crew. Tell them to drink up."

"That's great, Mooney. Thank you."

"The high school is getting a new scholarship fund to send poor kids to college."

I looked at him quizzically.

"I got it. It's on me. Check with your school board. They'll confirm it. Sent them the check yesterday." He thought for a moment. "Well, actually, they might not confirm it. I did it anonymously. I don't need the glory. Told them to keep my name out of it. But I can show you the canceled check when I get it if you want. If you need proof."

"I don't need proof. I trust people. You're a hell of a guy, Mooney."

"Yeah, I am. Think about a price. Everybody's got a price."

What was my price? I hadn't thought about that for a while. I'd have to cogitate over it.

I made the five-minute walk home up the Hill of Tears, ran Marlowe around in the yard, read some James Joyce, and fell asleep. I told myself I wouldn't think about Mooney's offer, or Mooney's question, until the next day.

I didn't feel like thinking just yet.

Chapter Seven

~∞

Strange and Wonderful Things

THE NEXT DAY, once again, thoughts of the increasingly enchanting Clara began to eclipse thoughts of Mooney and VelCro, and my walks past her house became even more frequent.

I walked by in the morning, and around noon, but at 9 p.m., I lucked out. It was dark, but lights were on both downstairs and up. I turned my head to the right, hoping to see a lovely face appear semi-magically out of a window. Instead, the lovely face—or at least the woman with the lovely face—tapped me on the shoulder.

There she was, Clara, holding a bag of groceries, carrots peeking over the top with their green leaves looking perky and fresh, just like she did.

"Hey," she said.

"Hey," I replied.

"Imagine running into you in this neighborhood."

"I just live up the hill."

"Well, then, it's your 'hood too. That must be why you walk by here twenty times a day."

We stood there. I smiled at her.

"Want some carrots?" she asked.

It would be hard to say no to her, so I said "Sure." In truth, I didn't like carrots.

"There's wine in here too. Wine and carrots?"

Now *that*, I had to say no to. "I'll stick to carrots, if you don't mind."

"How could I mind? More wine for me."

Soon we were seated on a comfy couch as Clara sipped chardonnay and I munched a crooked organic carrot. Penelope sang sweetly in the background. Our bodies weren't touching, but I could feel Clara's warmth and an occasional wisp of softness on my arm.

I didn't know what to say. I'm not great at small talk. I preferred big talk—who are you, why are you here, why am I here, what makes your essence, what moves your soul, what do you see as the true nature of God?

"Mmm, good carrot," I said.

"I'm a nurse," she replied. "Weren't you going to ask?"

"Oh, sure."

"I mean, isn't that usually the first question people ask—what do you do?" She giggled. "We've chatted before, but until now, we've never really tried to get to know each other. So, yeah, before you ask—I'm an emergency-room nurse."

"That's good. I like nurses. But somehow I feel like I already know what you do. You've raised a good kid, you chase birds around."

"What do you do?"

"Nothing. I'm retired."

"You run a movie theater."

"Yeah, I guess. That's mostly fun, a hobby. I don't consider that a job."

"And you chase birds around too." She smiled, revealing a small but endearing gap between her front teeth.

"I like birds."

"Me too."

We had birds in common. And carrots. And I liked her forthrightness, her graceful movements. Nothing self-conscious about her.

"I was there the night you died," she said.

And something else.

I did not reply.

"Yeah. You were dead when they rolled you in. They froze you. And then they stitched you back up."

"And here I am."

"And here you are."

And there we both were.

I took a bite of carrot. We both laughed. Her laughter was open and natural, musical. Like her.

"I was shot. One day on the damn job and I was shot. Nobody gets shot in Shelburne Falls."

"Is that why you retired?"

"That's why I retired as a cop. That's why I retired from pretty much everything. Dying pretty much takes the wind out of your sails. I was a cop for one day. Then I was a detective for twenty-five years."

She leaned forward, giving me a whiff of her clean scent— soap and maybe a scented shampoo. "What kind of detective?"

"A private one. A very private one. I was licensed for a few years. Then I let that lapse. I just couldn't follow rules anymore. Couldn't do much at all anymore. But, finding things? That I always could do. So I kept doing favors for friends. Sometimes they paid me. Sometimes they didn't. Now I'm retired from that too."

I could see her hesitation. Perhaps she didn't know how much to ask. Finally she asked, "What was it like to be dead?"

"Can we talk about birds some more?"

"No." She kept her tone light and playful, waggling an index finger and slowly shaking her head.

"Carrots?"

She inclined her head. "If you want."

"No. I'll talk about being dead." I crunched on the carrot before continuing, "It wasn't like anything. I don't remember anything."

"And how about coming back to life?"

"Nothing. I just woke up a couple days later with my chest sewed up."

"And life since then?"

"Same as life before then. It's life."

She frowned, a bit disappointed, perhaps. "No insights?"

"I'm alive. That's an insight. I could tell you that now I see every day as a gift, but that's too tidy, isn't it?"

"Too tidy for you."

"I always saw every day as a gift. That's not too tidy for me."

Penelope chirped. I took a bite of carrot. Clara sipped her wine.

"It's a miracle that I'm sitting here with you," I said.

"No, Frank, it's science. I'm a medical person. It's pure science that they knew where and how to stitch you up. They knew how to freeze a heart and unfreeze it."

"My heart's been frozen and unfrozen many times."

"Yeah, mine too."

"But yes, I understand about the science," I said. "That's not what I'm talking about, though."

"What *are* you talking about?"

Her hand grazed mine.

"That's what I'm talking about. That's the miracle."

She touched my hand again, stroked my palm and each individual finger. "Yes. There are miracles, Frank. But these things are not miracles."

"What are they?"

"They are strange and wonderful things."

"What's the difference?"

"Miracles are rare. They seldom, almost never, happen. Strange and wonderful things? They happen all the time."

I told her about my other miracle. "I was blind once," I said.

This statement normally shocks people, mildly at least, but not Clara. She just looked at me and said, "Okay, go on."

"I had a degenerative condition. My eyes got worse and worse. Then I went totally blind. I was blind for three years. Then one day I woke up and I could see. Just like that, I could see again."

She was still looking at me, and this time she did not have to tell me to go on.

"The doctors had no explanation. It was a miracle."

"Okay," she said, "maybe it was. I don't discount any possibility in this big, weird world. But as I said, I'm a medical person and I need to hear more scientific details before I can concede that it's a miracle."

"But it was just one eye, Clara. Only one eye regained sight. I'm still blind in the other one. What the hell is up with that? Are there half-miracles? Or are miracles like being pregnant— it's either a miracle or it isn't?"

"I can't answer that," she said. "Miracles seem to be your field, not mine."

"I don't know the answer either," I said.

We continued talking about miracles and strange and wonderful things.

Other miracles occurred that night.

We were sitting very close, and then we touched some more, and then we kissed.

Then, my shirt was off and she ran her finger slowly, gently, across the jagged scar running up my chest.

We lay there on the couch. I was close to another human, a beautiful one.

We made love.

Then it was morning and I left, fairly flying up the Hill of Tears.

Chapter Eight

~ѕ

Yes

REAL LIFE TENDS to crowd miracles away, and the next night I was sitting at the bar of the West End Pub. Mooney, who was there when I arrived, sat next to me.

It was a tiny L-shaped bar, and we were nestled in the corner next to the door they never use. Mooney handed me an inch-thick stack of white sheets of paper, bound together by two brass clasps. On the cover, it read *A SHOUT FROM THE STREETS—an original screenplay by Nicholas Mooney.*

"Read it."

"Okay. But why? I'm not making the film and I'm not a film critic."

"But you know film. I want to hear what you think of it. Anyway, if you accept my offer, it'll help you do your job. We're going to shoot the whole thing in town. You'll be able to spot most of the locations from reading the script. Besides, I'll fill you in on specifics as we line things up. Knowing the locations is important for what I want from you. So you can know what to look for in each one and be prepared."

"I like the title."

"It's from James Joyce."

"Funny. I was just reading Joyce."

"You know *Ulysses?*"

"As well as any duffer can. It takes a lot to really know that book."

"It's essentially Homer's *Odyssey* brought to early twentieth-century Dublin, with Leopold Bloom on a day-long odyssey through the streets and pubs. I've modernized it, set it in Shelburne Falls, and given Bloom a sex change. He's now a twenty-one-year-old woman."

"VelCro?"

"How did you guess?"

"Mooney, I gotta tell you, that sounds like it's gonna suck bad."

"It's good. I'm a good writer."

"I know you are. I love your stuff. But everyone has their limits. I mean … Joyce? Come on."

"Just read it."

As I sipped my club soda and idly stirred it, I was starting to come around. I could see VelCro pulling this off. She was that good. I couldn't picture anyone else doing it, though.

"Okay, if you got Bloom a twenty-one-year-old woman, who's his wife, Molly, and who does her soliloquy? That makes the whole book. How do you work that out?"

"Molly is Molly. Leopold, or Leonora in the film, is a lesbian. She's married to Molly. We have that now in case you haven't heard. Gay marriage?"

"Yeah, I've heard about it. I live in Massachusetts. It still sounds like it'll suck. Who plays Molly?"

"Julie. You, and most people in the world, call her VelCro. I call her Julie. People close to her call her Julie."

I thought to myself, *Maybe someday I'll know her that well*, and then I said, "Wait a minute. She plays both parts?"

"Who else could do justice to that soliloquy?"

"Nobody. But how are you going to do that?"

"They're not in many scenes together," Mooney said, "and

it's an easy effect to do. Remember Nick Cage in *Adaptation*? And did you see *The Social Network*? The Winklevoss twins? Fincher used the head of one actor but he had two different actors' bodies. He scrubbed out one of their faces and digitally superimposed the first guy's head. Filmmakers can work miracles now."

"I prefer to think of them as strange and wonderful things instead of miracles."

"No. We can do miracles."

"You're crazy," I said. "I see miracles everywhere. But not in the movies. Maybe in how people respond to movies. But not in making them."

"Trust me. We'll pull it off." He sipped his club soda before adding, "And I do miracles too. I can do anything."

He made good films. I still wasn't convinced about the miracles.

I was warming to the idea of this film.

"Actually, now you got me looking forward to seeing this thing, as weird as it sounds."

"I know. I can't wait. This is going to be the best thing I've done."

"Molly's soliloquy is like the sexiest thing I've ever heard," I said. "But, more than the sex, I see it as the most optimistic thing I've ever read. She brings Leopold back into her bed, she worries about his health, and she thinks about their first meeting, and she says 'yes' about a million times."

"She says it one hundred twenty-one times. I counted. They're all in that script you're holding."

"You do the whole soliloquy? All twenty-four thousand words of it?"

"Twenty-four thousand, two hundred seventeen words. I counted," Mooney said.

"You are insane. How long is this movie anyway? What is this, a twelve-episode miniseries?"

"No, I'm pulling your leg. We just do the end of it. I guess you don't get irony."

"I get irony just fine, thank you. I just don't know your sense of humor well enough yet to tell when you're being ironic."

Then I cleared my throat, and in my best Irish brogue, recited the last few hundred words of the soliloquy from memory.

"You mean *that* part?" I asked him.

"Yeah, *that* part."

"That's what I thought."

"You're not bad. We'll get you in this film too."

I thought, *There's no way in hell they'll do that*, and then I asked, "And a 'shout from the streets'—what does that mean?"

"Jesus. You mean you don't know? You seem to have the damn book memorized."

"No. Just the good parts."

"It's right in there. Dedalus challenges a student's bullshit argument using God as an excuse for anti-Semitism by saying that God is the shouts from the hockey game going on in the streets below them. God is in the common man. God *is* the common man. God is man. Man is God. God is everywhere. God is a shout from the streets."

"That's the kind of talk that got me thrown out of the monastery, Mooney. That's subversive. But you're smarter than you look. You're winning me over. I like subversive."

"I'm not telling you I believe that crap. I'm just telling you what's in the film. It makes a good story." He laughed. "And we're going to have singing and dancing in there too. That's all in the book. That's what happens in pubs—besides general bullshitting, which is also in the film."

"Singing?"

"Yeah. Like all those traditional Irish and English songs you guys sing. That stuff."

"Dancing?"

"Morris dancing will work."

"That's English, not Irish."

"Well, the story is no longer set in Ireland, remember. And I'll make it work. The word 'Moorish' is in the soliloquy—that's what Morris dancing comes from, right?"

"So some say."

"Your team want to be on the big screen?"

"I'll have to talk to the guys."

"Do that. Seriously."

"Okay, I'll do that."

"Good. I have a good feeling about this project."

"Yeah, a modernized, Americanized, lesbian, musical version of *Ulysses*, all set in Shelburne Falls. With dancing. *Folk* dancing. *Morris* dancing! And people sitting in bars discussing man and God. What could possibly go wrong with that? Sounds like Oscar material to me. Blockbuster stuff! Boffo box office!"

"Irony?"

I nodded.

Mooney replied to my nod, "Well, It's a crazy idea … but it just might work."

"It just might."

The sodas were almost gone. Mooney looked at me.

"Good, I'm glad you're on board. You *are* on board, aren't you? You never really gave me an answer. I'll call you 'security consultant' in the credits. What do you say?"

It was simply too good a setup, and I couldn't resist.

"Yes," I said. "Yes I will. Yes."

Chapter Nine

∿

Mayday ... Mayday ... Mayday

APRIL ENDED WITH the usual springtime monsoons. When they passed, May blossomed in its gentle greens and purples and all was well with the world.

There was hope in the air, and I felt blessed. I had compelling work to do—to watch over a person I felt might need to be watched over—and I had love sprouting in my life for the first time in many moons. Still, I felt some unease. For all Mooney's generosity and interest in me, both professionally and personally, there was something disturbing about him, and I decided to approach everything concerning him with caution. The dude scared me.

The first of May—Mayday—found me awakening well before dawn, donning my Morris whites, ribbons, and bells, meeting the Shelburne Falls Morris Men at the foot of the Hill of Tears for the trek, in full darkness, to its peak. There we would—as we had done each Mayday morning for the past thirty-five years—dance up the sun for no one besides ourselves.

Oh yeah, and for the two women walking dogs who met us there twenty years ago and have made it their own tradition too, now well into their third set of dogs, to make the Mayday climb.

Through the morning haze and wispy clouds, the first spears of sunlight reached heavenward. I stopped to record the *oo-wah-hoo* of a mourning dove as Danny began playing our traditional opening dance.

We did a couple rounds of dances. Satisfied that we had once again caused the earth to brighten, we walked back down the hill and found ourselves in front of McCusker's. After a few more dances, we returned to real life. We had been up since 4 a.m., and although it was still only late morning, it had already been a long day.

Clara and Sarah crossed the street from their home to watch and were joined by a few customers coming out of the store holding newspapers and coffee cups. Sarah, for some inexplicable reason, had fallen quite in love with Morris dancing and had insisted on going to school late just so she could see us.

We ran through some of our standard repertoire and then finished our dancing day with the whole team joining in on a massed "Nutting Girl." "The Nutting Girl" is normally done as a jig; that is, it is done by fewer than the six dancers who would normally be in a standard set—generally by only two. Today we got everyone in it, all twelve dancers, for a grand end to our Mayday. We liked this configuration. It was powerful and beautiful, and we agreed we would perform it this way instead of as a jig, at least for a while.

As we all joined in on the final "and what few nuts that poor girl had she threw them all away," we heard the usual polite applause from the small crowd, and a two-pinkies-in-the-mouth whistle from Sarah. Walking off, I literally stumbled into two figures standing at the foot of the dance set—Mooney and the eponymous Nutting Girl herself, both smiling and clapping.

VelCro was dressed in her usual sunglasses and scarf/veil,

strands of red hair creeping out the bottom and sides. She was wearing her Shelburne Falls Pretty Country-girl Milkmaid costume too. She even wore an amazingly cute floppy straw hat.

Mooney had cleaned up his act since the last time I'd seen him. His scraggly beard was gone, and his hair was shorter— no more ponytail. In this newly shorn springtime look, he seemed scrubbed, shaved, showered, shiny, and ready to go.

He greeted me with the words, "We shoot in two weeks." And then, "I liked that last dance. I want you to do that in the film."

"Won't work," I said. "That one takes all twelve of us, and I'm going to be otherwise employed, remember? You hired me for something important." I looked at VelCro, because she was that important thing I was talking about. She smiled back.

"How long did that dance take?" Mooney asked. "Three minutes, tops? I can spare you for three minutes."

VelCro piped up, "I think I'll survive for three minutes." And then, as if she had just recalled who I was, "Hello there, Mister Theater Man."

I replied, "Hello, Miss VelCro."

"Why don't you call me Julie? My friends call me Julie, and I hope that we'll become friends. That VelCro stuff, that's just for the press and publicity and all that stupid stuff."

"Okay. And you can call me Frank. Hello, Julie."

"Are you a Francis?"

"Yes."

"I think I prefer that. Is that okay?"

"Sure."

"Hello, Francis."

Now we were friends officially, but I think we were friends already.

Then I responded to Mooney. "Nope. You hired me to watch her. I can't watch her when I'm dancing."

"I'll dock you for the three minutes. No need to feel guilt."

"It's not the money. It's not the guilt. It's the job. Do you want me to do my job or not?"

"I want you to dance. That's part of your job now, okay? You're officially hired as a dancer."

Dancer and detective. I allowed as how I'd think it over.

Clara and Sarah came over to join us. Sarah was alternately staring at Julie expectantly and shyly shuffling her feet and gazing down at the sidewalk. I introduced Mooney to them, which generated only a weak handshake from Sarah. When I said, "And this is Julie," Sarah let out a poorly contained gasp and an "Oh, my God! I totally love you," followed by no handshake at all. Sarah had been instantly shuttled into another universe and had no idea how to react.

Julie was pure class. With a smile that stretched across her mostly concealed face, she said, "Thank you, Sarah. I get that sort of thing all the time. Normally I hate it."

Sarah replied, "Normally? You don't hate it now?"

"No. You seem nice."

Sarah smiled back. "I am nice."

Then it dawned on Sarah: there was something weird going on here, even weirder than the world's biggest star standing a block away from her house: that famous person seemed to be on friendly terms with the boring old dude who'd been hanging around with her mother.

"Wait a minute," Sarah finally managed to spit out. "You know Frank?"

"Yes, of course. He's my friend. And he's also a Theater Man. Also, he seems like a duck." She smiled when she said this and I had no idea what she meant.

"A duck? I've always thought of him as more of a parakeet. The day I met him, he helped us find my parakeet."

"Well, the day I met him, I was watching a bunny up on a movie screen, and yet I do not see him as a rabbit."

"Well, he's far more birdlike than hare-like," Sarah replied. "And yeah, I can even see the duck stuff. He's all calm and fluffy and soft on the surface, but underneath, those legs are churning and flailing away and going frickin' crazy. Yeah, he's definitely a duck."

Julie was really smiling now. "Yes!" she said. "That is *exactly* what I mean! I can't believe someone else sees that too."

"I see lots of stuff," Sarah said.

"Me too. Sometimes too much stuff," replied Julie. "It's like a curse."

The girls were clearly bonding here.

"That's probably why you're such a good actor," said Sarah.

"What do you mean?"

"Because that's the kind of stuff you have to draw on, right? To do character, emotion? The people you see, everything in your environment? The whole world. The whole universe. You see the whole universe, everywhere."

"I see the whole universe in everything—people's eyes, the sky, animals, birds, a peanut, a walnut …."

Sarah responded, "You know that William Blake poem? The one where he talks about seeing the world in a grain of sand, seeing heaven in flowers, holding infinity in his hand?"

"Yes!" Juliana said. "Exactly! That's perfect. That's exactly what I see."

"I see it too," said Sarah.

"So, you act?"

"Me? No. Come on."

"You were in that play in seventh grade, honey," chimed in Clara.

Sarah silenced her clueless mom with a glare, the sort of look that passed between them often.

"Well, maybe you should. You kind of get it. Better than almost all the people I talk to. Nobody else quotes Blake to me."

Sarah looked down at the ground, kicked the dirt a bit. "I'm not beautiful like you, though."

"You are too."

"Oh, my God!" Eyes wide, she cast about as if for confirmation. "VelCro, the most beautiful girl in the world, just said *I'm* beautiful!"

Sarah, despite her youth, did appreciate irony. She was being funny and everyone laughed. The girls had connected big time, over Sarah's humor and some shared understanding of the nature of the world.

We all chatted a bit more, and the Morris guys scattered back to their respective houses. Sarah and Julie hugged shyly and soulfully, and I walked Sarah and Clara across the street to their home.

Sarah could not believe what had just occurred. She had a new friend and it just happened to be the most famous girl in America.

She babbled, "She's gorgeous and so talented, and smart too. I never knew she was that smart. They never talk about that side of her. And that girl has done *everything*. She's had sex with Brenden Lassiter," who was, apparently, a current rock star heartthrob.

"Sarah!" Clara scolded.

"I'm sorry, Mom. I just can't believe this. Wait till I tell Stacey. She'll die."

It was then that I left Sarah and Clara—to die, or whatever else they were going to do next. I was tired enough to die myself, having been awake since 4 a.m. and jumping up and down dancing for much of that time. I was ready to trudge up the Hill of Tears.

After giving me a hug, Clara said, "Happy Mayday" and laughed.

I asked why she was laughing.

"I can't make up my mind if I think of Mayday as an ancient Northern Hemisphere spring festival or as an emergency procedure word."

I said, "Say it once, it's celebration. Say it twice, I guess it's still a celebration. But say it three times, it's distress. As a distress signal, it's always said three times to avoid mistaking it for a similar phrase that's less ominous. It's the repetition that makes it dangerous. But in any case," I concluded, "Happy Mayday!"

"Happy Mayday," said Clara, stepping on my line.

Which was followed, a little too quickly, by Sarah also saying, "Happy Mayday."

That made it three times. Three Maydays in quick succession.

I tried to write them off as mere echoes while I put one foot in front of the other and trudged up the hill.

But I couldn't.

Three Maydays. A distress signal had been sounded.

Chapter Ten

〜〜

Our Jewell of the Deerfield

MOONEY CAME TO that week's Morris practice to run through with the guys what he wanted us to do in the film. He brought along his director of photography, Dexter. And he brought along Julie, who seemed to be his constant companion. Safely out of the public's gaze, she took off her veil and sunglasses and stood there open and fresh and unhidden and oh so vulnerable.

We practiced on the stage in my theater. In this private spot, I was able to gaze upon Julie without her disguise. Under her frumpy public costume, she was wearing a loose-fitting blue t-shirt and the baggy sweatpants. But nothing hid that angelic face.

It was one of those moments when you realize that life is not fair and that some people are just from a whole other planet than the rest of us. She had a level of celestial beauty on a different scale from any other beautiful person you see in the real world. But it was another sort of charisma too, difficult to define. It took your breath away.

We did the twelve-man "Nutting Girl" dance over and over and over as Dexter kept framing us in his viewfinder, trying different angles, talking over lighting designs with Mooney. Meanwhile, the guys did their best to not trip over each other while staring at the stunning Julie.

That was the only dance we did that night, and by 8:30, quitting time, Mooney was satisfied with what he had.

As we were about to depart for the pub, Mooney came up to me and stage-whispered in my ear, "Julie doesn't want to get all disguised again. She's comfortable here. Let's stay."

"The guys will be wanting some beer," I told him.

He pulled out three twenties. "Send someone out for a few six packs. Let's hang out here."

So Stanley ran out to Good Spirits, and soon was back with a supply of IPA and chips. We settled in, some guys sitting in the front row and some plopping down on the stage itself.

Danny was playing tunes on his accordion, and the singing began. Mooney joined in wherever he could, Dexter chimed in gamely, and even Julie participated. She opened a beer and sipped from it. This made me nervous. She was of age, sure, but I had the feeling alcohol didn't mix well with her—I had already witnessed her in destructo-mode. I let it go, of course. Things seemed peaceful, the vibes were pleasant, and I wanted to give her a chance.

Everybody loosened up, and the guys were gently flirting with her. She was sharp enough to give it back to them, and the banter flew around the old hall. She was flirting in a harmless way, witty and cute, revealing yet another surprising dimension.

We have bats in the hall. I'm not sure how many. When they fly around during a movie, I tell people they're computer generated. One woke up and darted about, to everyone's delight.

As the beers started to kick in, we were surprised to see Clara and Sarah come in. They were about the only other people in the world who were also welcome here at this time, and we were all glad to see them.

Clara sat next to me in the front row of seats, and Sarah made her way to the stage. She sat cross-legged next to Julie, who welcomed her with a hug. I warily spotted Sarah take some sips from Julie's beer. The singing continued and the two girls gradually drifted off into their own private party, giggling and whispering in some secret world of innocent young womanhood.

Sarah, though very pretty, was not a classic beauty like Julie. She was also tiny, having inherited her mom's physical stature, so the two small redheads seemed a natural pairing, though Sarah's hair was straighter and more straw-colored as opposed to Julie's blazing hellfire curls.

I knew it was leading up to this, and sure enough, after enough beer had been consumed, Michael stood and cleared his throat. Holding his bottle of IPA aloft, he announced, "Ladies and gentlemen, in honor of our special guest this evening, this lovely lass sitting in the corner …."

Sarah stood up and bowed, which got its intended laugh. We all knew she was not the lovely lass Michael spoke of. Julie counteracted by making an exaggerated move to pull Sarah back down and then stood to take her place, bowing and waving, queen-like, to the hooting lads.

The two girls then put on a funny silent slapstick routine of fighting for the spotlight, each one pulling the other down in some different clumsy way and taking her place, bowing, curtsying, even doing a few tap dance steps. They looked for all the world like a practiced, old-time comedy team.

Finally they both stood together holding hands and erupting in uncontrollable laughter, Julie tilting her head and leaning it on Sarah's shoulders, doglike. They were freakin' adorable.

The dangerous femme fatale, the scourge of L.A., had morphed into a sweet, pure child before my eyes.

Michael took the floor again. He was about to sing his favorite song. The choice was inevitable, given its title, which played beautifully on Julie's name: "This is a very old traditional song, written by that guy over there."

He pointed at me. Yes, I wrote this song, a long time ago. The stuff about it being traditional was a joke.

"It's about," Michael went on, "our Julie of the Deerfield."

I wrote it as "Our Jewell of the Deerfield," and I have no idea what I intended it to mean. Like so many things in life, it just was.

It was a slow, sweet ballad about the river flowing through town, and it was simple enough that we continued to make up new verses, often spontaneously as we were singing it. That's the oral tradition at work. The tune wasn't hard to sing, but Michael had the rich, ringing tenor voice to make it sound spectacular.

> Rivers flow and people go
> down by the Deerfield
> Time moves slow
> and there's so much we don't know
> down by the Deerfield
>
> But the spirits rule
> when the air is cool
> and it takes a fool
> in the drowning pool
> to overrule
> Our Jewell of the Deerfield

By now everyone had joined in. The voices and harmonies were shaking the walls. The bat circled ominously, perhaps frightened by the volume.

To my surprise, as it felt like we were getting near the end, Sarah stood up and belted out a verse, clearly one she was making up spontaneously, in what was a surprisingly lovely, clear voice:

> Our Jewell swept in

on the springtime wind
and we knew she couldn't stay

Then, not to be outdone, Julie stood, and in an angelic voice—why had this girl never been cast in a musical?—completed that same thought, in rhyme, almost as if the girls had composed this in advance, which of course they had not:

She may have sinned
and her prospects dimmed
the day they swept away
that Jewell of the Deerfield

Then she added a heartbreaking and mysterious coda:

The bodies merge
with the river surge
Will there be a dirge
for Julie of the Deerfield?

It ended with an abrupt, sudden, and eerily complete silence. In the hall's still air, the bat was nowhere to be seen.

It was a strange verse to be making up on the spot. Was she afraid of being swept away by our river?

The mood was less jovial now. The odd verses from the girls resulted in a curious pause. The energy soon faded, and the guys began to file out into the late, dark, moist spring night.

All the Morris guys were gone. Dexter said his goodbyes too. Mooney, Sarah, Clara, Julie, and I remained. I started locking up and turning out the lights.

The theater was totally dark now, and the only source of light was the streetlamps shining in through the lobby window.

"Those last verses got a little weird," Julie said, "but it all makes me want to go see the Deerfield. Let's walk and talk."

So we did, all of us. It was a good suggestion.

Chapter Eleven

~

Not a Bad Deal

W^E WALKED AND we talked, and it was good talk, but it
ended suddenly, as if some greater force stood in our
way.

It was gloomy for a spring night, still cool, but summer's
warm promise was there too. The warmth and coolness met
up to create fog and mist so thick it was hard to see. There were
peepers chirping off in a distant swamp, providing us with a
rhythmic accompaniment. I recorded it. It was close enough
to birdsong.

The five of us headed down Bridge Street. Hardly anyone
else was around. Shelburne Falls shuts down early, even on the
most pleasant of evenings.

Mooney and Clara strolled ahead, turning off toward the
falls, and behind them the two girls walked on either side
of me. Then I did hear the birds—drawn out *seeps* and *chips*
from sparrows. They serenaded us until the roar of the river
overcame the birds and the peepers. As we got closer, droplets
of water from the falls began to splatter our faces like tears,
dampening the soggy night even further.

"I believe I'm going to like working here," Julie said to me as we walked by the yoga studio. Then she added, "What do you believe?"

She was probing me. She wanted to know more details about this guy who had been assigned to essentially not leave her side for a month. I figured I'd play along and go where she was leading me.

"I believe in a lot," I answered, "but not what they wanted me to believe."

"Who are 'they'?"

"You know—they. *They*—the ones who tell you what to believe."

"You mean like when you were a monk?

"Yeah. That's part of the 'they.' "

"Do you believe in God?" she asked.

"I believe there's something in all of us. And in everything—animate and inanimate. Is it God? I don't know."

"Something in all of us? That doesn't sound too radical to me."

"Well, it is when you think that maybe that *is* God. And that's all God is. That's kind of where I was at."

"Okay, now I get why you're not a priest anymore," Julie said.

"No, I was never a priest. I was a monk. There's a difference."

"And what is that?" Julie was staring at me with those green eyes in the black night.

"A priest is ordained. He can say mass, give sacraments. A monk is someone who dedicates his life to God by withdrawing from the world into a separate community."

"Okay. That's not a good job for someone who doesn't believe in God, is it?"

"I didn't say I don't believe in God, did I? I'm still sorting it out."

"Doesn't sound to me like you've sorted much out."

"Yeah, but I'm working on it all the time. They don't like people who work it out. They like people who know. And mostly people who know what they're told."

"Who do you mean by 'they'?"

" 'They.' The people who make the rules. The people who run monasteries. The people who tell you what you're supposed to believe."

"So 'they' sounds like pretty much everybody."

"Pretty much. Yeah."

"Have you worked out anything at all? Sounds to me like you haven't."

"I've worked out that the world is perfect. And that we're all basically the same soul. And that God works through us all. All the time. And if you're forced to pin it down, if they held a gun to your head or something, it would all boil down to the idea that God is love."

"Do you pray? How do you pray to God if God is love?"

"I pray. All the time. If indeed you accept what I do as prayer—many don't. Although that's not really necessary. No one has to pray all the time. You just have to pray till it works. Then you can stop."

"You didn't answer my question. How do you pray to God if God is love?"

"Well, that was the big problem with me there. They believed in what they call 'intercessory' prayer. That means accepting that the one who prays, in this case the monk, or in other cases the priest, acts on behalf of the person he is praying for. He pleads their case, if you will."

I was silent for a moment, wondering why Sarah didn't offer her perspective, but she was just watching the two of us curiously as if we were performing a skit and unaware of her presence. In a way, it was true. I was a little embarrassed to have excluded her—not that she seemed to mind. I wiped the spray from my face and picked up the thread.

"Me, I believed that all people are God. No need for anyone to act as intercessor. All each of us has to do is be aware of the presence of God in himself. The rest takes care of itself.

"So, I didn't pray the way they wanted me to pray. To me,

prayer is simply recognizing the presence of God. In any situation. Anywhere. Everywhere. And that's it."

Julie gave me a sidelong look, eyes narrowed. "Well, you're talking like you believe there is a God."

I shrugged. "You know what they say? 'Act as if ye have faith and faith will be given to you.' "

"That's from Mark, isn't it? Or is it Paul?"

"It's from Paul—Paul Newman. *The Verdict.* They use it like it's really from the Bible, but it's not. They wrote it for the film. Written by David Mamet, believe it or not. I like it. I act as if I have faith."

She nodded. "Good idea."

"Yes. When in doubt, be positive."

"Well, whatever," Julie said. "You pray. In your own way. Good for you. I don't. I don't know how to."

"Yes you do. I've seen you."

"You've seen me pray?"

"In your own way. I saw you dance. Same thing."

"I dance sexy. And I completely lose myself. Time doesn't exist. I just get caught up in the rhythm, the movement. I'm lost. How is that prayer?"

"When you dance—are you lost? Or are you found?"

She laughed at this. Yeah, it was funny, but I meant it sincerely.

Her next words kind of startled me. "I'm still going to hell though."

"What are you talking about?"

"You know. Everything I've done."

"What hell? Is there a hell? You're not going anywhere bad. You got too much love in you."

"I'm going somewhere. I can feel it. And I'm just along for the ride."

"So are we all. Some consider it being passive. Me, I consider it adaptation. We go with the flow. And we adapt to it. The important thing is to enjoy the ride."

Then I asked her, "You know everything can be undone, don't you?"

"You mean like all that born-again crap?"

"Well, only in the loosest possible sense. Sure, Julie, we all have to be born again. But it's got nothing to do with the way they usually use that term. We all have to change our souls. That's what 'born again' means. It's got nothing to do with accepting Jesus. It's got everything to do with accepting love. That's when you're born again. That's when the bad stuff gets undone."

"Forgiven … or undone?"

"Undone. Stuff gets undone retroactively. A bad action, a bad reaction, an illness, a sin. Enough love makes it disappear. I've seen it over and over and over. I hurt you, I lie to you, whatever. Then I give enough love—to you, to the universe in general—and it all vanishes. All is well again."

"Jesus," she replied, "I think that actually makes sense. Not sure why, exactly, but it rings true. Okay. Now I'm getting a better sense of what you believe."

"Well, then you're a few steps ahead of me. I don't know what the hell I believe anymore. I don't believe in suffering though."

"Jeez, I'm surprised to hear you say that. You seem like a guy who suffers constantly."

I was taken aback. It took me a few seconds to answer. "I'm sorry it looks that way to you. I don't believe in suffering. If I did, I'd be a Buddhist. They believe all life is suffering."

"Yeah, but don't they also believe that there is a way out of that suffering? By seeing things as they are? By accepting reality? They call it *dhamma*."

"Yeah, they do. And that's always been the problem for me— Christians believe in miracles. Miracles are the way out of that suffering. Buddhists believe in reality, dhamma. Dhamma is the way out of all that suffering. I like both beliefs, but I've never been able to reconcile them."

"How about this? You believe in reality. Things are real. Then a miracle happens. So then the miracle becomes real. So you got both. No problem."

I looked at her and we both laughed. This girl was smart. And she actually thought about things. Important things. I liked that.

I said to her, "These days I don't know what I believe."

"But once you were sure enough that you withdrew from the outside world for it, into a monastery."

"Yeah."

"Well, seems to me you've done that again. Not the monastery this time, but here—your damn Hill of Tears, your little house, your dog, your theater. Here." She made a slow turn, encompassing everything with her arms. "That's where you withdrew to this time."

I didn't answer. I couldn't.

"Yeah. I know," Julie said, "that's why we chose you."

We all silently looked at the water roar over the falls. We had been standing apart from Mooney and Clara, so I wasn't sure how much they'd overheard. Then Mooney said, "Did they toss you out of the monastery, or did you leave on your own? That was never clear. Nobody would talk about that. Nobody."

I replied without hesitation, "They tossed me. I was willing to stick it out. I'm not a quitter."

"They tossed you because they didn't like what you believed in?"

"That's about it."

He wasn't letting up with his intense interrogation. Eyebrows raised in skepticism, he said, "I would have bet they tossed you for drinking."

"No. I didn't drink while I was there. I drank before I went in and I started again when I got out, but in that respect, anyway, I was good there. It was a Catholic Franciscan order. I went in there when I was twenty and it took them two years to ask me to leave."

"What did you guys do in there?" asked Sarah. So she had some interest in this too.

"We meditated and we prayed—two things I don't do anymore, at least not the way I did then. And we raised German Shepherds, and we sang—two things I still do. Oh, yeah, it was pretty medieval in there, so we Morris danced. I still do that too."

"I thought Morris dancing was pagan. You guys were Christian," said Sarah.

"Morris dancing might be pagan and it might not be. It might be Christian too. Nobody knows. It's all lost in the mists of time. What we do know is that it's a ritual and they were big on ritual there. It's musical, and they were big on that too. And it relates to the natural patterns and movements of the earth; they liked that stuff too. I totally got that part of the monastery. If that's all we did there, they would never have tossed me. It's the other parts that I didn't get."

I thought on this a bit further. "Well, actually, I think I did get those parts too. It was *they* who didn't get it." I thought a minute, then with a laugh added, "At least I got a dog. They let me take a dog."

"That can't be Marlowe," said Sarah, "He'd have to be like thirty years old now."

"No, that one was Marlowe's great-great-great-great grandmother. That's four greats."

"That's funny," Sarah said. "We've been talking about God and now we're talking about a dog. And dog is God spelled backwards. Both concepts are extremely spiritual, right, Frank? In fact, I don't see much difference between the two."

"Well," I said, "there is one big difference."

And they looked quizzically at me before I went on to say, "The difference is that the dog comes when you call him."

After a few breaths, Julie asked, "And that's why you're here in this town instead of in a monastery, right?"

I did not even have to answer. We walked on.

"So all you got from two years in there was a dog, Morris dancing, a bunch of songs, a head full of doubts, and an urge to drink?" she went on.

This time I was going to answer, but before I could, as her face was stained by droplets of water from the falls, she concluded, "You know, Mister Movie Man, Mister Duck, that's not a bad deal."

"Not a bad deal?" I asked her. "And please don't call me Mister anything, especially not Mister Movie Man. You can call this guy that." I pointed to Mooney, who smiled at the title.

"Call me Frank. Or Frankie. Only my mother and you girls can call me Frankie. Or Francis. Francis works too. I've got a lot of names."

"Okay. No, it's a pretty good deal. Look at me, Frankie, I know a bunch of songs and I've got a head full of doubts and an urge to drink like crazy. But I don't have a dog and I don't Morris dance. So you're two up on me."

I smiled and shook my head. "Well, that's one way of looking at it."

"You're starting to make some sense to me now," she said. And then she gave me that devastating smile. "Everything is perfect and all will be well. You got a good deal."

"Yeah," I said, "but you're rich and famous and beautiful."

"Like I said, you're two up on me."

I thought about it for a second.

"Yeah, you're right. It's not a bad deal at all."

Chapter Twelve

∾

Sarah's Watch

THAT'S WHERE THE talking stopped.

It gleamed. Somehow, through the fog and mist, an object caught a sliver of light when a wedge of moon faded in through the gloom and it gleamed. My one working eye caught the spark and I ran toward it.

It was attached to the hand of a young man as tall and skinny as the still budding maple tree hovering over his head. The gleam was shiny and metallic and I heard it click. Once, then twice, then a whole series of clicks.

My first thought was: gun. This guy is shooting at Julie.

The kid saw me coming and ran. He pivoted and headed toward the stairs leading down to the potholes, where he leapfrogged over the gate and down the rocky cement stairs to the swirling waters below.

I followed. I couldn't vault over the gate as gracefully as the kid but I managed to crawl over it. He was not far ahead of me as I landed.

With the heavy rains recently, the waters were high and swift. Only a few rock ledges rose far enough above the river to be visible. The kid jumped from one rock to another. He was athletic, like a basketball player, and he was making progress downstream away from me, leaping like a leggy young deer.

I made the first leap from rock to rock, but barely, and my foot slipped and my whole left leg got soaked. I stumbled in the next attempt and fell completely into a swirling pool. It took nearly a minute to pull myself out. I was drenched.

Meanwhile, the kid was progressing farther down the river where the water became shallower. The rocks were more plentiful, and his path away from us easier. He was getting away. He was in his early twenties and I was in my fifties, and it was not a fair race, but—*dammit*—he wasn't going to get away if I had any say in the matter.

I pursued him gamely. Then he slipped and fell into the river, getting soaked head to toe. So things evened up a bit and I was getting closer, but he still had an advantage over me.

I was standing there trying to decide if I could make the jump from the rock I was on to the next one when another figure dashed past, leapt effortlessly from my rock to the next, and continued after the kid. It was Sarah.

The kid slipped again on a mossy rock. Sarah was on him in the water, pinning him against the rock, her arms locked around his in what looked like a practiced wrestling hold. He couldn't budge. The kid was a foot taller than she was and probably a hundred pounds heavier. Still, she had him pinned. Floating in the water like that kind of neutralized physical strengths.

By the time I caught up with them, she had him up on the rock, high and dripping. She was in total control.

Around his neck, on a strap, was a camera with a long lens. Sarah had his arms pinned, so I slipped the camera off his shoulders and scrolled through the shots. The outer parts of the camera had gotten wet and the lens was probably broken forever, but the innards still worked. He had dozens of pictures of Julie from the past several days, none of them clear. She was always covered up with scarves and veils, or distant or with a barrier in the way and not recognizable.

The three of us stood on that rock in the fog with the peepers peeping and the sparrows seeping. He squirmed. "Jesus Christ, girl. Let me go. I'm not hurting anybody."

"That could have been a gun. I thought it was a gun," Sarah said to him.

"It's not a gun. Who do you think I am anyway? It's a freakin' camera."

I tossed the camera into the river, where it immediately disappeared.

"Not anymore," I said.

"Oh, fuck, man," he said. "That's worth a lot of money."

"The pictures were crap."

"I've sold worse."

"Well, you won't sell those."

"I have more cameras, and more pictures. And I'm just the first. They'll be hundreds of guys like me here soon."

The kid was right. We all knew that. Sarah let go of her grip.

He looked at her and held out his hand to shake hers. "I'm Lorenzo," he said.

"I'm Sarah."

"For a while, I thought you were her and I was real excited, you being all uncovered and all. I thought I'd get some great stuff."

The three of us made our way downstream, and up the stairs to the deck. Julie was standing in the shadows away from us, lying low. Mooney walked up to us.

"Who do you work for, kid?" he asked.

"Nobody. I'm freelance."

"How did you find us?"

"I have my ways."

"You're the first. You're good."

"Yeah, I am."

"Still … you let a teenage girl catch you."

"Yeah. I didn't expect that." He turned to Sarah. "You're one fierce girl."

"Don't you forget it either," she replied. "Nobody fucks with my friend."

"Don't swear," I told her.

"Sorry."

By now, Julie had wandered up to us. She took off her scarf, her red hair pixilated in the fog, merging with the haze. She smiled at him, that deadly smile.

"You want some good shots, Mister Photo Man?"

"Oh, yeah. That's why I'm here."

She started unbuttoning her peasant blouse. She was halfway down and it became clear she was not wearing a bra. She paused and began to pose for him, bending, showing cleavage, smiling seductively, swirling that gorgeous hair around.

"Oh, man," the kid moaned. "Let me get a camera."

He stepped back into the shadows, where he had set a small case down earlier, and came back up with a smaller, cheaper digital camera.

Julie vamped for him and he snapped away. The kid was drooling.

It was the return of Bad VelCro. She was the girl with the curl—very, very good or very, very horrid. No in between. And she could apparently switch from good to horrid in an instant.

"You got enough?" she finally asked him.

"I could never get enough of you. But yeah, thanks. This is fucking amazing!"

Mooney glared at Julie and she looked back at him and said, "The cat's out of the bag anyway. It's just a matter of time. Might as well have some fun. Nothing the world hasn't seen before."

Sarah grabbed the camera out of the kid's hands and threw it over the fence and into the river. A ninety-five mile-per-hour fastball. Right on target.

"No. Not on my watch. And you, Julie, you shouldn't do shit

like that. It gives these guys the wrong idea. No more fucking pictures like that, okay?"

I forgot to tell her not to swear.

Julie bowed her head almost reverently and looked at the ground. Then she looked up into Sarah's eyes, into mine, and then back into Sarah's. And she said, quietly, under her breath, "I'm sorry."

Chapter Thirteen

∽

Staying on the Path

LORENZO PICKED UP his bag with the rest of his equipment and left, muttering to himself.

"You guys make a good team," Mooney said to Sarah and me.

"I've never worked in teams," I replied. "I'm a loner, or haven't you noticed?"

"Yeah, I noticed. I also noticed her run past you like you weren't there. And I noticed her ditch those pictures that could have screwed us royally. Jesus Christ, it's hard to insure a movie with this girl in it. Shit like that won't help. She's got a rep and she's gotta tone it down. Christ! That's the stuff that gets her in deep shit. And now it spreads to me and I can't have that."

He turned to Sarah. "Good work."

Sarah was very pleased with herself.

"I guess I'm losing it," I said. "I've never needed help like that before."

"Yeah," Sarah was smiling, "but I'm eighteen and you're like eighty. Of course you're going to need help."

"I'm fifty-five," I said, "but I get your point."

We left the falls, crossed the street, and started toward the

Bridge of Flowers. It was lush and ripe, and the air was filled with resin and sweet smells. It seemed we could not escape that roaring, tear-filled river, which bubbled under our feet with waves approaching the bridge itself.

I couldn't help but notice the signs saying PLEASE STAY ON THE PATH. I was going to point them out to Julie, which would have been useless, since she seldom, if ever, stayed on any path for long. She was deep into her own head, walking slowly by herself, brooding but still pausing frequently to look at and smell the flowers. Sarah was walking alongside me.

"I didn't know you had that in you," I told her.

"Yeah, I ran cross-country for three years. I'm stronger than I look."

She picked a just blooming tiny purple flower, which the sign identified as an Osteospermum, off its branch. You're not supposed to do that—pick the flowers—but I let it slide. I was kind of turning into a pain in the ass. She stuck it into her hair, which was pulled back into a ponytail, where it somehow beamed at me.

She continued, "It gets me sad though. I know she won't be here forever. Once she's back in Hollywood with all that glamour and excitement, I'll never hear from her. She's a very special person, and everybody wants something from her."

"Maybe you're special too. Ever think of that?"

"Maybe I am. I guess I am. But come on, she's from another world."

"Just be her friend while she's here, and let the future take care of itself. Live in the present."

"I do that. At least I try."

Sarah and I slowed our pace. The others were gaining on us. Then Sarah stopped.

"I want to help you take care of her," she said.

"I'm not really supposed to do much except watch. She's got behemoth, monster guys for the actual physical bodyguard stuff. You know, all I need to do is stay alert, look for things out of the ordinary, sense danger. A lot of that will be just eyes and ears and intuition. Like just then, when I saw that glimmer."

"I'm real good at that stuff. I've lived here all my life and I know where everything is and how everything should be, just like you. I'm fast and strong, as I've just demonstrated. And I've got intuition like crazy."

"I'm sure you do. Okay, you're hired. I'm sure Mooney will go along."

"She's very vulnerable, Frankie. She scares me."

I knew what she was talking about. "What are you feeling, exactly?"

"I don't know. Something."

"Okay. Let's work together. We'll both keep our eyes and ears open. And our intuitions."

Sarah picked a burnt orange Asiatic Lily and stuck it next to the Osteospermum. "I've never seen the river higher," she said.

"I love the high river!" Julie had come out of her trance and joined Sarah and me.

"I love the way it roars and the high waves with their white peaks and all the power. When you're as small as me and you feel like you could fall into nothingness, you react to that kind of force."

"How could you ever 'fall into nothingness'?" asked Sarah. "You're like the most important person ever."

"No, I'm not. I'm nothing. I'm the nothing girl."

I was staggered. The Nothing Girl. The Nutting Girl. It became even more clear now why I called her that in my mind. We both saw the possibility of her being gone, becoming nothing.

Julie went on, "I'm not important. Except in the sense that we all are. You know?"

"You're way smarter than everybody makes you out to be. And way nicer too," replied Sarah.

"And you're way smarter and nicer than me. So what does that make you?"

"You're gorgeous."

"You are too."

We were in the middle of the bridge. In the hazy night, the flowers faded into the background and into the faces of these two young women.

Sarah said "I love you, Julie."

Julie replied, "I love you too, Sarah."

I saw no reason to speak. I was honored to be present at this moment.

Chapter Fourteen

~∽

All Will Be Well

WHEN CECIL B. DeMille was shooting his epic *The Ten Commandments* he would shout "Cue the hordes" before filming those immense crowd scenes, or so legend has it.

Someone must have shouted "Cue the hordes" in Shelburne Falls, because the hordes descended with a vengeance.

The film crew invaded town with vans, trucks, bigger trucks, more trucks, coils, enough space-age equipment to land a person on the moon, grips, gaffers, best boys, carpenters, set decorators, producers, cameras, cameramen, assistant cameramen, assistant-assistant cameramen, location managers, cranes, props, costumes, makeup artists, publicists, assistant directors, art directors, music directors, director's assistants, craft service people, wranglers, agents, walkie-talkies, boom mics, boom men and women, sound engineers, sound recordists, editors, actors, extras, and assorted hangers on.

They re-did the town. They took down road signs and replaced them with road signs that said the same things but looked better. They changed storefronts. They parked different cars on the streets. They poured gravel where there was pavement and they paved where there was gravel. They re-planted plants and re-painted walls and re-re-did it all over again just for the hell of it.

Then the paparazzi arrived, with high-powered cameras with big lenses and video and microphones and furtive glances and slick hair. Thousands of them, it seemed, swarming our narrow streets and leaning out upstairs windows, cruising the village, searching for VelCro's green eyes, ready to pounce.

I saw the headlines:

> WHERE IS VELCRO?
> VELCRO ABDUCTED!
> TOO STRUNG OUT TO SHOW HER FACE?
> BRENDEN & VELCRO SECRETLY MARRIED IN NEW ENGLAND HAMLET!

The official title of the movie was now *Untitled Nicholas Mooney Project.* That's a common practice when making a film whose ultimate title they want to keep secret. Since I was one of the few non-crew members to have read the script, I knew its real title and its story.

The rains came, biblical in proportion.

For seven straight days, it poured. The river, already high from late northern snowmelt, rose, threatening the natural and man-made banks and the Bridge of Flowers and the Iron Bridge. The falls were magnificent and horrifying. On Thursday, the river overflowed onto Conway Street, washing a small ranch house off its foundation and floating it down the street like an ark—until it was halted by a tree, the impact splitting it in half.

Basements and first floors were flooded. Power was lost for two days, longer in some places. Doors, lumber, couches, tires, and TV sets washed onto the streets, and when the water finally receded, there they remained.

The paparazzi roamed the barren but wet streets searching for the elusive VelCro.

She was safe and hidden at Clara and Sarah's house. Julie was sleeping in the bedroom of Clara's nineteen-year-old son Matthew, who was attending Oberlin College. She had gathered blankets up to her neck on these warm spring days. She ate next to nothing and talked to no one but Sarah, her ally and confidant.

As shooting approached, she grew distant and weary and moody. Mooney wanted her to participate in rehearsals, but she said she couldn't.

Doc Fitzgerald could find nothing wrong and prescribed rest.

Mooney flew in her personal physician from the coast, a woman whose sole purpose in life was to declare VelCro healthy for insurance purposes. She diagnosed "exhaustion" and agreed with Doc Fitzgerald's prescription.

Aside from Julie's being harmed by nefarious strangers, this was Mooney's worst nightmare—VelCro's reputation confirmed. Though there were no signs of alcohol or drug abuse, there would now be delays, difficulties, and perhaps even problems that could bring a premature end to *A Shout from the Streets,* aka *Untitled Nicholas Mooney Project.*

Of course, the problems went much deeper. Mooney felt genuine affection for his young star, as we all did. We were concerned for her health, and even for her life, for she looked pale, weak, and at times near death.

The West Coast doc wanted to send her to a hospital, not the closest one in Greenfield, but to her usual one in L.A. Julie would have none of it. She insisted on staying in Shelburne Falls, in Matthew's bed, in Clara and Sarah's house.

Sarah never left Julie's side. She nursed her, held wet cloths to her forehead, read to her, and coaxed her to eat home-made chicken soup.

Julie's illness was not in itself creating shooting delays. They could not have filmed in the deluge in any case; a power outage meant they couldn't even shoot interiors not involving Julie. Though Julie was in virtually every scene.

So we waited. And we waited. It rained and it rained.

Then it stopped, the rain and the sickness both.

Like a faucet being turned off—it was that quick. The sun reappeared; the waters receded. The fever broke. And Julie lifted her head.

"Wow," was her first word.

Sarah hugged her friend.

Soon Julie was up and about, eating and talking, though mostly in secret to Sarah. She had lost weight and looked even paler and more fragile than before.

She would not leave Clara and Sarah's house. Mooney brought in other actors for minor rehearsals. There were no other stars of note in this film; it was all riding on Julie's bird-like shoulders. Mooney was not the sort of director who believed in a lot of rehearsing anyway.

The press continued to wander the now-dry streets in desperate search of a glimpse of VelCro. Their frustration was palpable, and more rumors sprouted. Some said she had died, and a lot of internet bandwidth was devoted to this possibility.

Mooney was quoted everywhere assuring the world that shooting would begin soon and VelCro was not dead.

A date was set for the first day of principal photography— the following Monday. The film crew renewed their re-making of the town. The magic and unfathomable resources of a Hollywood production put the damaged town back together. Carpenters, environmental rescue companies, and throngs of cleaner-uppers appeared almost magically and worked around the clock. By Sunday night, Shelburne Falls had never looked better.

Mooney paid us a visit. He was traveling around in a stealth vehicle—a beater of an old Subaru with a driver in jeans and gray work shirt—and came around the back entrance to the house. Mooney could easily walk here from the big rented estate on Maple Street where he was staying, but he was avoiding being seen on the streets too.

Julie was looking pretty good. Mooney gave her a kiss on the cheek.

"How you doing, babe?"

"I'm good. Ready to go."

"Okay. That's great. We really only lost a few days and we can make those up quickly if all goes well, which it will, right?"

There was slight admonition in his voice, but only slight.

"You know me. All will be well. That's what I'm all about."

Mooney gave her a call sheet, and he passed one along to me too.

"And now that you're up and about, we can move you into that big house we got for you next to mine," he told her.

"No, I like it here. I'm staying."

"Come on. We got you the most spectacular house in town. With a private caterer. And a full staff. It's gorgeous and it's private and I'm right next door. You'll love it there."

"I love it here."

He could see she wasn't going to budge.

"Okay. Fine. Suit yourself. We can make this work too."

He turned to me. "The first shot of this whole damn picture will be you Morris guys doing your dance in front of McCusker's. We'll get to Julie's stuff in the afternoon. Let's start her off slow."

"Nicky, I'm up for anything," she said. "I can go anytime."

"Let's get these Morris guys first, and then be done with them and they can go drink beer and sing songs or whatever the hell they want to do. Then we'll do that scene in the West End since we'll be right there. Won't have to move far at all."

"Cool. Totally cool."

Mooney asked me, "You guys all set?"

"We're psyched."

"Okay. See you bright and early."

With that, and another hug and kiss for Julie, Mooney and his driver left.

Julie said, "I'm going to be there to watch you guys shoot your scene."

"I wouldn't do that," I told her. "That's the only time in this whole film I won't be able to watch you. Stay here. Only come out when you need to work."

"I want to see the Morris dancing. I'll be fine. I'll have bodyguards up the ying-yang."

"And I'll be there too," said Sarah.

I didn't feel good about this, but I didn't want to stifle her either, especially after all she'd been through.

"Well, okay," I said. "Sarah, I'm counting on you."

"I'm all over this, Frankie."

The girls smiled.

It was late. I needed my rest. We had a 7 a.m. call. I wasn't going to leave Julie's side until this film was over, so there would be no trekking up the Hill of Tears for me for a while. I had put Marlowe in the kennel for the duration, and I would sleep at Clara's.

I was heading upstairs and about to say my goodnights when Julie stopped me.

"Francis …" she began. "You said I could call you Francis, right?"

I nodded, and she went on, "When all this is over, I need to talk to you some more."

"We can talk now."

"No. I've been through enough of these to know—you have to concentrate on the film to make a good one. This is all I'm going to be thinking about for the next month or so. But still, we need to talk, okay?"

"Well, yeah. Sure. But can you give me a clue?"

"No clues. That wouldn't be concentrating on this movie."

"Okay. But I'm all ears when you're ready."

I took the first step up the stairs.

"Francis?"

I paused.

"I saw a lot of things when I was sick."

I wanted her to talk. "Tell me about them."

She shook her head.

"Not now. Another day, in another town. Get some sleep and dance well tomorrow. All will be well. Will you remember that?"

She walked away into Matthew's room.

I would remember what she told me, but I would not sleep that night. Not a damn wink.

Chapter Fifteen

∾

Break a Leg

MONDAY DAWNED BRIGHT and crisp, a perfect New England spring morning. I was not the only one who had not slept, or at least not slept well. The excitement of the first day of shooting had cranked up the whole household. Clara made waffles for us. I sipped coffee. Julie studied her script at the breakfast table and ran lines with Sarah.

Julie and I were not the only people with dual roles in the making of *Untitled Nicholas Mooney Project.* Sarah was now detective and stand-in. Mooney had agreed to my hiring her as my assistant in guarding Julie, and he had also latched onto her as the perfect stand-in for his star.

Movies employ people the approximate size and coloring as their major performers to stand on the set, in the identical costume as the real actor, while the camera and lighting departments spend interminable hours setting up shots and tweaking the lighting, thus saving the *real* actors for the *real* work.

While Julie had a much more perfect, in fact an almost impossibly perfect, look, she and Sarah both had red hair, pale skin, and were pretty much the same size.

So, on this fresh morning, the girls were dressed identically in the costume that Julie would wear for her first scene—a rather outrageously short, tight purple skirt with a mismatched orange silk blouse, leggings with horizontal black stripes, red high-top Converse All Stars, and an orange bandana matching the blouse. It was not clear what look Mooney and the costumer who had arrived at dawn to dress the girls were going for, but they did look striking. They were not yet "made up." The make-up person would arrive closer to the actual shooting of Julie's scene.

How could two young ladies, the same size, the same coloring, dressed identically, look so similar from a distance, but so different up close? At this morning's breakfast table, Sarah looked like a teenage student from Shelburne Falls, while Julie looked like a drop-dead gorgeous movie star.

Safely sheltered inside Clara's home, eating our waffle breakfast, we were oblivious to what was going on just outside our doors. Clara's house was on the side street heading up the Hill of Tears from McCusker's, and the streets directly in front of McCusker's were where we would be dancing for the first shots. We could have spit out the window and hit the hundreds of people who had gathered there—the film crew, the paparazzi, and locals just hanging out to observe the filming.

That is exactly what I saw when I peeled back the curtain and took a glance. The police had blocked off the streets. Yellow tape and orange cones corralled the roads, and high-tech equipment and its operators were everywhere. There was even a sixty-foot crane on a large flatbed truck parked in front of the church. And hundreds of hungry people. Hungry for what, I did not know.

Frick and Frack arrived. They were two behemoth linebackers from UMass, one black, one white, weighing in at six hundred pounds between them, dressed casually in polo shirts and shorts. These guys were Julie's bodyguards—pure muscle, little brain—and they did call themselves Frick and Frack. It wasn't until much later that I could determine which was which.

Jenna was with them—VelCro's "assistant," whose job was to be her filter, to deflect attention from her, to relay questions and instructions to her. She was one of the few deemed important enough to talk directly to VelCro, other than a few very important luminaries. The rule was you had to go through Jenna. Mooney, Sarah, and I had been granted special dispensation.

When Clara and I exited to the streets, I was "kitted up" in my Morris whites, bells strapped to my legs, bedecked with red and silver ribbons and sporting the team's trademark bow tie. The throngs gave us a cursory glance, saw we were nobodies, and went looking for bigger game.

The girls and Jenna and Frick and Frack snuck out the back door. They cut through neighbors' yards, entered a waiting Cadillac limo, and drove around aimlessly before emerging in front of McCusker's. All to keep their starting point a secret. They could have walked to McCusker's in ten seconds, but the trip took ten minutes.

Sarah exited the limo first amid much gasping, photo clicking, and buzzing. The crowd surged toward her but was halted by the police. It took a few minutes before the peons realized she was not the impossible-to-find VelCro.

Then the real VelCro emerged from the car, preceded by Frick and followed by Frack, or vice versa, and the buzzing and surging began again, this time doubled in volume and intensity. Jenna emerged too with no discernible effect on the onlookers.

"We love you, VelCro!" shouted a female voice. Some poor male admirer tossed a bouquet of roses. Julie waved politely and ignored the flowers.

The Morris guys were in front of McCusker's, Danny playfully cranking out tunes on his accordion. I joined them. Soon VelCro and Sarah and Frick and Frack and Jenna were at our sides. Mooney seemed lost in the multitudes. He was wearing one of those cool black Greek fisherman's hats. With his youthful face and newly shorn locks, he did not have the look of a powerful Hollywood director, and few in the crowd had any idea who he was. One of his producers, a man slightly older with a far more distinguished appearance, worked the periphery—a more likely director than Mooney. I could see people pointing and staring at him, apparently under the mistaken impression that he was Nick Mooney—the real Mooney's intention, no doubt.

It takes forever for these Hollywood types to get their act together. Though we were about ten minutes early for the 7 a.m. call, it would be a few hours before the shooting would begin. While the rest of us stood around, tech guys were hauling cable, monitors were being set up, and some poor sonofabitch was perched up in the apex of the crane. People were grabbing breakfast burritos from the craft service table set up in front of the West End, and Mooney and Dexter were consulting with the lighting and sound people.

Our twelve-man "Nutting Girl" takes about three minutes to dance, but they had allowed four hours to shoot it. I was guessing only a few seconds would make it up there on the silver screen, if that. We would have to do the entire dance at least five times to allow for the five different angles requested by Dexter, who would need multiple takes for each shot. It was also possible that we'd have to do at least parts of it over for some cut-ins.

The twelve of us stood on the streets in front of McCusker's in what would be our dance configuration while Dexter set things up with Mooney. Dexter would have his camera set up halfway across the street, on the mid-street stripe and on a dolly for the first take. The crane shot would come later.

As we were preparing, Sarah and Julie, with their constant companions Frick and Frack and Jenna, established an encampment on the other side of the street near the fence along the river. As much as possible, I kept my eye on Julie while at the same time assessing the crowd for things and people out of the ordinary.

It was a hard job. Frankly, I had never worked under conditions like these before—this many people, this much confusion. And Mooney and Dexter were demanding a lot from me; my attention was often pulled away from Julie. My assignment was not starting off well.

I was reassured by the two brutes on either side of her, and by Sarah, but Sarah seemed to be more involved in whispering secretly in Julie's ear than in observing the crowd. While the linebackers did appear to rotate their heads and search, it remained to be seen how much these two guys were capable of noticing.

One thing anyone with eyes and ears would notice, however, was the power of the swollen river. It rushed and roared, as high as it could get without overflowing its banks. Whitecaps reached up to the windows of the building across the street. The sound guy gazed forlornly at his console. Shaking his head, he said we'd probably have to go into a studio and record new sound for this scene later, but he'd do his best to capture it live.

At long last, it seemed we were ready to go. All was in place. The police held back the great unwashed. An assistant director herded twelve dancers into position with Danny and his accordion at the head, facing the storefronts. We dancers faced the streets. A young woman clapped a clapper, announcing the scene number and the fact that this was take one. The assistant director called for silence, the production assistants passed this request politely on to the crowds, and they hushed completely and suddenly, as if shot dead en masse.

From my spot in the dance set, I could see Julie and Sarah repositioning themselves at the riverbank edge. On that side of the bank were a few benches and a concrete wall about three feet high. It was topped by a black iron railing another foot higher than the wall, right at the very edge of the river. With

Frick on one side and Frack on the other, Julie hoisted herself up onto the railing and Sarah, next to her, did the same, so that Julie was on my left as I watched, with Sarah on her right and Frack next to her on her left. Frick was to Sarah's right.

It was a bizarre sight: the two tiny girls perched like matching red birds on the fence flanked by the behemoths who towered over them. It was made even stranger by the raging of the river behind them, dangerously close. The waves literally washed over their matching red heads, close enough that droplets splashed their freckled faces. Jenna stood directly in front of them, a human shield trying to make it as difficult as possible for the throngs to stare at and photograph VelCro. The problem was that she was also making it difficult for me to watch over VelCro, but I had to dance anyway, so it didn't make much difference.

As crazy as everything had been, it was now suddenly settled, silent, and safe. We were getting the late morning slanted sunlight. Mooney whispered a few words to Dexter and backed off to sit under an awning where he would watch the scene unfold on a monitor, just as the camera was seeing it.

The assistant director reiterated her call for quiet, made sure the sound and cameras was ready, and said, "And—"

Julie interrupted her, shouting out, "Break a leg, Francis!"

Had it been anyone other than the film's biggest celebrity, she would have been unceremoniously tossed out, but Mooney ignored it, even sheepishly grinned. A few crew members laughed aloud, having been given permission to do so by Mooney's smile.

I chuckled, and the assistant director finished her call, "Action!" Danny started playing, the Shelburne Falls Morris Men started dancing, the dolly grips started pushing Dexter and his camera and his focus puller infinitesimally closer to us at a deliberate pace, and the music swelled. We were dancing beautifully, and I did not break my leg.

Then the really, really bad thing happened.

Chapter Sixteen

~∿

A Dirge for our Julie of the Deerfield

A T SOME POINT during the dance, I gave up. I stopped trying to do two things at once. I decided that I was now a dancer and not a detective and that's where I would focus my attention and energy. I jumped as high, and as beautifully, as I was capable of doing, sweeping my arms up over my head to get full hankie extension toward the almost cloudless heavens.

I occasionally glanced over to the riverbank and saw the two identical redheaded figures sitting on the iron fence.

We were near the end, where we finished up in a long line of twelve guys, each facing in an alternate direction, arms up in the air and hands clasping those of the guys next to us.

Danny, on the accordion, stomped his foot to the rhythm of the tune and put some extra oomph into it. We were looking good for the camera.

I glanced at the girls on the fence.

"And what few nuts that poor girl had …" we sang. I momentarily turned away from Julie and Sarah but I saw the two heads there as I made the turn.

"She threw them all away," we finished. And we concluded with a loud, "Hey!"

I was now facing the two girls again, holding Michael's hand on my left, young Sam's on my right. We all smiled, then began our patented, circular walk-off.

As I began walking off, I saw there was only one redhead on the fence.

I stopped walking and blinked, as if that would change things. Then there are no redheads on the fence.

I started running—toward the fence, toward the redheads who were no longer there.

They were gone, both of them. In an instant. *Poof.* Just like that.

It seemed like no one else on the fence, or nearby, or anywhere, noticed their absence except me. Everyone else was still watching the filming play out. Some were even clapping.

Then Frick, or Frack—the black one—climbed up on the fence and dove into the water. This was heroic but not smart.

I was now at the fence myself, staring down into the river. Nothing was visible down there but swirling white waters from hell.

Then the hordes started to notice that something had happened. Slowly, a few at a time. There were raised voices, screams.

And then, instantly, they all knew. The police momentarily lost control of the crowd that had gathered for the filming and the crowd rushed to the riverbank, hundreds of them. No one called "cut." For all I knew, Dexter was still shooting all of this.

Sirens started to wail and red flashers flickered more brightly than the sun. I held on to the top rung of the fence and looked down at the roiling stew down there—and looked and looked. I wanted to jump in. But it would not help.

Then I saw Frick—for I was later to ascertain that it was he and not the other one—bravely paddling but barely keeping his head above water, pretty much helpless, being pulled along toward the falls on a wave.

At this point in the river, it flowed directly toward a dam

owned by the electric company, a dam leading to the falls over which the river drops to create the Glacial Potholes. There was one redhead bouncing, ghostly white and vacant-looking, in the waters approaching the dam.

To hell with it. I jumped in, bells and ribbons and hankies and all. The river swept me along like I was a twig flying in a hurricane, like I might vanish, like I was nothing. I was totally out of control, but it was taking me directly toward the blanched face with the lifeless eyes and the sopping red hair.

It pushed me right into her, bumping her motionless frame with a painless thump, and I grabbed her around the waist. I had no idea which one she was. We were both rammed against the flashboard on the dam, and I held on to that with one hand and the girl with the other. A few feet to our right, Frick was in a similarly helpless position.

The three of us clung there desperately and it took all my strength to not let go of the girl or the flashboard. The power of the river was mightier and more profound than I had ever given it credit for, and I was ready to die, or pass out, but I would never let go.

I did not die. I did not let go.

An orange polypropylene rope appeared and then I let go. I let go of the dam and grabbed the rope. At the same time, a small green boat began to approach, as tossed around by the waters as we were, with two hooded souls aboard. Somehow the rope—powered by several extremely strong people or more likely a winch—began to pull us sideways toward shore, even as the boat approached from the rear. I could see Frick also receiving a rope.

We were pulled onto the shore. I saw yellow-clad firemen, Chief Loomis, some earnest young people, gently handling us, stretchers, a white ambulance. The ambulance had probably already been in position in case it was needed for the movie.

Cold, wet, tired, scared, empty, drained, I was still conscious, but barely. My face was buried in the green grass on the shore but I was thrilled to see its blades in front of me, parting gently as my breath blew upon them, and to feel my heart beat.

I woke some time later in an antiseptic-smelling hospital room with Frick in the bed next to mine.

Who knew how much time had passed? There was no nurse, no doctor. Just a TV set playing MSNBC soundlessly and Frick asleep, or unconscious, or dead. I had no idea which.

I had tubes in my arms. I gathered them up and left the room, and in my flimsy hospital gown, walked into the hallway. I saw the nurse's station at its end, but no nurse had as yet spotted me. I wandered to the room to my left in which I saw two older men on two beds. One eyed me with curiosity, the other slept.

I walked into the adjoining room to my right, where one redheaded young woman lay quietly and motionlessly in a bed identical to the one I had just risen from.

One. Only one.

The bed next to hers was empty.

Her head was tilted away from me, but I could tell by the color of her hair who it was.

In her unconscious state, she groggily rolled over until I could see her face and be absolutely positive that indeed it was Sarah.

I was relieved but also stunned. Stunned at the empty bed. Stunned by there being only one of them. Stunned that a really, really bad thing had happened, and happened on my watch. I had been hired to protect the most famous girl in the world, and I had failed. She was gone.

I stood there and saw Sarah toss and turn, her red hair winding around her neck, heard her breaths coming in and out, softly, weakly.

A nurse found me, took me by the arm, and said, "Mr. Raven, you're awake. You have to stay in bed. Come on."

She tried to lead me back to my room, but I resisted. I had little strength, and my resistance was for naught. As she led me out of the room, I twisted my torso and looked back at the girl on the bed. She looked startlingly peaceful.

But I was not peaceful. I did not take failing lightly.

At this moment the nurse was stronger than I was. She forced me out of the room, even as I tried take in one more minute of the breathing, living Sarah.

But it was just one. One girl.

A tune began playing in the back of my head. I tried to shut it off but I failed. It droned on.

It was a dirge for Our Julie of the Deerfield.

Part Two

where there is darkness, light

where there is sadness, joy

Chapter Seventeen

~∽

She Was My Friend

JULIANA VELVET NORCROSS, our Nutting Girl, VelCro, was gone—by all appearances, swept away by the angry river.

Sarah and I, and Frick too, paid only a small price for having tried to save her. We were treated for hypothermia and shock and some not serious abrasions and were out of the hospital in a few days. By then, the town was insane. If we had paparazzi before, now we had become ground zero for a ravenous and gluttonous media orgy that made our little village unrecognizable.

They were everywhere—networks, cable stations, bloggers, radio stations, commentators, analysts, medical experts, river experts. And police of every stripe—local, state, federal, private. With dogs, helicopters, boats, high-tech thermal-imaging equipment, and divers.

They were everywhere, but VelCro was nowhere.

It was universally agreed that, barring a miracle, no one could have survived that fall into the river and subsequent flushing downstream. The river was raging furiously, and beyond the dam, there was nothing but rocks and more fierce and turbulent waters. A tiny body like Julie's would have no chance.

Still, no body was found. They searched for a mile down to the Gardner Falls dam, where they dredged and found nothing. They went another half-mile to Wilcox Hollow, where they found nothing. They went on and on, where they found nothing.

They gave up.

The spot across from McCusker's where she went over became a spontaneous shrine. Flowers, poems, photos, stuffed animals, and DVDs of VelCro films appeared. Each evening, for a week, a crowd gathered right there on the sidewalk, spreading out in the parking spaces and into the street, with young people playing guitars and singing songs about dead young girls and anything else sad. The Morris guys joined them instead of attending our usual Tuesday night practice. We led the group in some dead baby songs, and everyone wept.

Then, after a week or so, it was over. The world moved on to its next zeitgeist, to something newer and sexier.

Untitled Nicholas Mooney Project was over, most likely forever. The film crew was gone and the streets of Shelburne Falls were once again empty and quiet and boring.

Things were not over for me, however. What hits you at a time like this is not despair, nor is it sadness. Way beyond sadness, it's a gnawing feeling that the universe has been thrown off its course. This was wrong. The world was wrong.

There was no denial. Hell, she was gone. There wasn't even any anger. There was no bargaining and certainly no acceptance. There was numbness and emptiness and that was about it.

Sarah was inconsolable. She was in a constant state of agitation. She obsessively walked the river every day, along its banks, onto its rocks, sometimes wading into it, waist deep. One day she did it all wearing Julie's colorful peasant skirt.

She continued doing this for two weeks. I had moved back home but I was spending a lot of time at their house.

One day I was having lunch there with Clara when Sarah walked back through the door. She was clutching a six-inch swatch of orange silk that she had found on the banks of the river off of Bardwell Ferry Road in Conway, a good three miles from the spot where Julie had disappeared.

She went into her room and came back with her orange silk blouse from the day of the shoot and held the piece she had found against it. It was identical.

It was the only trace of VelCro anyone had found. "Take it to the police," I said.

"No," replied Sarah. "She was my friend, not theirs."

"It might help them find her," I said.

"No," she said. "She was my friend. I'll find her."

"I'll help," I said.

"I don't need your help. But you can if you want. I'll find her."

She went back into her room and did not come out for a long time.

Chapter Eighteen

~•~

Work to Do

I COULDN'T ARGUE with Sarah. But I was burning inside as much as she was and I was going to put every bit as much heart and soul and passion into this. I had a job to do, to protect her, and I failed. Here was a young woman who had told me all would be well, and all was not well. I could not help but feel that it was my fault.

She might very well be dead. Dead or alive, Juliana Velvet Norcross would be found.

What had happened to her? Did she jump? If so, why? Did someone push her? If so, who? And why? And how?

Sarah didn't emerge from her room until the next morning. She was dressed in the orange silk blouse, in fact wearing the entire outfit they'd both had on the morning Julie disappeared: the short, tight purple skirt, black striped leggings, red sneakers, and orange bandana.

I was sipping my coffee. Sarah was making a bowl of oatmeal. Clara was reading the morning paper.

"How are you doing, Sarah?"

"I'm okay. I'm good."

"Are you?"

"Yeah, Frankie, I am."

"Sarah, I really think we should take that piece of cloth to the police."

"I told you, no. I found it. It's mine."

"They can run tests on it. There's all kinds of stuff they can find. They could find DNA on it indicating someone else was involved."

"Nobody else was involved."

"How can you be so sure?"

"Frankie, I was right there. I was right next to her. Hell, I jumped in to save her. One second she was there, and the next, she was in the river. She jumped."

"Were you watching her all the time? I mean *all* the time?"

"Yes."

"You didn't turn away for a second?"

"No. I was watching her."

"You weren't watching the dancing?"

"No."

"Not even for a few seconds?"

She answered with a more emphatic, "No." Pausing for a few seconds, she said, "Well, I guess I did watch the dancing for a while. But she did too. We were both watching."

"Could someone have come up and pushed her?"

"No way. I was right next to her. We were touching."

"There were a million people around, Sarah. People were passing back and forth. Couldn't someone have slipped in there quickly and pushed her?"

"No."

"Well, okay."

"Frankie, Jenna was right in front of us. Her whole job was to keep people away. And Frack was on the other side of her. No one was going to screw around with Frack right there."

"Okay. But why would she jump? You knew her better than anyone. Did she ever talk about killing herself or anything like that?"

"No, never. And don't talk about her in the past tense. She's still alive."

My heart broke. I wanted her to be alive. We all wanted her to be alive. But no one I talked to thought it was even remotely possible.

I touched Sarah on her arm.

She pulled away. "Don't patronize me, Frankie," she said. "I'm not a baby."

"I'm sorry. I want her to be alive too."

"I don't *want* her to be alive, Frankie. I *know* she's alive."

She didn't finish her oatmeal. She walked out the door. She was clutching the orange swatch of material.

"I have work to do," she said.

Chapter Nineteen

~∾

Losing My Religion

THE RIVER WAS still. It was hard to believe it was the same body of water. Two weeks of dry weather, and it was low and lazy and lavish with hints of early summer warmth. People were swimming in the usual swimming holes. Recently it had swept away the world's most famous girl; now it was gently hosting swimmers.

I walked its banks every day, not looking for clues or bodies or anything at all except newly sprouted green and pink buds and birds whose songs I could record. I was searching for signs of life.

And I was thinking. I was doing a lot of thinking.

The Shelburne Falls Morris Men's season was over. We only dance out in the spring, and summer was almost here. We did have our usual cookout in someone's yard.

The newly married Michael and Angela, whose wedding marked the beginning of all this, invited us to their recently purchased, rambling old fixer-upper on the Buckland side, right along the riverbank, with a spacious, fenced-in yard and a stone barbecue pit. We had lots of beer, hamburgers, soyburgers, hot dogs, pet dogs, tofu pups, buns, condiments, and chicken. A lot of wives, girlfriends, kids, friends, and former dancers showed up, and we were doing a good job of carrying on—telling funny stories, playing music, singing, eating, and drinking. There were about twenty-five of us. Clara and Sarah were my dates, and they were gamely playing along, as if life were normal.

And if you pretended hard enough, it was. Julie had not been a part of our lives until a very short while ago, so her absence did not create a big gap in existence as we knew it. Or at least, it shouldn't have. I recorded the *churr* and *buzz* of a wren in the distance.

Off at the periphery of the party, sitting in a lawn chair facing the river, wearing the same Yankees cap as when I first met him at the wedding, was Harvey, Angela's grandfather.

I told Michael that it was good to see the old dude. Harvey's wife Emma had died shortly after the wedding. It was sudden, and Harvey took it hard. He started losing it a little more than before, and Michael and Angela had moved him into the tiny apartment in their new house. He could live independently, but they could keep an eye on him and help him as needed.

"He still does pretty good," Michael told me. "He takes care of his own place. We never have to go in there. He comes over to visit, and he eats with us a lot. He's still pretty sharp, but he has some blank moments. And, well, he wants to get out and see as many people as he can.

"He's on his way out," continued Michael. "Lung cancer. Terminal. He smoked Luckies for like eighty years. Go up and talk to him. He remembers you. He actually likes you, even if he thinks you're some kind of hippie or something."

I walked over to the river. With my back to it, I crouched down and faced Harvey. Thinking he was asleep, I sat there for a minute. He opened his eyes, blinked, and looked at me.

"You're that cop. The one at Michael's wedding. Or whatever. Some damn hippie."

"Yeah. That's me. I remember your wise words about chicken."

"Hell, I don't have wise words about anything. Screw it all, anyway."

"Yeah. Sometimes I come around to your way of thinking. Screw it all. And I'm not a cop, by the way. I was once, but not now."

"Or are you the priest? Somehow I thought you were a priest too. But you don't have the collar."

"No, I was never a priest. I was a monk."

"Oh, right," he said. "I think I remember that now. You withdrew from the world, or some damn thing."

I ignored this and asked, "How are you doing?"

"I'm okay, I guess. I like sitting here, looking at the river. Michael lets me sit here all day some days. It just flows by. It never stops."

"Yeah," I replied. "That's why we like them so much. They never get tired. They flow and they flow and they roll and they roll. But me, I get tired."

"Not me. I'm sick but I'm not tired. I have lots of things I still want to do."

"Like what?" I was curious.

"I'd like to find that missing girl," Harvey replied. "That's one of the reasons I sit here watching this damn river. She's in there somewhere."

"What's she to you?" I asked.

"Not a damn thing. Just a pretty little girl. She used to walk along here with that other red-haired girl. They seemed nice. And it's a damn shame what happened." He paused, then added, "You're a cop. You should find her."

In my mind, I said I would. Out loud, I said nothing. Clearly his memory was going.

The river kept on chugging along. Harvey was looking at it. I was looking at Harvey. I turned to stare at the river.

"That damn river," said Harvey. "It never stops. It rolls and it rolls and it rolls. Can you get me some chicken? And a beer. Get me a beer."

I got Harvey a paper plate with a big, slightly burnt and crispy chicken breast. I piled potato salad on there too. And brought him one of those monster twenty-two ounce Berkshire Traditional Pale Ales.

The first thing he did was sip the beer.

"Mmm, that's good," he said. "You want some?"

"No. I don't drink."

Harvey was sipping thirstily, stopping just short of gulping. The river was mesmerizing as it flowed by over the mossy rocks.

"Yep. 'Ol' Man River.' That was a good song," he said. "Funny how much those words can mean."

"I know. That's why we all sing so much."

"I heard you guys singing before. All you sing about is dead babies and dead dogs. That's for the birds. Rivers make more sense."

"We sang those dead songs when I was in the monastery. That's where I learned them."

"You're not in the monastery now?"

"No."

"Why not?"

"I was losing my religion."

Harvey laughed. "That's a song too."

"You know that song?"

"Yeah. Emma and I saw REM play at Amherst in the late eighties. What was it—eighty-six, maybe? Eighty-seven? We were the oldest people there. It was fucking great."

"I thought you hated hippies."

"They weren't hippies. That was alt rock. I hate that hippie shit—Grateful Dead, Phish. That shit totally sucks. Self-indulgent bullshit is what it is."

Harvey was turning out to be an even more remarkable guy

than I had imagined. He was downing the beer quickly and working hard on the chicken and potato salad.

"So you lost your religion. Me ... I watch the river flow."

"That's a song too."

"Yeah, I know. Dylan, right?"

"Yeah."

He passed me the beer. I was tempted to take a drink but I didn't. I just wordlessly handed it back to him and he continued, "Yeah. I watch the river flow and wonder about that lost girl." He drank some beer. "She looked up and her eyes met mine that day."

"What day?"

"The day she fell in."

"You saw her?"

"Yeah. I was sitting right here."

"She was alive?"

"Oh, she was alive, all right. I saw her eyes. They were open."

"Dead people's eyes can still be open."

"No, this girl was alive. I could see the life in those eyes. She looked right at me."

"Jesus Christ!"

"She just flowed down that damn river. Like a raft. Or a salmon. Bouncing around on those waves."

I tried to digest this. It was not easy. It gave me hope.

"And then I saw her again after that too," he said.

"What?"

"I think so. I think I remember seeing her after that. I think."

"Where?"

"Where? I never go anywhere. Had to be here, I guess."

I was stunned. I asked Harvey to elaborate.

"I just remember her hovering around here," he said. "She was just sort of floating around. All over the place. For like a week."

"Are you talking about a ghost, Harvey?"

"Oh, fuck ghosts. There's no ghosts."

"Spirits? You believe in spirits."

"Spirit. They were a band too. Remember 'I Got a Line on You'?"

"Yeah. Great song."

"You got that right."

"Tell me about that girl some more."

"Nothing more to tell."

"Try."

"I saw her floating down the river. She was smiling. Then I saw her floating all over the place. Here, there, and everywhere. That's a song too."

"Beatles."

"Yep."

"That's it?"

"That's it. You need something to do. I don't know if you're a fucking cop or a damn priest or a monk or a singer or a damn hippie or what the hell you are. But you should find that girl. If I was in better shape, I'd do it myself."

As if to emphasize this last point, he coughed a violent dry hack without covering his mouth.

I walked over to the river and looked downstream. From this angle, you could see a long way down. There was little winding in this stretch. I tried to imagine Julie being swept helplessly away. How far could she go? Could she be alive? Where would she end up?

"There was something missing in her, in her eyes," Harvey said. "She was alive, but she was distant. Do you know what I mean?"

I didn't and told him so.

"She wasn't connecting with me. She was all alone," he said. He went on. "Do you have any idea what I'm talking about? I could feel the distance between us. She wasn't with me. She wasn't me. We were different people."

"Aren't all people different?" I asked.

"You don't believe that, do you?" Harvey said.

"I'm asking you."

"I'm me. You're you," said Harvey. He was getting fed up with me. "That girl was that girl. Everybody at this shindig is themselves. We're born alone and we die alone. I should know. I'm going to be the next one to bite the dust." Then he laughed and said, "Yeah. Another one bites the dust." He looked me straight in the eye. "And I'll bite the dust alone. Even with Emma and Michael and all the rest of you guys."

"Then why are you getting so misty about that girl in the river? If we're all alone, then who cares?"

"I didn't say I liked it. I said that's the way it is. We're all alone. We're all fucking alone."

"You're full of shit, Harvey. That's how people lose their religion. That's why they tossed me out of the monastery. We're all the same person, Harvey. We're all part of one big damn beautiful soul."

"You think too much about stuff nobody cares about. Screw all that stuff. Just find the girl."

I had said too much, so I shut up and walked back to the party. Harvey was right. About one thing anyway. I would find the girl.

Chapter Twenty

∿

A Quest

THE NEXT DAY, I had a second girl to find.

I did not need a second girl. One was enough. Too much. But these two were connected, which was the only reason I had any interest in finding the second girl.

I needed distraction. I was back at the West End, working on a Reuben and my third root beer of a long night. It was slow there, drawing only the lonely single guys—two others from the fraternity were also there, a space between each of us as propriety dictated.

The root beer had a bite to it and the Reuben had turkey, which bartender Tyler said made it not a Reuben. What the hell, it tasted good.

Of the few remaining seats at the bar, she chose the one next to me. That made me feel important because she was a real looker. She could have sat next to one of the younger, hunkier guys. But I was old and safe.

I merely nodded at her as she tried to order a Pabst Blue Ribbon, which they don't carry. She ended up with a twenty-two-ounce River Ale, which is a lot of beer and costs way more than a Pabst.

I didn't try to talk to her. She was not there to talk to the likes of me.

She took a sip of beer, turned to me with a welcoming smile, and said, "That's good beer."

"Better than a PBR?"

"No, I like Pabst."

"Back in the day, so did I. But now we have a lot of great small local breweries."

She was not a large person, but she had a big feel to her. It came from her mind or from her heart. In there, she was big, tall, strong, muscular, in terrific shape, an athlete perhaps, grounded and connected to the earth. So unlike our dear vanished Nutting Girl, who at times, despite her act, seemed to be pure spirit and more connected to heaven than earth.

But in her physical manifestation, this woman was short in stature with long, wavy black hair drifting down her back, a sharp nose, and black-framed glasses. She was pretty in a smart, geeky kind of way. Pleasing to look at. I would have enjoyed talking more to her, but she seemed preoccupied, so I let her work on her ale while I worked on my root beer.

It was slow, and Tyler wasn't busy. He hovered over her, solicitous, being an extra-good bartender. He was already a good one. Soon they were engaged in friendly chatter, and I was relegated to mere listener. I had learned to listen. That's what detectives, and monks, do.

Tyler ascertained that our visitor was from Boston, just here for a while, a lawyer, *blah blah blah*. He seemed pretty enchanted with her. She was asking him local details—places to stay, eat, the usual. He told her she had to visit the Bridge of Flowers and the Glacial Potholes. He said the West End was the best place to eat. She said she wasn't sure how long she was going to be around or if she'd have time to do touristy things. Tyler asked if she was here on business. I wondered what lawyer from Boston comes to Shelburne Falls for business.

She said it wasn't typical business. Tyler did not probe further, but this piqued my curiosity.

She asked a question: who was the best person around to find something that was lost?

Tyler suggested the police.

She said, "Besides them. We've gone to the police and no luck. They can only do so much, then they stop."

Tyler asked what sort of thing was lost.

She said, "Well, I'd rather not get too deep into details here."

Tyler did what I was afraid he was going to do. And what I was afraid he was not going to do. He pointed at me and said, "Well, there's always this guy. He finds things."

She looked at me with those big eyes and I saw that I was in trouble.

"Used to," I said. "I'm retired."

"I heard you were un-retired," Tyler said.

The woman's big eyes looked through me.

"Well," I said, "semi-sorta, temporarily, kinda but not really retired. At least I think."

The wavy-haired lawyer from Boston said, "You know, don't you, that retirement is not necessarily permanent? I've heard that director Nick Mooney talked his Uncle Lyle out of retirement, and he was working for him, at least before all this other horrible stuff happened here."

Nick Mooney? Now she really had my attention.

We had moved from the bar and were sitting at a table on the glassed-in porch in the back. She was on her second River Ale and I was still nursing my third root beer. We could see people pass by outside on the Bridge of Flowers, but neither of us were interested.

"Do you know Nick Mooney?" I asked her.

"Not personally. But my sister does. Or did. She knew him quite well."

"He's good at talking people out of retirement," I said.

"He's good at talking people out of a lot of things. And into a lot of things."

"What do you need me to find?" I asked, knowing what the answer would be.

"My sister," she replied.

Edith Marie Pasternak was her name—her sister's name. The curly-haired lawyer was named Amy. Her sister was an actor recently moved to the West Coast, recently hooked up with Mooney, and part of the entourage that followed him into Shelburne Falls.

Edith had kept in close touch with Amy by phone and text until just a few days before VelCro disappeared. The messages abruptly stopped. Then there was silence.

The police had been useless. "She's an adult," Amy said. "She can go away if she wants and not talk to her sister. No laws against that and no sign of foul play. So they say. So here I am, looking for someone who can help me."

"I'm retired," I said.

"No you're not," she said. "Look at your eyes. You're not retired. Not when it comes to Nick Mooney. That guy's got something on you."

She was right. If there was an answer to what happened to Julie, it went through Nick Mooney. If there was an answer to what happened to Edith, it also went through Nick Mooney. That was too much coincidence to ignore.

Other than the fact that she was a human being, and all humans deserve respect and love, I had no interest in Edith Marie Pasternak. I never knew her.

But there had to be a connection between the two young women who vanished and had relationships of some sort with Nick Mooney.

So I would find Edith Marie Pasternak. Maybe it would help me find Juliana Velvet Norcross.

Amy gave me a professional headshot of Edith—the subject was carefully posed to not look posed. Black and white, but you could tell her hair was red. Slim, pretty, abundant freckles not airbrushed out, just this side of beautiful. On the back were her acting credits, painfully brief.

I folded that lovely picture and stuck it in my pocket.

I gave Amy one of my old business cards from my wallet. I hadn't dug one out for ten years at least. I still had the same phone number, so it would work.

So would I. I would work at finding the girls. Both girls.

This would be more than a distraction.

This would be a quest.

Chapter Twenty-One

∾

The Mean Streets of Shelburne Falls

CALLING THE STREETS of Shelburne Falls *mean* usually drips with irony, but now they seriously did seem mean. Innocent young women were vanishing here.

I had no idea how to find Julie. The whole world, including Sarah, was working on that. What more could I do?

But finding Edith? That seemed more human in scale, like something I could do. I had found missing people like her before. I had never found someone with the fame, and soul, of Julie.

Both were connected to Mooney somehow, but Mooney himself had vanished. No one had seen him since that fateful day. So, with nowhere else to turn, I concentrated on what I know best—the streets. The mean streets of Shelburne Falls.

I knew the drill. I made my rounds, store to store, gallery to gallery, café to café, bar to bar, headshot in hand. Everyone thought they might have seen her, but no one was really sure. Of course, everyone had seen the Hollywood invasion, but those folks all blended together. Some thought they *might* have seen Edith.

By the time I got to the Blue Rock, it was five o'clock and they were just opening for dinner. Alice was sweeping the sidewalk and George was behind the bar, which is where I sat and ordered what was for me a rather elaborate dinner—a scallop and shrimp dish.

George was smiling and friendly. The guy always cheered me up with his relentless and unceasing optimism. I like that kind of attitude. He showed me some shots on his phone of a painting he was working on. He was a fine artist. Everyone in Shelburne Falls was some kind of artist.

He poured me a refreshing club soda and lime, and I unfolded Edith's photo and showed it to him.

He immediately grew quiet, very unusual for George, and then conveniently was called back into the kitchen while I sat there and sipped.

When he returned, I thought he had forgotten about Edith as he busied himself cutting up lemons and mixing elixirs of various flavors for later when the bar got busy.

But he hadn't forgotten. He came back in front of me and said, "Yeah, sure I remember her. She was in here a couple times."

"Can you fill me in?"

"Yeah. She came in with the director and that whole gang. And then one night with only the director. I won't forget that one."

"No?"

"No way. They made quite a scene. Nobody saw it but me though. It was real late just before they took off and I locked up."

"What happened?"

"Well, the director, Mooney, he was all over her. They were back there in the corner, alone, sitting real close and kind of whispering. I turned the music up loud because it was none of my business and I didn't want to hear anything. Know what I mean? That's the bar business. You become invisible when you have to. So I cranked up the sounds. And I still could hear them."

"What did you hear?"

"Mostly it was just voices. I don't remember specific words. At first they looked real sweet and cuddly, but after a while, *man* did they go at it—*mad*. Or I should say she was mad. Royally pissed. She threw a drink in his face. One of those real expensive ones—Duke of Cuke, maybe. I had to mop the floor later. A mess. Pieces of cucumber all over."

"What did he do?"

"It was hard to tell. They were back in the corner and I was trying to not stare. None of my damn business. I just wanted it to play out and be over."

"And did it?"

"Yeah. Eventually. They ended up walking out, with him holding his arms all around her like he was trying to restrain her. He tossed me a twenty as they walked up the stairs. That was my tip. He had already paid for dinner. "

"Or maybe it was your bribe," I replied.

"Bribe for what?"

"Keeping your mouth shut."

"Well, he'd have to be a little more explicit about that, wouldn't he?" George said. "He didn't say anything. And you're asking. You're a nice guy who I've known for like forever. So I'm talking."

"Have you seen her since then?"

"No. He's been back in, but not her."

I was finishing up the club soda, playing with the lime.

"Do you remember anything else?" I asked.

He thought for a while. "Not from in here."

"What do you mean?"

"After I cleaned up, I had a drink myself and locked up. I was walking home, and I decided to walk across the Bridge of Flowers instead of the Iron Bridge. I like that. Even at night when you can't see much. It smells sweet.

"So, I'm walking along and I see someone coming toward me. As he passes by, I see it's Mooney. No big deal, right? But he was alone. No girl with him."

"Maybe she went home. What was weird about that?"

"Nothing. Except that's a narrow path on the bridge. I got water on my shirt just passing him there. Dude was dripping wet."

Chapter Twenty-Two

~⌒~

Frack, Frack, Where Did You Go?

THERE ARE SEVERAL ways to get wet. In this case, the obvious, most likely possibility would be a dip in the river. Seemed like everyone was taking a dip in the river.

Why Mooney would do this, I had no idea, but I was slowly inching my way toward progress, painfully minuscule as it was. I had learned a little bit more about Edith and her relationship with Mooney. I would let this tidbit simmer for a while because my instincts told me it was now time to get back to the main event and the one thing that was really driving me: finding Julie. I would return to Edith soon.

I decided to have a chat with someone official and see if I could learn a little more about any progress with the Nutting Girl search. They don't usually tell you much of import, which is why I didn't try this earlier, but once in a while they slip up.

I walked over to the police station and found Chief Loomis, glasses on, writing notes in a ledger.

"Hey, Frank. How's it going?"

"About as well as it could be, given the circumstances."

Neil Loomis had been chief when I'd been on the force—the one day. He was about ten years my senior, rumpled, a little seedy, not as fit as he used to be but not paunchy, with most of his hair, all of it white. A receding hairline and a lot of wrinkles in his forehead.

"Yeah, me too," he said. "I'm glad this whole VelCro thing is finally fading away. It is, you know. Hardly any reporters or photographers around now. Pretty soon someone else famous will die and then they'll all be gone. Thank God."

I asked him what he could tell me about the investigation. Technically he couldn't tell me anything, but he'd known me for many years and was aware I had an interest in the case.

Basically, there wasn't much to say. After this much time and no clues, the police were writing her off as dead. Well, we did have one clue—two, if you counted Harvey's observation. But the chief didn't know about them, and I was not going to tell him. I doubted they would change anything. The police were no longer dredging the river or searching its shores. They had given up.

"She's dead, Frank," Loomis said. "I hate to be the one to break that to you, but really, what else is possible?"

"All kinds of seemingly impossible things happen every day, Neil."

"There's about a one in a million shot she survived. If all the bounces went just perfect and hit her body in just the right places, or missed her completely, and her head was not under water for too long at any point, maybe, just maybe, she could be alive and breathing somewhere. Actually, the fact that the river was so high is a factor in her favor. A very small factor. It would kind of raise her above the danger, insulate her as it swept her along. There's some small hope, Frank. But it's very small and I'm not buying it. My advice? Consider her dead. That's the kindest thing I can tell you."

Time crept by. Numbness set in, but life went on. We were showing movies at the theater on weekends. Sarah had finished school for the year. Before Julie disappeared, Sarah had been talking about finding a summer job, but that idea had fallen by the wayside. Her obsessive searching for Julie slowed down.

I had a quiet dinner with Clara and Sarah on one of the first really hot days in June. We barbecued burgers out in the yard. Sarah whipped up a fresh green salad with an oil and vinegar dressing. Matthew was home for the summer from Oberlin, but he was never around. He was off with his buddies and had a girlfriend.

The Hill of Tears going home was a slow slog, but Marlowe's joy at seeing me cheered me up. I tossed some sticks around the yard for him. The days were much longer now, and it seemed like darkness might never come. I was wanting it to come so I could bring a suitable end to the day and go to sleep.

Bringing Marlowe back in through the porch door, I checked the mailbox. Among the bills and magazines I never got around to reading was a thick, 9 x 12 envelope hand-addressed to me. I ripped it open with a paring knife.

Inside was a series of five sharp, clear color 8½ x 11 photos. They were from the day of the ill-fated film shoot. Together they made a progression, told a story. They were in sequence.

The first showed four figures sitting on the iron railing next to the river with dozens of others milling around, a very small section of the full panorama that day. Whoever shot these was good. He or she was focused right on Julie, with Frack directly to her left, Sarah to her right, and Frick on Sarah's right. Jenna was in front of them, but Jenna is quite short, and the picture was shot from a high angle so she didn't obstruct anything. The girls were caught mid-laugh, big grins, directly facing each other. Frick and Frack looked grim and hard at work, Frack gazing off to his right and Frick staring straight ahead.

The second picture was blurrier because there were two passing bodies caught in mid-motion, but they were off to the sides and did not block anything. There was an unobstructed view of the four figures on the fence. Not much had changed there, except Frack had turned so that his gaze was directed at Julie and his arm was coming up and captured at about her shoulder level. His arm was moving, thus creating more blur effect. Julie was still looking directly at Sarah.

The next photo was startling. It was like seeing that frame from the Zapruder film where JFK's head essentially gets blown off. Frack's arm was still blurry, now a little lower than shoulder height. Basically you could see Julie's purple skirt and her leggings pointed out horizontally and only a tiny flash of her orange blouse, blurred like Frack's arm. You could see her face too, barely, right at the edge of the frame.

She was falling backward, into the river.

The fourth picture was one of chaos. There were more people coming into the frame and they were in motion. Some were pointing, some clearly captured mid-run. All were looking at the river. You could see just the smallest piece of smudged color where Frick had been. He had jumped into the river, and this was all that was visible as he vanished from the frame. There was an empty spot where the two girls had been sitting.

The fifth and final was a wide shot of two bodies fighting the surge of the river. The figures were tiny. One was far ahead of the others and near the lip of the dam. The other was closer to shore but heading toward mid-river.

I knew that three bodies had gone into the river at this point, which meant that one of them had already gone over the dam. The two remaining bodies were Sarah and Frick. Julie was gone.

The empty spot where people had been perched on the iron railing was now concealed by the backs of many heads, some hoisted up on the concrete base of the rail.

Among them, clearly seen because he was dressed all in white with bells still strapped to his legs, was a guy looking, even from behind, indecisive. Me.

That was it. No note. No return address.

I stared at them. I got up and walked around the house, then went back and studied them some more. I tacked them up on the wall behind my couch, in sequence, at eye level. They were like stills from a movie. Maybe that's what they were.

They told me one very important thing—Frack's arm had moved up toward Julie's shoulders just as she was about to fall into the river.

I didn't sleep that night. The first thing I did the next day was try to find Frack.

Frack, Frack, where did you go?

Chapter Twenty-Three

~

Finding Frack

Finding Frack was not easy. I had no one to contact from the aborted *Untitled Nicholas Mooney Project* shoot. I never got any phone numbers. My only encounters with Mooney took place in bars, initiated by him. So that avenue was closed to me.

I didn't even know Frack's name. It was extremely doubtful that it was Frack. He and Frick both had been introduced to me as linebackers from UMass, but I wasn't sure if that was meant metaphorically or actually.

A visit to the UMass Athletic Department website gave me the answer. There was a group shot of the football team followed by larger individual shots of each player accompanied by a quick bio. It wasn't hard to find Frack. The photo showed a grinning, buzzcut, innocent-looking white kid. The caption read:

> Frederick "Fritz" Frackman—6'5" 310 lbs—linebacker. Junior, communications major, Meyers High School, Wilkes-Barre, PA. This gentle giant has professional aspirations, if not on the gridiron, then maybe on the

silver screen. Watch your back, Arnold. And he plays a mean guitar too."

A phone call to the university was no help. Any and all information about students was confidential. School was out for the summer, so I wouldn't be able to find him on campus anyway.

Or would I? I called Jerry McElroy, my old friend who covers sports for the Springfield Union. Jerry told me the football team never really stopped practicing. This time of year, they would be lifting and running once a day, and sometime later in the summer, they'd begin "two-a-days," or two practice sessions each day. I'd have a good chance of catching him if I dropped by the gym or track.

Jerry made a few calls of his own and told me my best bet was to hit the track early in the morning. So, the next day, there I was, watching huge boys run around a dirt track at 8 a.m. as the birds chirped and a couple of older guys in shorts with whistles yelled at them.

There were dozens. They all looked pretty much alike, except some were black and some were white—although, big as they all were, few were as large as Frack. So I just looked at the most monstrous of the behemoths, searching for his familiar face.

I didn't see it. I watched them run around the track a couple of times and still, I did not see it.

Then, while looking even more intently, I was tapped on the shoulder by a positively Brobdingnagian black kid. I turned and found myself looking into the face of Frick.

"Hey, Mr. Raven, what are you doing here?"

I reached out to shake his big paw. My hand was buried, just short of being crushed.

"Oh, hey. I was just looking for you guys."

"How are you? Are you all right?" he asked.

"Yeah, fine. I wasn't hurt really. You?"

"Yeah. The same. I'm okay."

"Where's your buddy?" I asked. "Is Frack around?"

"The Frackster, man. I wish I knew. Dude's vanished. I heard he left school."

I told him I'd like to discuss all this further. He said he'd be busy until near noon, so we made an appointment to meet for lunch at the Amherst Brewing Company.

"I'll buy you a beer," I said. "You're twenty-one, right?"

"Yeah," he said. "Coach won't like it, but I'll let you buy me a brew." He looked me in the eyes, "I'd love to talk about that day. It was fucking crazy, man. And I haven't talked to anybody about it yet."

Chapter Twenty-Four

~⁊

My Lunch with Frick

"So, what's your real name?" I asked Frick.

We were seated in a pleasantly dark booth in the corner of the massive but mostly empty pub.

"Bernard, but I don't mind Frick either. I kinda liked the Frick and Frack duo stuff. I liked that Frackster dude. He was my bro."

"The school called him Fritz."

"Fritz? I don't know why they listed him like that. I never heard anyone call him Fritz. Maybe in high school. Here he was Frack. And I was Frick. We were buddies, a team."

"I'm going to go with Bernard, if you don't mind."

"That's totally cool, Mr. Raven."

"Yeah. And you can call me Frank."

"Awesome."

Bernard was sipping a tall, frosted traditional ale. I was working on a root beer. He was just getting started on a twelve-course lunch spread. I had a grilled cheese with tomato and onion.

"How badly were you hurt?" I asked him.

"I was hurt but nothing was broken. Had a lot of bruises

and cuts. And hypothermia. My head got clunked and they thought it might be a concussion, but it checked out okay. Good thing, because they don't let you play for like forever if you're concussed. They got a whole protocol you gotta follow. Thank God I wasn't. You're okay too?"

"I'm a lot older than you, but I guess I'm made of rubber. I got bounced around but no permanent damage."

"Good. How's that girl?"

"She's okay."

We paused while he vacuumed a side of french fries.

"Too bad about VelCro. Man, that's all I saw on the TV for weeks. And to think I was right there when it happened."

"And Frack?" I asked. "What's up with him? Have you talked to him?"

"No. I haven't seen or heard from the dude since that day. And he was my best friend around here. I've got some good buds back in New Orleans, but he was the guy here."

"That's where you're from—New Orleans?"

"That's my home. Way different from here."

"You like it here?"

"It's different, but I like it. People are good. Hate the snow."

He started on the first of three cheeseburgers.

"What makes you think he left school?"

"I don't know. Coach said he was gone. Haven't seen him. I gotta move on too. No time to be sentimental, much as I like the guy."

I marveled at the speed he was devouring that burger. "Where would he go? Did he ever talk about going somewhere? Some place he always wanted to visit?"

Munching thoughtfully, Bernard said, "He talked about New Orleans a lot, said it sounded cool. He wanted to play music, and he heard that was a good music town."

"He was a musician?"

"He played guitar." He paused, then added, "Or, well, he claimed he did. Dude was just learning, but he wasn't bad."

"What kind of music?"

"All kinds. He liked the blues. White dude wanted to sound black. Wasn't too bad. He hung around with me, after all. Learned from me. Didn't even own his own guitar though. Dude had no money, Mr. Raven. He came from a poor town in Pennsylvania. The only thing he had going for himself was his scholarship here, and now he's blown that."

I smiled. "Call me Frank."

He thumped himself on the head. "Oh, yeah, Frank. Sorry."

"So, how did you guys get hired for that movie gig anyway?"

Bernard took a long sip of ale before answering. "Frack always wanted to be in the movies. This director dude came to practice looking for big guys to be bodyguards and he and Frack hit it off. The guy promised to get Frack in the movie somewhere. Even said he'd get to speak a line or two, which would have been great since then he'd get paid more. And residuals too. He said he'd get residuals.

"Then he dragged me along. I didn't care about the damn movie, but Frack wanted me around. Like I said, dude was my bro."

He finished the third burger and began working on dessert— hot fudge brownie with vanilla ice cream. He was on his third ale too. Beer and ice cream together. He came up for air. This lunch was going to cost me a fortune.

"You think VelCro's dead?" he asked.

"I don't know. I still have to hope for the best."

"Me too. I was raised to look on the bright side."

Frick wiped his mouth with a napkin. Finally he said, "It's a damn shame what happened. Dude should never have pushed her. I don't know what got into him."

"You think he pushed her?"

"I saw it."

"I've seen pictures. That's sort of what it looks like, but to me it's inconclusive."

"Dude pushed the girl. I saw it."

"He raises his arm and it goes up near her chest, then she falls in. That's all you see in the pictures."

"Well, that's what I saw too. But I know he pushed her."

"Why haven't you come forward about this?"

"Nobody asked me. And none of my damn business anyway."

"Didn't the police talk to you?"

He shrugged. "Sure. But I don't talk to police. I don't count them. I just told them I saw nothing. That's one thing I learned in New Orleans. Police talk to a brother? Don't tell them anything. You get instant amnesia. Besides, I didn't want to get the Frackster in trouble."

"Why would he push her? Did he have some problem with her?"

"No," he said quickly. His brow furrowed. "I don't know."

"Could he have been doing something else and she just fell in? She was small. A good breeze could have knocked her over."

Bernard raised his hand, as if to silence me. "I know what I saw. Dude pushed her."

It didn't make sense, so I persisted. "You were two people away. Sarah, who was right next to her, didn't see anything."

"All I know is what I saw."

I finished my grilled cheese and asked, "Did you see anything else?"

"Yeah," he said. "That girl was smiling when she fell in."

Chapter Twenty-Five

~⌇~

The Nutting Girl Smiles

A T HOME, I took the photos off the wall. Sitting on my couch, I held each one above my head, moving them about to change the perspective until they seemed to be circling me like ominous vultures. The third picture, the Zapruder still where Julie went overboard, was my main focus. Frick was staring straight ahead. He was not looking to his right, where he would have had a clear shot of what was happening with Frack and VelCro. His certainty about Frack's pushing her was highly questionable.

There was more intriguing stuff in that third photo too. Julie was nearly out of the frame, leaning backward, falling. Her face was mostly obscured. But yes, there was the smallest hint of a smile on Julie's lovely face if you really examined it. Still, it was hard to tell with her head at such an angle.

I was blind once and my vision is lousy. This is not a good trait for a detective to have, but I always made up for it in other ways, like being able to see things others could not. I did that by intuition, and by persistence. I never gave up on anything, back in the day.

I tacked them back up on the wall at eye level. I had to stick my face up close to the photo to really see what was going on with Julie. I was wishing whoever shot these could enlarge that one further. My nose was almost touching the photo, and Julie's face was filling my poor vision like the big screen in my theater. I was so close, all I could see were smooshed up colors. The image wasn't even human.

I went to the West End for a drink. A root beer drink.

The root beer had a bite to it and all twelve seats at the bar were filled, one by me. Then the cute old couple next to me got up and left.

A tall, skinny Hispanic kid sat next to me and ordered a martini. I watched him play with the olive.

"You like the pix I sent you?" he asked.

Startled by his question, I took a closer look and realized it was Lorenzo, the kid photographer Sarah had chased down the river.

" 'Like' is not the word I would use."

"Let's say, was your curiosity piqued by those pix?"

"An unhesitating yes to that question."

He nodded. "Mine too."

"How did you get them?"

"I had the best seat in the house—McCusker's rooftop. I climbed the fire escape and hoisted myself up the last few feet. Had a perfect view."

"You could sell those, you know."

"Yeah, I know. They would pull in a bundle."

"Okay. So don't you want to make a bundle? That's what you do, right? Sell pictures."

"I've already sold a lot of pictures from that day. I've already made my bundle. Now I want to find out what happened to her."

"What's that to you?"

"I shoot famous people all the time. Mostly they're assholes. I mean, sure they're going to be assholes to me. But I mean, they're assholes to everybody. I see them when they're not 'on,' you know? Believe me, ninety-five percent of them are complete fucking assholes. But I liked that babe. There was something different about her. And I liked that other girl too. So I want to know what happened."

"You had the best view of anybody. And you were watching it all through a telescopic lens. What do you think happened?"

"You know, when I'm working, I'm working. You don't really *see* anything. I was just snapping away. All I know is what those pictures tell me."

"And what is that?"

"I don't know. That's why I sent them to you—a detective."

"Retired detective."

He rolled his eyes. "Bullshit. I can see it in your face. You're not retired. Not from this job anyway."

I sipped my bitter root beer. He sipped his martini.

"Lorenzo," I said, "I presume you've got those pictures on your computer?"

"Yeah. Sure."

"So you can blow them up bigger, right? So we can look at details?"

"Sure. They're real high res. You can blow them up monster big."

Lorenzo was staying at a bed and breakfast on Church Street. We finished up our drinks and took the quick walk over the bridge and to the house.

The proprietor was playing her cello in the living room when we walked in and Lorenzo led me upstairs to his room. We could hear the Vivaldi from her cello as Lorenzo turned on his laptop and found the pictures from that day. She— appropriately, just as if we were in a movie—was providing us with a soundtrack behind which we could say our lines.

I had him pull up the third picture, the Zapruder one, the last one where Julie's face was visible.

He expanded it until Julie's face filled the screen. The quality was superb. It didn't get grainy or out of focus. He zoomed in on her mouth, where the lips were upturned and there was a glow about her face.

There was no doubt about it. Our Nutting Girl was smiling seconds before she hit the river—an angelic, beatific, but subtle smile.

Chapter Twenty-Six

~⁓

The Nutting Girl's Smile

S HE WAS SMILING, but I had no idea what that meant. Lorenzo printed out an 8½ x 11 copy of the big smile and gave it to me. Unlike the photo of Edith, I didn't want to fold this one, but he had large envelopes and some stiff cardboard, so he packed it up securely for me. I would take it home and tack it to the wall above my couch with the others in my gallery.

I was ready to leave but wanted to see that grin again. *Grin* was the wrong word, but none of the synonyms for *smile* fit either. In fact, *smile* was not quite right. It was something else.

I took the picture out of the envelope and studied it. It wasn't a smile of happiness or joy or excitement. It was an expression of determination, of resolve, mixed with peace and contentment.

Lorenzo looked at it too. Then he wordlessly held up his index finger in a silent plea to "wait a minute." He dashed downstairs and returned a few minutes later with something in a fancy stemmed glass that looked like a martini and a bottle of ginger beer. He handed the ginger beer to me and sipped the martini.

"Don't go yet," he said. We both stared at the close-up of our

Nutting Girl's mouth. "We have more to talk about. What does that picture tell you?"

"Not a damn thing," I answered.

We looked at it some more.

Then we stopped looking. I had hardly even tasted the ginger beer. Lorenzo had finished his martini and gone downstairs for a second one. Now he sat on the edge of the bed while I sat on a stiff wooden chair. Vivaldi on the cello filled the room.

"Who are you, Lorenzo?" I finally said.

"I'm just a guy who's always liked movies. I've been around them all my life. My father produced some films you've probably even heard of, and I worked for him since I was eleven. I did just about everything you can do on movies. I started as a production assistant, ran for coffee, made copies, shit like that. When I got bigger, I did grip work, gaffer stuff, assistant camera. And I worked in the office for my dad. I studied photography, and he wanted me to be a cinematographer. But I found out I preferred pictures that don't move. I like to do the moving and have the pictures stay still. And I like the fun of sneaking around. It's like the excitement of being a thief without having to steal anything and get arrested."

"Except their souls, right? Some people think by taking their pictures you're stealing their souls."

"Only when I'm doing it right."

We sipped our drinks.

"You know the business," I finally said. "How does this all work?"

"What do you mean?"

"I mean, what happens now? This movie is dead, right? What happens to Mooney and all the elaborate stuff he set up here? Where does he go? What does he do?"

"Frankly, my dear, I don't give a flying fuck," Lorenzo replied.

I laughed at the *Gone With the Wind* reference, but Lorenzo looked serious.

"What do you mean?" I asked.

"I don't give a flying fuck what happens to Mooney. I never liked that guy."

"You know him?"

"No, I don't really know him, but I've been around his movies before and I hear all the scuttlebutt. He's a total sleazeball."

"What do you mean?"

"I mean VelCro's dead and Mooney's better off than he ever was. He's got the money to make a dozen films now."

I didn't say anything. I just looked at Lorenzo and he knew I needed more.

"You don't know how this works, do you?"

I shook my head.

"When you got somebody like VelCro in your film, you have to insure it up the wazoo. With her history? She's a major risk factor. It's real expensive, but no one will let you shoot without it. With her gone, it pays off big time."

"So he actually *made* money on this."

"Yeah, a lot. And he didn't even have to make a movie. More even than if this was a hit. Unless it was the biggest fucking hit ever."

"Well, this film was not going to be a hit. I read the script."

"It sucked. Or so I heard."

"It sucked. I read it." I thought all this over.

"Did anybody on this film get paid?" I asked.

"Yeah. Everybody got paid for whatever little work they'd already done on it. But they only shot one day. Not even. Just a couple hours. So it didn't add up to much. Except for VelCro, of course."

"What do you mean?"

"A star like her gets paid up front. She already got her fifteen mil, or whatever it was."

"So Mooney and VelCro both get monster paydays and everybody else gets nothing?"

"That's about it. It's fucked up."

I asked Lorenzo if he had any idea what happened to Mooney since the shoot ended.

"I don't know. I guess he's back out west. Probably planning to make a real movie this time. The guy has talent. He's got great stuff in him."

"But he doesn't have VelCro this time."

"No, but he's got his other dozen hot redheaded girlfriends. Maybe he can make one of them a star. The next VelCro."

I had no idea what Lorenzo was talking about.

"You know. All those girls? All those redheads?"

I looked at him stupidly.

"The 'A' girls? At the girls' dorm?" Lorenzo laughed and said, "Dude's got them lined up. Waiting."

Then he showed some mercy to this uncomprehending old man.

"They're all over town," he said. "Don't you see them?"

I did not respond.

He said, "For a smart guy, you don't know much, do you?"

I allowed as how I didn't.

"Well, they're everywhere. He had a million girlfriends, that guy. Women love him. But then really, deep down, he only had one. You know what I mean?"

I took a wild guess. "VelCro?"

"Bingo. He loved her. Even with all these other babes around, she was the only one he really wanted."

"I never saw that," I said, feeling stupid.

He laughed. He actually laughed. Then he said, "I mean … duh! What are you, fucking blind?"

Chapter Twenty-Seven

∿

To Paradise

I SEE A lot, but there is much I do not see too.

I knew Mooney was sleeping with Julie. Hell, it seemed like half the men and maybe a quarter of the women in Hollywood were having sex with her.

Yeah, I knew it. I just couldn't admit it. Not till now, when it was shoved in my face.

It didn't sit well with me to have it spelled out explicitly. It added another dimension, and I didn't need more dimensions. Could Mooney have set up Frack to kill his star and pocket the insurance? Would the possibility that he was sleeping with her make that more, or less, likely? Romance gone bad, maybe? That causes more nasty things to happen in this world than just about anything. Frack and Mooney were both missing. Julie too, actually, though the longer she was gone, the more dead she seemed.

I had a lot of questions and almost no answers. But I also had one more thing in my life relating to the whole Nutting Girl case, and that was something I had been ignoring while I accumulated all this new data. Sarah.

She had become sullen and basically paralyzed. I wasn't sure what she was doing each day but it didn't seem to be much of anything. She stayed in her room a lot. Maybe she was online, or reading, or meditating, or praying, or thinking. Maybe she was crying. Most likely she was just sitting there.

Clara was concerned. But hell, Sarah was a teenage girl and not inclined to pay much attention to what Mom had to say— even less inclined to pay attention to what a boring old dude who was hanging out with her mom, and possibly even having sex with her, had to say.

One June night, I decided to talk to the girl. I had enjoyed a calm and quiet dinner with Clara. Sarah had come into the room, silently picked off a couple of carrot and celery sticks, and retreated back to her sanctuary. I nodded at Clara and went over and knocked at her door.

She was lying on her bed with her computer in front of her. "Hey," she said.

"Hey back. How're you doing?"

"I've been better."

"Yeah. Me too."

I was standing off to the side. She tilted her computer screen toward me. Julie's face filled it. Sarah pushed a button for the slideshow to begin and a series of pictures of Julie taken from the web began to parade across the screen. Publicity stills, candid shots, headshots, body shots, each one lovelier than the last. None of the nudes or semi-nudes that were all over the web. Just pretty, heartbreaking shots of an unearthly beauty.

Sarah pushed a button to stop the slideshow.

"That's how I'm doing," she said.

"It takes a long time to get over something like this," I told her.

"I'll never get over it," she said. Then she looked right at me, or through me, and continued, "And neither will you. Look at your face. You look just like me."

There was no denying it.

So, despite my better instincts, I proceeded to relate

everything I had recently learned—from Harvey's observation, to the pictures on my wall, to Frick's report, to Lorenzo's story.

Her reaction was curious. I saw no hint of the excitement of the hunt, or of renewed hope of getting answers, or of anger or dejection or any of the emotions I had considered possible.

Instead, I saw an unchanged, blank expression.

She closed the lid of her laptop.

"Frankie," she said. "I wish you had told me all that before."

"I wanted to deal with this myself."

"I'm involved too. She was *my* friend."

"I know. But what more could you do?"

"Jesus, Frankie! Well, first of all I can look at those pictures. I can't believe you didn't bring them right to me. Second of all, I pretty much knew all that crap anyway. What do you think I've been doing on this computer? Besides looking at her pictures, I mean. All that stuff about the insurance is all over the web … if you dig deep enough, anyway. And I do. Mooney is making out like a bandit on this fiasco. Third … him fucking her? Tell me something I don't know. Anybody with eyes could see that. Fourth … Frack is in New Orleans. I already figured that out too. You and me are going to go visit him. Fifth … nobody knows where Mooney is. He's missing too. He's not in Hollywood. He's collected the insurance money and he's in parts unknown now. My money's on New Orleans, with Frack. Sixth … smiling when she went into the river? Hell, I knew that. I was right next to her, looking into her eyes. And it was more than a smile, Frankie. It was the kind of look I think terrorists get when they know they've sacrificed themselves for God and they're on their way to paradise. If I didn't know her so well, I'd think it was scary. And seven … you march me up that fucking Hill of Tears right now and show me those damn pictures."

I didn't tell her not to swear. I marched her up the fucking hill.

Chapter Twenty-Eight

∿

Shattered Glass

SARAH DIDN'T HAVE much to say about the photos. She looked at them carefully, but she said little.

Then she said, "Frankie, you have a cousin in New Orleans, right?"

"Right."

"How big is his house?"

"Not very big. He's got a wife and kid."

"Room enough for some visitors?"

"He's got a guest room and an office. And a couch. Sure."

"How much do flights cost?"

"I don't know. A couple hundred bucks. Maybe three. Maybe four."

"How soon can we be on a plane?"

I held up my hands, palms out. "Come on. Slow down, Sarah. We don't even know what we're looking for."

"I know what I'm looking for."

"*I* know what you're looking for—your friend Julie. She's not in New Orleans."

"Isn't she?"

"No."

"How do you know, Frankie? At least it's a place. At least it's *something*. Some place to go. Something to do. I want to *do* something. I *have* to do something."

"I'll grant you that there's a good chance Frack is there. And I'd love to talk to him. But I don't think that's compelling enough to make me—and you—dash off halfway across the country. I don't have a lot of money, Sarah. And you don't have any, as far as I know."

"Well, what do you want to do?"

I thought this over. "I want to talk to Mooney," I said.

"So do I," said Sarah. "He's probably there too. I'm feeling pulled there."

I don't usually quarrel with people when they say they're pulled somewhere or somehow. I was feeling pulled there too.

I called my cousin, Tommy. He had room for us. I went online and checked into tickets. They were fairly inexpensive and available. We could be basking in the New Orleans heat real quick, if basking was what we wanted. But *asking* is more what we wanted to do. We wanted to ask that son of a bitch Mooney what the hell was going on, not only with Julie but with Edith.

New Orleans is a big town. I had no idea how we could go about locating Mooney or Frack there. Shelburne Falls was one thing. I know everything about this burg and I know how to find anyone or anything here. New Orleans was a different story.

Tommy could be a big help. He'd lived there forty years playing in bars and painting houses, so he knew the place inside out. But still, it was a crapshoot, a needle in a haystack.

I needed to think it over more before I committed to going. I convinced Sarah to sleep on it. We would decide tomorrow.

I wanted to go for a walk. Alone. Or alone with a dog. Night had settled in and the neighborhood was quiet. I put Marlowe on his leash and headed out. Instead of going into town, we headed the other way—up the Hill of Tears, a direction I didn't often go in.

Just a short way beyond my house, the paved road ends and turns into a dirt road and the houses get farther and farther apart. Very quickly you are no longer in a village but in the country, seemingly deep in the woods. It gets dark and lonely and completely still.

We heard some bird songs I stopped to record. A Northern Mockingbird serenaded, or mocked, us with an endless string of *chew chews*. No cars passed by and we were lit up only by the sliver of the moon shining through the veil of the birches above our heads.

Marlowe was distracted by a rabbit and gave the leash a pleading tug. The rabbit passed and he tugged no more. There was no one around, so I let him off the leash and he dashed about happily, sniffing and picking up sticks. I tossed a few for him.

All I could think of was Mooney. I had never really been able to get a real grasp on the guy. Alcoholics can do that to you. We know how to keep a distance, how to reveal a little but never too much, never enough.

Was he capable of killing a young girl, his lover, to collect insurance money? Could he be that much of a monster? Could anybody?

And what the hell was up with this whole Edith Marie Pasternak thing? These two gone girls were related somehow.

Mooney was key. Once I found him, I could then move on to finding the Nutting Girl, if indeed there was anything left of her to find.

Edith was a throw-in. I knew Julie. I had been hired to protect her and I had failed, so making amends meant everything to me. I never knew Edith, so that intense personal connection was not there. But now I had been hired to find her too, and when I am hired to do something, I do it, so finding Edith meant a lot to me too.

Close to the peak of the Hill of Tears, Marlowe and I approached the old Snyder property—a sprawling estate with a two-hundred-year-old farmhouse at its center with more recently built spokes extending out from there. It had long since been converted to a mini artist's colony. The spokes had been filled with dorm-like rooms and studio space, and a barn out back converted to a performance center. The old place was just on the verge of crumbling, but it still appeared to be salvageable. It was in need of a buyer and a little loving care.

The now faded "For Sale" sign had fallen off its post and was leaning against the mailbox. It had been on the market for years—a magnificent place on a magnificent spot, but too costly for anyone around here to afford. Eight hundred thousand. It had sat vacant for a long time.

I was surprised to see a light on in the living room. I crept up to see if I could look in, but the curtain was drawn, and all the other windows were similarly cloaked. Was anyone in there or had someone just left a light on?

Marlowe ran around the perimeter, sniffing, wagging his tail, excited to be on a hunt. Truth be told, so was I.

It was quiet, still. No one was home. The quest was over. For now. I headed farther up the Hill of Tears, toward the peak. Marlowe followed reluctantly.

We were almost out of sight of the place when I heard something smash behind me—a shattering sound, glass. I turned. Marlowe ran toward the sound.

I looked.

It was Mooney. Standing outside the Snyder place porch. Looking down at the large flat rocks that lined the walkway. Looking down at a broken bottle.

"Raven, you sonofabitch," he hollered. "Come on in for a fucking drink."

Chapter Twenty-Nine

∿

Ashes to Ashes

MOONEY HAD ALREADY had a few. More than a few.

The house was furnished in a "staged" manner, the way realtors do to make a place look homey and almost lived-in but not quite. But this place looked really "lived in." There were empty pizza boxes everywhere and other takeout wrappers. Lots of empty bottles. A few were still filled.

It had been about a month since Julie floated down the river. I would be surprised to learn that Mooney had shaved, slept, or bathed since that day. By the looks of him, I would add "eaten" to that list too, except for the evidence of the empty food packages.

He had been drinking, though. That much was clear.

We were into June now, and the weather was getting warmer, but no windows were open. It was stuffy, sweaty, and smelled like a locker room.

And Scotch. It smelled like Scotch too.

Mooney staggered to the sofa and sat down with a groan, motioning for me to sit in the overstuffed chair next to him, which I did.

He poured three fingers of Scotch into a water glass and held it out to me.

"No thanks," I said.

"Okay, it's mine, I guess," he said, and started sipping from it.

"You've already got one," I pointed out, noting the similarly filled glass on the floor in front of him.

"Oh, hell. Can't have too much now, can you?" He laughed.

I laughed too.

The Muppet Movie was playing silently on the TV in front of Mooney.

He finished the drink in his hand and reached down for the one on the floor.

"This film is genius, by the way. Someday I'll make something this good. So, what brings you into these parts?"

"I live here. This is my 'hood."

"So do I. This is my 'hood too. I bought this place. We're neighbors."

"The 'For Sale' sign is still out there."

"Yeah. They left it there. They also left me this furniture. Nice, huh? I'll take it down tomorrow … the sign, I mean. Have a drink."

"No thanks."

He was watching Kermit play his banjo on the TV and singing "The Rainbow Connection."

"You know what, Raven? There really aren't that many songs about rainbows. There's only forty-two of them. I sat down and counted them yesterday. That's all I could come up with— forty-two. And I used Google too."

"That's not an insignificant number," I said.

"You know why there are songs about rainbows at all? Because everybody is looking for something on the other side. Just like Kermit says."

"The other side of the rainbow, as in pot of gold, or the 'other side,' like life after death?"

He cocked his head, took another sip. "I never thought of it that way. I guess it's ambiguous. I was thinking 'pot of gold' all the way. Everybody's looking for that damn pot of gold. And you know what, Raven? It's not there. There is no fucking pot of gold."

"Yes there is."

"No there's not."

"I gotta believe there is. There is something at the end. If, in fact, there is an end. I'm not even sure about that. But there is something somewhere."

"I gotta believe there's not."

"That's the difference between you and me, Mooney."

"I don't think so. There's no difference. You lost your religion. I lost mine. No difference. We end up the same."

"You're right about that. We're the same. We're all the same. It's the same damn soul, Mooney, everywhere."

"So, if we're the same and I'm drinking, you should have a fucking drink with me."

Hard to argue with logic like that. He poured three more fingers of Scotch into the first glass and handed it to me.

I accepted it, looked at it, smelled it, and set it on the table next to me. I didn't drink it though. Not yet. But I thought about it.

"We're the same guy, Raven," he said, "We both like redheads. You got your redheads. I got mine."

"I got two of them. How many do you have?"

"I got a houseful of them, Raven. A whole fucking houseful. A stable. I keep spares in case I run out. Same as you. And they all end in 'A,' same as yours. Just like your Sarah and your Clara."

"What is it about that sound, anyway?" I asked him. "It's somehow comforting."

"It's the very sound of comfort," he replied. "It's that casting out of your breath. *Ahh*. It's release. It's relief."

I had never heard anyone else talk like this. Or think like this. I'd figured I was alone. I was getting a little nervous.

He went on, "We're the same, Raven. In lots of ways. Maybe in every way. We're alcoholics. We see everything. We sense everything. We're tuned in. And we like redheads who end in 'A.' "

I thought this over. "There's one difference," I said. "You killed her. I didn't."

At this, he laughed. "Did I?"

"You did."

"Or was it you, Raven? I think it was you."

We were silent for a long time before Mooney went on, "There's no other side, Raven. No pot of gold. No life after death. There's nothing. When we're gone, we're gone. When she's gone, she's gone. And that is *it*. That is fucking all there is."

"Is she gone, Mooney?"

"She's gone, Raven. Just like Hall sings in the song. Or is it Oates? Never could tell the difference between those two."

"It was both, Mooney. They harmonized."

He walked to the corner of the living room. The place was sparsely furnished so there was nothing there really, except a small pile of something I couldn't quite identify—gray and black, maybe a couple feet in diameter, a couple inches high. It was chunky, lumpy, with a few sparkles of color mixed in. And I could see that the wide oak floorboards below it were scarred, burned.

"Ashes to ashes," he said as he stood over it. "It's an altar."

He ran his fingers through those ashes as if he were looking for something in there. His fingers were getting black as the ashes sifted and drifted back onto their spot on the floor.

"Pictures, Raven. Cards. Letters. Some people still write things on paper and send them through the mail. Poems. Some people still write poetry, Raven. Some people still do beautiful things. All Julie's. All for her. I couldn't stand to see them anymore. I couldn't stand to have them around."

"It didn't work, did it Mooney? It didn't get rid of her, did it?"

"Yes it did."

"Did it?"

"Yes, Raven. She's gone. Just like in the song. And now all traces of her are gone." He jutted his chin at the full glass beside me. "Drink up."

I looked at the drink he'd poured me, staring at me from the table. The stinging, bitter smell of it, and what had been spilled around here the past month, burned my nose and turned my stomach, not to mention my heart. I looked at the pyre in the corner.

Mooney was a wreck. He was the one I was looking for, and I had stumbled onto him, but his sorry state wasn't telling me much. Was he falling apart because he was missing Julie? Or because he had killed her? Maybe both.

"Why is she gone, Mooney?"

"She's gone because she's gone, Raven. There is no why."

I considered this. "Okay," I said, "is there a how? How is she gone?"

"Because she fell into the fucking river."

"Fell … or was she pushed?"

He didn't answer. He finished his drink and poured another. Then he staggered out of the chair and got real close to me, right in my face. As if to demonstrate, he pushed me. Hard. I pushed him back. Hard. Then he sat back down.

"Have a drink," he said. "It smells good, doesn't it?"

I had to admit, it did.

I looked Mooney in the eyes. "Are you okay, Mooney? I mean seriously. You look like you need some help."

"No, I'm not okay. But I don't need any help."

"Seriously, man, if you keep this up, you're going to die. I've seen this stuff before."

"I know you have. I know everything there is to know about you."

All I could think of was that I did not know enough about Mooney. I didn't know enough to know what he was capable of doing.

He sipped his Scotch and continued, "So, tell me Raven. Where have you seen this stuff before? Why is it so familiar to you?"

I didn't speak. Mooney let out a laugh.

"Yeah. We both know, don't we?" he finally said. "This is how alcoholics die."

"And sometimes we don't die. Sometimes we come back," I replied.

"Yeah," Mooney said, and then he added, with emphasis, "*Sometimes*. Sometimes they die and come back to life, right?"

I could not answer this. He laughed.

"Yeah. You know what I'm talking about, don't you?"

I did.

"They die and sometimes they come back to life. Has that ever happened to you?"

I let his question hang there. But we both knew the answer was yes.

Then he went on, "But you know what, Raven? They never come back the same. Something changes."

We sat there. Marlowe sat on the Oriental rug in the middle of the room with his head perked up, alertly scoping out the space with great interest.

"They're never the same, are they?" he repeated.

I had to agree. I shook my head.

"Have a drink," Mooney urged.

I was weakening, but I said, "No thanks."

"That's what happened on Lavender Street. Right?"

I remained silent. Then I said, "Wrong, Mooney. You don't know anything about Lavender Street. That's not what happened on Lavender Street. You're way off base. Anyway, there is no Lavender Street."

Mooney laughed. Then he said something else. "She was pushed. "

I looked at him.

"She was pushed," he repeated. "If I tell you how, will you have a drink with me?"

"No," I said. But I looked down and saw that I was holding the drink in my hand.

He laughed again. "Actually, I think you will," he said. "You pushed her, Raven."

"I was nowhere near her."

"You pushed her. You pushed her with all your crazy talk."

"What?"

"That talk about everybody being the same person. That 'God's in everyone' talk. The same stuff you were just telling me."

I couldn't respond.

"You pushed her, Raven. You killed her."

The drink was heavy in my hand. The next second it was feeling light. And now it smelled good.

"You know what I'm talking about, Raven?"

I put the glass to my lips. "Yes," I replied.

Mooney jumped off the couch and slapped the drink out of my hand, spilling the liquid over my face and onto Marlowe and the nice rug. Marlowe started lapping it up where it pooled.

"No, you don't want to do that," he said. He sat back down. "We'll find what we need to, Raven," he said. "So you gotta stick around for that."

"I thought you said she was gone. And that there's nothing on the other side. Nothing to find."

"For a guy so fucking smart, Raven, sometimes you are real fucking stupid. Yeah, she's gone and there's nothing on the other side of that fucking rainbow. Nothing. Nada.

"But you're not really listening to that frog on the TV, are you? He's not singing about the rainbow. He's singing about the *connection*. That's what matters, Raven. The connection. And that's what we'll find. *That's* what matters. That's *all* that matters."

"Now you're sounding like me, Mooney."

He poured me another drink and handed it to me.

"I'm gonna explain it to you real simple," he said. "All your talk about everybody being the same. And all that God bullshit."

I responded, "Everybody is the same, Mooney. And everyone is God. That's what I believe. That's all I believe. That's all I've ever believed."

"You're real close, Raven, but you're slightly off. You and me? We're both the same. That's the fucking rainbow connection. But it doesn't go further than that. It's you and me, buddy, that's the same. It's not all of humanity. We're not all the same. Everybody else is different. But me and you?" He took a thirsty sip. "Me and you? Two peas in a fucking pod." He held out his glass for a toast and said, very softly now, "Drink up."

"Fuck you," I said.

"You pushed her. You killed her. You, Raven. I saw her face when she listened to you talk. I saw how she changed on this shoot. I saw her when she was sick. She was off in never-never land for weeks, Raven, and when she came back, she was different. And it was all because of you. You pushed her."

"Me?"

He laughed. "Yes, you."

And then I took a sip.

Chapter Thirty

~∽

Day Zero

I HAVE REASON to believe I took many more sips that night, but I remember none of it.

Then I woke up. That I remember.

I woke up on Mooney's couch. Marlowe was licking my face. I felt like shit. Was it the next morning? Or a week later? A month later? A year?

I could hear Mooney snorting from the downstairs bedroom, a snorting just short of a snore.

I pulled myself up. I was unsteady on my feet, but I succeeded in rising. Marlowe was pleased to see me still among the living. He wagged his tail and sniffed me curiously.

All I wanted to do was to get the hell out of there, so that's what I did. I stopped twice to throw up on the walk back down the Hill of Tears to my house. At home, I collapsed on my own couch and continued my interrupted night's sleep.

When I awoke again, it was dark out. A plaintive wavering whistle *klee-klee-klee-klee* greeted me from my window—the mating call of a kestrel.

A mating call. I peeled off my clothes. There was hardened vomit on my shirt and pants. I was going to toss them into the laundry, but I choose the garbage instead. I managed a shave and a shower. Then I managed to eat some scrambled eggs.

Next, I managed a walk down the Hill of Tears to see Clara.

How did she know? I thought I had cleaned myself up. But she knew. She knew I had slipped up. Slipped up bad.

"Jesus," she said, "look at you."

She poured me a blessed cup of coffee.

What was she seeing? I didn't think I looked that bad. I was showered and shaved and I had on clean clothes.

"It's in your eyes," she said. "They're hollow and drained. I've never seen your eyes look like that. There's even less life in them than usual."

I started to tell her.

"Stop," she said. "I don't need to hear it. I don't want to hear it. Unless you really want to tell me, that is …."

So I shut up.

Sarah came in. She looked at me. "Jesus," she said, "what the hell happened?"

"I had a bad night."

"I guess so."

Clara cooked some food for us. I don't even remember what it was, but I devoured it. It tasted good and I was starting to feel human.

It was nighttime. I had lost a full day.

Clara touched my face kindly and said little.

I ate food and drank more coffee and then decided it was time to go home and start over. So I rose from the table and touched her face and kissed her on the cheek and headed for the door.

"Day one," she said. "Today is day one."

"Day one?"

"That's how they count it in AA. One day of sobriety."

That didn't sound right to me. This wasn't any kind of day. This was one of those periods—sometimes they last a day, sometimes a year, sometimes several years—when you are in the twilight zone. You go through the motions. You are breathing but you are not alive. It's purgatory and it's not worthy of any number at all, especially the number one.

I explained that to Clara.

She asked, "What would you call it then?"

I thought for a minute and said, "Day zero."

I headed up the hill with a tear in my eye.

Chapter Thirty-One

∾

Day One

Day zero mercifully came to a close, and I awoke to Day one.

I had survived. I went back to Clara's.

She was sipping tea and sitting on the couch where we made our first strong connection not that long ago. I joined her. It took a while for the words to come out, but they finally did.

"I'm feeling shame," I told her.

"I can understand that, but that's not productive. It's over. Start over. If you couldn't make yesterday day one, make it today. Live in the present, not the past."

"I know. It's not easy."

"No one ever said this stuff would be easy."

We sat there a while and neither of us spoke.

Then she asked, "Why did you drink, Frank? You know you can't do that."

"I thought you wanted to move on. Are you trying to make me re-live it? Isn't that living in the past?"

"No. This is the present, right now. And you're not going to drink right now. That's all I care about. But maybe knowing why you did it can help you not do it again."

I thought for a long time before I replied. "He said I killed Julie," I explained. "And it made sense."

"That's crazy talk, Frank."

"No, Clara. I don't think it is. I made the mistake of telling her some of the stuff that runs through my head, and I think it set her off somehow. That's all my own stuff. I had no right pouring it out on someone else."

"Your stuff is good stuff, Frank. That girl was unstable. Everyone knew that. If something set her off, it was inside her, not from you."

I couldn't meet her eyes. "She had a spark inside her. It could have brightened up like the sun, or it could have exploded like dynamite. I lit the fuse. I shouldn't have done that."

She laid her hand lightly on my leg. "Frank, you did what you had to do. It is what it is. What she did with it was her responsibility, not yours."

I held a cup of tea but was not drinking it.

"All I ever wanted to do was help her. All I ever wanted to do with anything was help people. That's why finding things has always meant so much to me. That's why I loved being a good detective. I had a knack for finding things and that helped a lot of people. I did a lot of favors for friends. And now that's all backfired on me. Now trying to help someone might have killed her."

"You didn't kill her, Frank."

"Didn't I?"

"No." After a while, she went on, "You're scaring me, Frank. You gave up on life once before, and now it sounds like you're going to do it again. Don't."

"It was different before. I had two miracles happen to me. My sight came back and I died and was reborn. Those two things came pretty much back to back and it was exhilarating, for a while. Then life got to be routine. No more miracles. Life went on, day to day, moment to moment. I got bored. I got tired. Even finding things for friends didn't help."

"That's when you gave up," Clara said.

"Yes."

"And you got born again when you ran into this crazy movie guy and this sad young woman who fell into the river, and set out on a search a lot bigger than anything you were ever on before."

"Yes."

"You needed all this, Frank. You didn't kill her. In fact, it's almost the exact opposite. She brought you back to life."

Did she have to die to do that? I didn't speak that thought aloud, but it ran through my head.

I answered my own question. *No, she didn't have to die. She didn't die. I didn't kill her.* In fact, if I was going to honor her gift of bringing me back to the living, I owed her something, and that was to find her—to bring her back to the living too, if that's what she wanted. I knew that maybe that wasn't what she wanted.

But that would be her choice. My job was to find her.

I had been silent a long time.

"Are you still there?" Clara asked.

"Yes," I replied.

"Good," she said.

She touched my hand then. I realized how much she had been touching me ever since I met her.

I kissed her. I touched her. I thanked her.

I walked back up the hill to gather enough strength to face day two.

Chapter Thirty-Two

∿

Day Two

D AY TWO STARTED with my filling Sarah in on what had occurred. Clara was at work, and Sarah was sitting on the porch with her computer on her lap. It was the end of June, and a hot humid summer seemed to be settling in. The air was dense but the sun shone through; some deep clouds and thunderstorms were forecast for later.

"I can't believe that fucker is living right up that goddamn hill," she said. I had long since stopped trying to stop her from swearing. "And he's accusing *you* of killing her?"

"He means it metaphorically. At least I'm pretty sure he does. But it still hits home. I know what he's saying."

"He's crazy, Francis."

"I know. But still, if what he said didn't make any sense, things wouldn't have gotten so out of hand."

"You got to let go of that stuff. You can't allow what a crazy person says to affect you like that."

"I know."

"And you can't ever drink again."

"I know. You're just like your mom. She told me basically the same thing."

"I want to go up there and talk to him," she said.

"I knew you'd say that. But what's it going to prove?"

"I want to see his eyes. Just like I saw your eyes the other night. You can tell a lot by looking someone in the eyes."

"I think he killed her, Sarah. He was a mess, a total wreck. There wasn't much left of him. Only a few things can drive someone like that back to the bottle. Murder is one of them."

"How about the death of someone you love?"

"Yeah, that's one too."

"We know he didn't *actually* kill her. He was nowhere near when she fell in."

"He could have paid Frack to do the dirty work."

"But Frank, if he loved Julie, how could he kill her?"

"He's a psychopath, Sarah. He doesn't love anyone except himself."

"That's why I want to see him. I want to look into those eyes. If he's a psychopath, I'll know it."

"You've seen his eyes before."

"A lot has changed since then. I've grown up a lot."

It wasn't long before she had her chance.

There he was, over my right shoulder, walking on the lawn, stepping around the garden, approaching us. He still looked like shit—beard scraggly, hair greasy, clothes still the same as two nights ago. He reeked of foul body odor and alcohol seeping through the pores.

He sat on the edge of the porch, his back toward us. Sarah could not see his eyes from here. But we could hear his voice. "I try never to leave my house, but sometimes I need supplies. And who do I run into but you two guys?"

He turned around and we could see his eyes.

"Just the two guys I wanted to see."

Chapter Thirty-Three

◦◦◦

Do Not Go Gentle

"Y OU HAVE ANY booze in the house?" Mooney asked Sarah.

To my surprise, she got up, went inside, and came back with an almost full bottle of Jameson. She handed it to him.

After cracking it open and taking a substantial gulp, he said, "I'm on my way to Good Spirits to stock up. But that's a long walk."

"Yeah, like a block and a half. Can't walk that far without refueling along the way," I said.

He wiped his mouth and replied, "Yeah. I need my fuel."

Sarah was glaring at him—and staring into his eyes.

"Thanks for the drink, sweetie," he said to her.

"I just got it for you so you'd stick around long enough for me to study you," she replied. "Otherwise, you could go fuck yourself."

"Hey. What kind of way is that for a nice young girl to talk? Raven, you're not doing your usual job."

"I gave up."

Sarah grabbed the bottle out of his hand. "That's enough,"

she said. "I've seen enough to know who you are and I don't like what I see."

Mooney looked stunned, but also sincere.

"I'm the best friend you got, girlie."

"Don't call me girlie, asshole. Or sweetie."

"Okay, sorry. Jeez, I am an asshole, aren't I?"

Sarah did not hesitate to answer, "Yes."

"But I'm still the best friend you got."

"I don't know how many friends like you I could stand."

"Don't you want her back?"

She didn't have to answer this time. She just looked at him.

"I'm the only one around with the resources to do that," he said.

I had to jump in here. "Mooney, two days ago you told me she was dead. Not only dead but that I killed her. Now you want her back? What the hell are you talking about?"

Sarah was still holding the bottle. Mooney made a wave to her and she handed it back to him. He took a swig.

"Maybe she is, maybe she isn't," he said. He took another drink and looked down into the bottle as if there were answers in there. Maybe there were. "I want to know for sure."

"You seemed pretty damn sure when you were accusing me of murder. *Murder*, Mooney. That means the person is dead."

Raising his head, he looked me right in the eyes. Then he did the same to Sarah, and said, "I think she's dead, you guys. I *know* she's dead. And it breaks my fucking heart."

And here he did a funny thing, especially for a psychopath; he began crying.

He was sobbing and shaking. Then he took another drink, which seemed to stabilize him. He appeared stone cold sober when he repeated it. "Yeah. It breaks my fucking heart." He paused a long while before continuing, "And I want you guys to find her. If she's alive. I know that if anyone can find her, if she's alive, it's you guys."

I responded, "Mooney, we're already doing that. At least we're working on it."

"I can help you," he said.

"Good. We need all the help we can get," said Sarah. She grabbed the bottle back. "But before you can be any help at all, you have to give this up. Again."

Mooney grabbed the bottle back. "No. You know, I've only been drunk twice in my life—once for two years, and once for three. I started young, when I was seventeen. Now I'm on the third time around, and this one's going to last a while, just like the others did. You gotta give me this one, because I have a lot to give to you."

We didn't have to respond because the obvious question hung in the air like a lynched thief.

"Money," he said. "I can provide you guys with all the money you need. To go anywhere, do anything."

We looked at him.

He cried some more, then said, punctuated by a hiccup or two, "I hired both you guys a month ago and I've never fired you. You're still on the payroll. Only you've got new duties this time. You have to find Julie."

"We want a raise," Sarah said. "Two hundred dollars a day, plus expenses. Apiece."

"Done. You got it," Mooney said.

"No," Sarah said. "That was too easy for you. Make it three. Three hundred a day. Apiece."

"You got it."

"And a down payment," she added. She was a hard bargainer. "Two thousand dollars."

If you looked into his eyes now, you'd think he was sober.

He nodded to Sarah, wiped his eyes, took another drink, handed the bottle back to her, and started walking into town.

"You know where to find me," he said. Turning around, he looked at me and chuckled. "Yeah, I'm a burnout. Have a good laugh." Then he *really* looked at me, right in the eyes, and said,

"At least I'm not fading away. I'm raging, Raven, raging, raging. You're going gentle. Into that good night. And with that, I bid you both … a good night."

Then he was gone.

"I don't know what to think," I said to Sarah. "You don't hire someone to find a person if you killed that person."

"I do," she replied. "I know what to think. But I'll take his money anyway. Pack your bags."

Chapter Thirty-Four

~∽

Keep Kicking Mister Duck

H<small>ALF AN HOUR</small> later, Mooney was back on the porch clutching four bottles of Jameson, all fifths. Somewhere in town he had found one of those big white canvas bags with the name SHELBURNE FALLS on it in large green letters, in which he had packed the booze. A normal paper bag would have broken under the weight. Despite his shaky condition, Mooney was still resourceful.

Sarah took one look at him, let out a deep sigh, and ducked back into the house. She couldn't stand the thought of talking to him again. I wasn't wild about the idea myself, but I did have some other things I needed to discuss with him.

"Mooney," I said, "let's change the subject a little. What can you tell me about Edith Marie Pasternak?"

He cracked open one of the bottles and took a healthy swig. "I do not know an Edith Marie Pasternak."

Mooney wiped his mouth. He looked as if he preferred this subject to Juliana Velvet Norcross, so I pulled out the now crumpled and creased photo and held it in front of his face. There was a flash of recognition.

"Oh, Victoria. Victoria Diamond. Sure, I know her. She was going to be in the movie."

"Her name is Edith."

"I know her as Victoria. Victoria is her professional name. Her acting name."

"Well, this is her headshot. This is used professionally, right? And it calls her Edith."

"She changed it when she signed on. She's Victoria."

"Okay, whatever. So you know her?"

He held the bottle out toward me, but I ignored him. He took another chug.

"Well, sure. I hired her. I hire all the actors. A casting director finds them and sends them to me and I hire the ones I like."

"You liked this one?"

"I like a lot of them. I like girls, Raven. If you haven't figured that out yet."

"Have you seen her lately?"

"No."

"You know anything about her—where she's staying? What she's doing?"

He heaved a ragged sigh, and his face turned oddly petulant, like an aggrieved child's. "What the hell are you bothering me about this girl for, Raven? Who gives a good goddamn?"

"I give a good goddamn," I replied. "I give a lot of good goddamns."

He let out a laugh and accidentally spit out a mouthful of whiskey. "You, Raven? You give a goddamn about something? Good for you, man. You're coming around."

I did not react to his needling. "So … I'm waiting. What do you know about her?"

"Not much. I hired her in L.A. and haven't seen her since."

"I've heard she was with you here in Shelburne Falls."

"With me?"

I made a broad gesture. "With all of you. Here in town. Part of that whole gang you were going around with."

He scowled. "You heard wrong, Raven. I haven't seen that girl."

"You sure?"

"Yes, damn it." He was close to shouting. "How many times do I have to say it?"

"She's a good-looking gal."

He gave a derisive huff. "Is she? In Hollywood, she's plain. If not below average."

"Not to my eyes."

"You're the one who's blind, Raven."

"Okay." I let it drop.

"Maybe she was here with all the others," Mooney conceded. "I can't keep track of every redheaded girl who shows up."

"Maybe?"

"Yeah, maybe. Forget it, Raven. Forget all this shit, except finding Julie. That's your job now."

"This is my job too."

"How many damn jobs do you have anyway? When I met you, you didn't have any jobs. Now you got more than you can handle."

Despite the bloodshot eyes, the stench, and the occasional stifled hiccup, he acted almost sober and remained eloquent. I contemplated his face, trying to discern how much was bluster and how much truth.

Finally, I said, "Jobs seem to find me."

"That's funny, Raven. You're supposed to be the guy who finds things. Now things are finding you."

Mooney was drinking, but he was still gazing at the photo of Edith. He was seeing something there, so I made one more attempt. Eloquence aside, this guy was a wreck and I thought he might break a little.

"You sure you don't know anything more about Edith Marie Pasternak, aka Victoria Diamond?" I asked him.

"Didn't we go through all this like a minute ago? I'm positive. What else do you want me to say?"

"I want you to say the truth."

"Truth? What is the truth? The truth is that this whiskey tastes good."

He pushed the bottle toward me and I ignored it again.

"Truth, Mooney? Truth is seeing things as they really are. In Buddhism they call it dhamma. In Christianity, it's what God is. Along with love. And a few other qualities that I'm blanking on right now."

He raised the bottle as if toasting me. "Thank you, Mister Lost His Religion, for the lovely sermon."

I nodded. "You are most welcome, Mister Lying His Ass Off. You don't know anything else about that girl? I've heard different."

He took another swig, avoiding my eyes. "You can't believe everything you hear, Raven. You know that."

"I know all about belief."

"And lack of belief."

"I only believe about fifty percent of the things I see—"

"Well," he broke in, "that's because you're half blind." He was still looking off into the distance.

I continued, "And maybe ten percent of the things I hear."

"How's your hearing?" he said, staring at me now.

"Not too bad."

"Good. At least one of your senses works."

"My sense of taste is okay too. And some of my other senses are all right, mostly the ones that can't be measured. For instance, I believe one hundred percent of the things I feel."

He laughed at this and replied, "The trick is figuring out *what* you feel, right? Once you figure it out, you can believe it. It's the figuring out that's hard."

"You're smarter than you look, Mooney."

"That's one of my skills. Looking dumb. Comes in handy sometimes."

He drank up and then he broke the silence. "What are you feeling about me, right now?" he asked.

"You mean besides feeling like you're an evil sonofabitch?"

"Yeah. Besides that. I already know that."

"I feel like you know more than you're saying about that Pasternak girl."

He stared me down. "What do you believe?"

"I believe you know more than you're saying about that Pasternak girl."

More derisive laughter. "Belief is a bitch, isn't it, Mister Lost His Religion."

"Yeah. It's a bitch all right. I guess I haven't totally lost my religion. I've actually prayed about this thing. About Edith Marie Pasternak."

"And about anyone else?" he asked.

"Yes. You know the answer to that."

"Juliana Velvet Norcross?"

I nodded.

"Prayed to whom?" he asked.

"That's one of the best questions you've ever asked me."

"What's the answer?"

I never did answer his question. Instead I asked him one. "I've heard you had some kind of encounter with this Edith, or Victoria, at the Blue Rock one night. Care to comment on that?"

He mimicked my voice surprisingly well as he replied, "No. I don't 'care to comment.' I don't respond to rumors and third-hand innuendo."

"Why not?"

"Well, for one thing, in Hollywood, if you commented on rumors and third-hand innuendo, you would have time to do little else, and I have things to do. Important things." He took a gulp from the bottle, pointed at it, and said, "Like this." He continued, "But mainly because I don't have to."

"There are very few things we humans *have* to do," I said.

"And answering your stupid questions is certainly not one of them."

"Don't you sometimes do things you don't have to do?"

He examined the bottle as if he might learn the answer from the label. "Sometimes."

"Then why not do this one? For a pal."

His smile was half sardonic sneer. "Are you my pal, Raven?"

I stared out into the distance. "I don't see you having any pals, Mooney. You had lots of people bowing to you and lots of beautiful women all over you, but I don't think you ever had any real friends." I looked directly at him. "And now? Now you really don't have any friends. Except for that bottle. You sit alone in that big house with the bottle. I think you could use one. Toss me a bone and I'll be your friend."

I did not want to be this guy's friend. But he was weakening. I was getting somewhere.

He laughed. "You're not that easily bought. I wish you were." Then he changed the subject and said, "You think you're a smart guy, Raven, but you don't know anything about me."

"That's the damn problem, isn't it?"

"It's not a problem. Nobody knows me. But I'll help you out here. Because I really do need a friend."

And then, Mooney, for maybe the first time in his life, said something sincere. "I don't think you're easily bought, Raven. But I think you're easily fooled."

"Are you trying to fool me now?"

"You'll have to figure that out for yourself, my friend."

So I waited. And he sipped his drink.

"Okay," he said, bowing his head as if in surrender. "I knew that girl pretty well. We got pretty close. And yeah, we made a small scene in the Rock that night. But that was it. She couldn't get what she wanted from me and she split, just like I'll do once I can pull myself together, and once all this bullshit here is over, much as you folks amuse me. She went back west, as far as I know, and I haven't heard from her since. She's gone."

"Did you go for a swim that night?"

"No. What are you talking about?"

"Just heard some reports about you getting wet is all."

He frowned. "Your reports are wrong."

"You know what really bugs me about this conversation?" I said to him. "You just lied to me, Mooney. Sure, you ended up telling the truth, but you preceded it with a lie. How am I supposed to believe anything you say?"

"That's your problem Raven. You're the belief guy. And the feelings guy. Go with your feelings."

"Feelings and beliefs are inextricably intertwined."

He laughed, and then he drank. "You talk funny. But I like you, Raven, I really do." As he took still another drink, he said, "We're buddies now."

I saw red for a split second. It was blind rage. Then I got myself under control.

"A couple days ago, you said I killed Julie. Now you love me. What the hell is going on?"

Drinking can simultaneously crank you up and calm you down. Now Mooney was calming down.

"Take a walk with me, Raven," he said. "I like your flower bridge. Let's walk and talk."

The Bridge of Flowers was just across the street from Clara's house. Mooney was on the verge of telling me something, so I went along.

It was in full bloom now. It smelled sweet, and bees buzzed around us. Mooney was drinking, I was walking, and we were silent until we got to the center, when he paused in front of one of the stone benches. He stepped up on it and gazed across the relatively still river. He should have been unsteady from all the booze, but he stood straight and solid.

"I like the river too," he said.

He climbed down, back onto the walkway, and we continued our stroll. We must have looked like two old friends instead of two guys who each suspected the other of murdering someone he loved.

"I like your bridge and I like your river, Raven," he said. "But given my druthers, I'd always stay on the bridge. I don't get wet."

"Never?"

"Well, hardly ever."

"When was the last time you got wet, Mooney?"

He actually thought it over. "When I was baptized," he finally said.

I was surprised. "You were baptized?"

"Yeah. Holy roller stuff. In a river with a preacher."

"Okay, now I understand what you meant when you said you lost your religion too."

"I did. You know, I was raised by hippies. Parents had no use for religion. But me, I was a rebel, you know? I rebelled against them by reading the Bible. I had to do it surreptitiously. I'd read it under the covers in bed with a flashlight. Other kids looked at porn. Me, I read the Bible. I was a closet Bible reader."

"So what happened?"

"I got older than twelve is what happened. But not before I went out and got myself baptized. In a friggin' river."

"And you haven't been wet since then."

"No. Don't even like water. It's okay to look at it but can't stand to jump in."

"That's the difference between us, isn't it Mooney? You don't commit to anything. You look, but you're afraid to jump in."

"Raven, what the hell are you talking about? You haven't jumped into anything in years." We stopped walking, and he went on, "But now you're at least starting to get your toes wet. Next comes the feet. Then up to the knees. Then you're in waist deep. You might as well jump in all the way at that point."

Mooney was right. I had started jumping into things, and it all started to happen when he showed up in town.

"Yeah, Mooney. I'm a duck. I'm always wet."

He laughed. "Funny you should say that. That's what Julie calls you—a duck."

"I know." I winced a little, but only inside.

"Lots going on under the surface. I see it too, Raven."

He stopped at the end of the bridge, near the gate, and said, "Keep kicking those legs, Raven. That's the only way you're going to stir up the waters."

"A duck kicks his legs to move, Mooney, not to stir things up."

"How far are you moving, Raven?"

"Not very far. Not very far at all."

Did that bother me? I didn't think so. Moving forward hadn't been a goal for a long, long time.

"Well, maybe you should keep at it then."

"Maybe I should."

As he walked away—no sign of a stagger—he said, "Keep kicking, Mister Duck, keep kicking."

Chapter Thirty-Five

~⁀~

Not Leaving on a Jet Plane

SARAH HAD TOLD me to pack my bags, so I did, but we would not be leaving on a jet plane. Not just yet.

Clara was coming too. She would not let her eighteen-year-old daughter and me go running off to a strange town, so now there were three in our party.

We had three tickets to New Orleans, leaving from Hartford with a two-hour stopover in Atlanta. I was traveling light—one small bag and my daypack. Sarah, for a teenage girl, surprised me by packing as lightly as I had. Clara was just as efficient. It was an early flight—7:15 a.m.—and about an hour drive to Hartford. We were giving ourselves plenty of time to be delayed at the airport, and we allowed time to stop at the truck stop in Whately for breakfast, all of which meant it was about 4 a.m. when we loaded up my old Subaru.

Officially known as the Whately Diner Fillin' Station, it was a classic American silver boxcar-like diner right on Rt. 91 and yes, at 4:30 a.m., it was lit up bright and red and neon and its lot was filled with long-haul tractor trailers.

The three of us sat at the counter. I ordered scrambled eggs and toast and home fries and sausage and coffee. Sarah had a monster stack of blueberry pancakes. Clara had an omelet. The clientele was virtually all male, except for Sarah and Clara.

I was sipping my second cup of coffee and reading the *Boston Globe* when Sarah left for the restroom. Too much time passed.

"She's been gone a while," said Clara. "I'm going to check on her."

Clara left and I read some more. Then I realized that she had been gone for a long time too. So I folded the paper and headed toward the restrooms myself.

On the way I found Sarah and Clara, sitting in a booth with a bald, burly guy in a flannel shirt, all sipping coffee and deep in conversation. Sarah looked up as I approached and waved at me. She motioned for me to sit down, which I did, next to the guy.

"And that's why I hate to haul potatoes," he finished up.

Sarah laughed like this was the funniest thing she had ever heard. The bald guy looked pleased with himself.

"Bert," she said, "this is my dad. You can call him Frankie."

Bert stuck his hand out across the table for a handshake. He had a firm grip.

"Pleased to meet you, Frankie. You've got a nice family here. On your way to the Big Easy?" he said. "I love that town."

"Yeah, me too," I replied.

"Business or pleasure?"

"We're visiting my Uncle Tommy," Sarah said.

Bert seemed like a pleasant and amiable enough guy. Still, I wondered why they were sitting there with him. But I played dumb, not hard for me.

We chatted for a while. I even had another cup of coffee, which Bert said he would pay for. Bert told us about his wife and two kids back in Ohio. We were making a new friend. I had no idea why.

Sarah kept Bert enchanted with her wit and intelligence, while Clara and I sat there almost completely silent. We were going to be late for the flight if we didn't leave soon, so we politely said our goodbyes and headed back to our seats at the counter to pay up.

We were almost there. Sarah was nudging me, elbowing me silently. Then she pointed behind us with her thumb, indicating that I should turn around, which I did.

What I saw was Bert rising from his seat and reaching into his back pocket for his wallet.

In his other back pocket, sticking out two or three inches, was an orange bandana identical to the one worn by Julie on the morning of the shoot.

Chapter Thirty-Six

∿

A Good Life

YOU HAD TO go up to a cash register to pay your bill. Bert was in the front of the line, and there were two other customers between him and us. I recognized the bandana.

Sarah furiously whispered in my ear, "Yeah, I see this old dude coming out of the men's room and I see that bandana in his pocket and I had to talk to him. So I just walked up to his table and smiled. I said could I talk to him a minute; I needed to get away from my asshole parents for a while. He let me sit down."

"That is so dangerous, Sarah."

"Yeah, right. But what else was I supposed to do? This is important. This whole damn thing is dangerous."

"Those bandanas are pretty common, aren't they?"

"No. Not those bright orange ones. They're real hard to find. I was all over the internet looking for them. There's some knockoffs around, but that's the real thing there. I can tell."

Bert paid his bill. The two customers between us paid their bills pretty quickly, and then we had to decide what to do. Bert was leaving the diner and heading toward one of the big tractor trailers.

Did we want to confront him? Someone who might be a kidnapper, a murderer?

Yeah. We did. Because whoever he was, he knew something. At least we were pretty sure he did.

He was almost to his vehicle. Sarah trotted up to him and tapped him on the shoulder. He turned around, appearing a little startled. He smiled at her.

"You in a hurry, Bert?" she asked.

"No. Not really. I'm running ahead."

"So are we," she lied. "Let's talk some more."

So we all went back in for more coffee.

He did seem like a good guy, a little shy, not really sure why these strangers were wanting his time, but he was curious and bright, and willing to play along and see where this was going.

Sarah idly stirred her coffee and got right to the point. "Bert, that's an interesting orange bandana you've got in your pocket."

"Oh, is that even there? I totally forgot about it. Don't usually carry one. I've been using it to wipe the mirrors."

"Where did you get it?" Sarah said.

"Well, that's a weird story. Couple weeks ago, I'm driving this same route, moving potatoes down south, and I'm right here at this diner. Just about this time of night too. Or morning, whatever. I drive all night. Hard to tell what time of day it is. It was still dark. Just before dawn, I guess. Like now.

"Anyway, I'm sitting there drinking coffee just like now. And this girl comes up to me, just like you did. In fact, you kinda remind me of her. How many times does an old fat bald dude like me get approached by two pretty young girls?"

"She looked like me?"

"Well, no, not really. She didn't have that red hair. Hers was dark. Black. And kind of short, trimmed up like a helmet around her head, you know what I mean? But she was about your size. And you remind me of her somehow. The way you talk, the way you move."

"What did she want?"

"A ride. She asked where I was going. I was going all the way to Jacksonville, Florida. She said that was close enough."

Sarah asked, "Do you always take hitchhikers?"

"Well, she wasn't technically hitchhiking. She was just asking sweetly. We're not supposed to. Not good for insurance. Usually I don't, but sometimes it gets pretty lonely on the road and I appreciate somebody to talk to."

As good a guy as he seemed to be, I was starting to have doubts about old Nice Guy Bert. He seemed to read my mind.

"Hey, I'm happily married. I don't mess around. Especially with young girls. If I give someone a ride, it's just to help them out and find somebody to talk to, okay? Jeez, I've picked up guys, old folks, all kinds. I'm no sleazebag. Okay? Do we understand each other?"

I allowed as how we did and he continued, "It's sixteen hours to Jacksonville and I did it straight through."

Now I was having doubts about this dude again. "That's a lot of coffee," I said.

He caught my drift. "Yeah. A lot of coffee. And a lot of other stuff too. We all use them. Little pills—red ones, green ones, yellow, white. I've learned how to not abuse them. Only use them when I have to, and only on the job. I'm careful.

"That Jillian, though, wow, that gal was not careful. She could scarf them down like Skittles."

"Jillian? That was the girl you drove."

"Yeah."

"What else do you know about her?"

"Funny you should ask. When you're popping speed with somebody for almost a full day and you're stuck in a small space like that, all you do is talk. And that's what we did, we talked. I must have told her my whole life story like three times. And my thoughts on every freaking issue from sports, to politics, to movies, to religion, to family, to love, to the best pie on 95. There's really no good pie on 95 anywhere now, by the way, not that we stopped. None of it's really homemade anymore."

"So what did she talk about?" Sarah asked.

"Well, as I said, I talked about a lot. And she talked a lot too, but I honestly don't think she talked *about* anything. I mean she said a lot of words, but I don't remember her revealing anything at all about who she was. It was like she was reading from some kind of script, you know what I mean. I mean, she was a great character. She was cute and funny, and wow, really, really pretty. I'm not blind. But I have no idea who she was deep down inside or anything like that."

"Where was she going?" Sarah asked.

"Miami. To see her grandmother. She said that much. Jacksonville was right on the way."

"When was this?" I asked.

"Not long ago. A couple weeks."

So it was quite a while after the day Julie got taken by the river. No wonder he was not connecting the two events. I had seen enough of her performances—those not up on the big screen—to know what a chameleon she could be. She was a good enough actor to get so totally immersed in a character, both physically and emotionally, that there was no reason this guy would ever suspect he was transporting the world's most famous missing person.

Sarah needed more than he was giving us. "I don't get it," she said. "You guys were in there for sixteen hours and all you did was talk. What *did* you talk about? She must have said *something*."

He thought a moment, his brow knit in concentration, eager to please. "Well, she said a lot. But just kind of superficial stuff. She told me about her boyfriend, some kid named Bruce if I recall. Sounded like a nice boy—basketball player. Talked about high school, her favorite subjects—she liked math and science. She had a dog—a corgi named Rufus. Talked a lot about Rufus, throwing him sticks in her yard."

"You picked her up here," Sarah asked. "Where did she start out?"

"She said she was from Shelburne Falls. Born and grown up there."

"How did you get that bandana?"

"Just found it on the seat after she got out. It was down behind the cushion. Actually, I didn't find it till she was long gone or I would have returned it to her."

"Did she seem nervous? Scared? Happy? Sad?" I realized Sarah would do just fine in an interrogation room.

"Wait a minute. Who is this girl to you?"

Sarah took a deep breath before answering, perhaps realizing she needed to tone down the intensity. "She was my friend," she said in a calmer voice.

"What happened? Did she run away or what?"

"We don't exactly know yet."

We had learned about as much as we were going to learn from Bert. And we had missed our plane, but that was okay. There would be other flights to New Orleans if that was still where we wanted to go.

But Bert wasn't done yet. "You know I said this girl was a mystery and I meant it. She gave me all this generic high school talk and she looked the part too. But she also said one thing I didn't quite get.

"It was just when she was getting out. At another truck stop, just off 95 in Jacksonville. Maybe her defenses were down by then. Anyway, she turns and looks at me and I say my goodbyes, all the usual stuff about how it's been fun, wishing her the best, etcetera, etcetera. And she looks me right in the eye. And, Jeez, those eyes can pierce right through you. You guys must know what that's like. So I say, 'Have a good life,' which is what I always say to people, you know.

"And she says something like, 'I've had a good life. And I thought it was over. And it still might be. At least this life.' Then she got out. And that was the last I saw of her."

I paid for Bert's coffee this time and we headed back to the parking lot with him. We walked him back to his truck. He pulled himself in and cranked down the window.

The roar of his engine rolled over us and we were just about back to my Subaru when he pulled up next to us, heading toward the exit.

He had to shout to be heard over the cacophony. "Hey, I almost forgot to say have a good life, you guys."

Sarah hollered back to him that he should have a good life too.

Then he added one more thing, "That Jillian was cute and smart but she might get lost. I've been all over Jacksonville many times. And there's no Lavender Street in that town."

Chapter Thirty-Seven

∿

Hints of Traces of Ghosts

WE WENT BACK to Shelburne Falls. I had no idea what to do next. Thanks to Mooney, we had all the money we needed to go anywhere and do anything, but I did not know what these places or things should be.

We were going to New Orleans because we believed Frack was there and that he knew something—or perhaps had even pushed Julie into the river.

Now we were sure that Julie was still alive, or had been alive a couple weeks ago. She had survived the fall into the river.

But her curious words about her life, and yes, about Lavender Street, echoed loudly.

It was one of those nights when I could not fall asleep. We now had a hint of a trace of the ghost of our dear missing Juliana Velvet Norcross, and that was exciting and invigorating news. But there was another missing girl—Edith Marie Pasternak, aka Victoria Diamond—and I was obliged to find her too. She had slipped far into the back of my mind, and I felt bad about this.

I still kept her crumpled photo in my pocket. I would un-crumple it and look into her eyes on occasion, and then recrumple it. And I had never stopped looking for her.

I mean that in its broadest sense. I was looking everywhere, but since Julie was my major concern, my looking for Edith occurred in the everywhere places I would go anyway. I was not digging deep. I was not asking people about her anymore. Hell, I had asked everybody who might know anything long ago. I was not going anywhere special to look for her. I was living my life and hoping she still had a life to live, hoping the two would intersect somehow.

Then they did. At least I thought they did. And shortly after that, I knew they did.

I was lying in bed, heart pounding, wide awake. Midnight turned to 1 a.m. turned to 2 a.m. and I tossed and turned. I finally got up and found my smart phone to play back some bird songs. They usually calm me down.

That was all I had on the phone—a series of bird calls that by now added up to about forty-five minutes of songs, some more relaxing than others. But to me, they all sounded soothing, even the cackly, piercing ones.

I listened to the *chideep-chideep* of the barn swallow. Penelope was on there with her fateful *fweep-fweep*. But it was the *oo-wah-hoo* of the mourning dove that made me freeze up.

Lying there, yearning for unconsciousness in the middle of the night, I listened with unusual concentration. All was still and very quiet. Marlowe sat soundlessly, furry head on his paws. The mourning dove voice was clear and loud.

This was recorded on Mayday, just before we danced at the top of the Hill of Tears, just before Danny had started playing his accordion, just as the blinding sun was peeking over the trees and light was overtaking the darkness.

I had picked up some ambient sound behind the bird, barely audible.

It was a voice. A female voice. It must have been one of the dog walkers. There was no one else up there besides them and the guys on the team, and it was a woman's voice, soft.

I was near sleep when I heard it. There were some garbled words, sentences, and then it ended with two unmistakable words: "Victoria Diamond."

Chapter Thirty-Eight

∿

Sisters

I DID FINALLY doze, but sleep was restless and brief. Now I had someone else to find—the dog walkers. I had no idea who they were. I'd seen them one morning a year for twenty years or more, but that was it—one fleeting morning. And I had no idea who they were.

But I had a good lead—I knew the dogs, or at least what they looked like. Yes, I had reached that pathetic point in my life where I paid more attention to the way dogs look than the way women look.

A lot of people walk by my house, it being on the Hill of Tears. It is a popular route, since it starts in the village and quickly turns into countryside, and village people like to walk in the countryside.

So there I was, sipping a weak cup of coffee and staring out my window, when one of the dogs walked by—a spunky, cheerful black and white border collie mix, led by a nondescript fortyish woman bundled up in more jacket and hat than was necessary on this day, which would probably become warm but was now chilly.

I walked out to greet her, coffee cup still in hand, hair

uncombed, still rumpled from my basically sleepless night.

"Hello," I said.

"You're one of the Morris dancers," she said.

We continued in this vein for a while. I had never spoken to this person, despite seeing her each Mayday morning for twenty years. A shame. She seemed like a lovely lady.

Brief intros were finished as were cute comments on the weather. I wasn't quite sure how to approach the subject, so finally I asked directly, "Oh, hey, by the way, do you know Victoria Diamond?"

"Well, yeah. Do you?"

"Only in a manner of speaking."

She didn't press me too much on this vague statement. It turned out that this woman, whose name was Cheryl, had met Victoria when Mooney and his crew had first come to town. Cheryl had been a fashion designer in New York at one point in her life, and Mooney found her and approached her about costuming for the film. She had met with some of the actors and done some preliminary measuring for costumes. One of the actors was Victoria Diamond.

They had developed a bit of a friendship, meeting up for coffee a few times, but then Victoria had gone back out west. Or something. In any case, Cheryl had stopped hearing from Victoria and had not seen her for a long time.

Until last month, when Cheryl had seen Victoria from a distance, passing on the street, not near enough to speak to.

"And that's what I was telling Molly about that day we saw you guys dancing—just us girls catching up."

So Edith, or Victoria, was here in town and alive, at least as recently as last month. That was good news. I would have called Amy right then, but I wanted to have a confirmed personal sighting before I did that. And it was possible they had re-established their own communication anyway, since it seemed Victoria had rejoined the living.

My own personal sighting occurred soon after. When

circumstance and good luck find you, they find you in bunches, just as bad luck does. I must have been having a streak of good luck.

I was walking in town, on Bridge Street, at about noon when there she was, big as life, walking toward me. She would have bumped right into me, had I made a quick leftward turn.

So I didn't turn leftward. I tried to make eye contact and it worked. She looked right into my eyes. It was enough to make her stop in her tracks, right there in front of Mocha Maya's.

She said, "Do I know you? How do I know you?"

"No, you don't," I said. "But I know you. Sort of."

A few very convincing words from me and we were soon occupying one of the window seats inside Mocha Maya's, where we could watch the town stroll by as if on a big movie screen. And talk.

"I've been looking for you for a long time," I said.

She was smiling, with sweetness bursting out of her pores. She was a kind soul. "I'm not hard to find."

"Yes, you are. You're elusive. And evanescent."

"You use funny words."

"I'm a funny guy."

She smiled. "Yes. I can see that."

"Where have you been?"

"I've been back in L.A. I was in a commercial. I even had a line. It was for Toyota. Very cool! It's going to play nationally."

"Congratulations."

She sighed, her bright green eyes pleading with me to understand. "I was so close to giving up. It's so hard to make it in this business. You have to sell out so much. I'm an artist. I'm an actor. Smiling and being sexy to sell cars sucks. But I got paid. Pretty well too."

I echoed her enthusiasm, my tone chipper and encouraging. "And now you're back. You were going to be in the movie they were shooting here, right?"

"Yeah." She laughed, a pretty, tinkling sound, a bit rueful.

"That was going to be a big deal. It could really have helped my career. Mooney was promising the moon." Realizing what she had said, she laughed again. "Mooney … moon." I gave a polite laugh, hoping to keep her talking, and she did, "I'm never sure how much to believe from that guy, but he does real good stuff, or at least he did. Who knows what he'll do now." She looked around the café, as if he might walk in at any moment.

"Why did you come back?" I asked gently. "This movie is dead, right?"

She picked up her water glass and took a drink. "Well, yes. But I don't have anywhere else to go. No other work lined up. We've got a place to stay here that's paid up for a while, and a bunch of the other girls are still here. So there's that."

She paused, and then said, "And, of course, Mooney's here. He's kind of falling apart, but he's here."

"You're pretty close to him."

She actually blushed a little.

"Well, sort of. For a while. He gets 'close' to a lot of his actors. If you know what I mean."

"The female actors."

"Yeah. Mostly." Another blush. She had freckles. A lot of them, even down her neck.

"I heard you guys had a bit of a scene at the Blue Rock one night."

She looked a little startled that I knew, her green eyes widening, but quickly recovered. "That was bad," she said. "But then it ended up okay. We made up and we even went for a midnight moonlight swim in the river. That was amazing."

"I heard Mooney doesn't swim."

"Oh, no. That's crazy. He loves to swim."

"Fully clothed? The guy was dripping wet all over."

She narrowed her eyes and tensed slightly. "Wait. How do you know? You weren't there, were you?"

"No. I just heard."

She exhaled a sigh of relief. "No. We went swimming in the

nude. Then we got dressed. We were fooling around, pushing each other and teasing, you know? Then I pushed him in in his clothes. He grabbed me and pulled me in in my clothes. It was fun! We were playing there in the river with all our clothes on and the moon real bright overhead. It was like a magical night. I'll never forget it."

She sounded wistful. We chatted some more. Wistful, yes— but she also seemed relatively happy and healthy.

Our conversation was over. We both stood up. She shook my hand. Then she hugged me. I hugged back.

Finally I said, "I hope you've been in touch with your sister. She was worried about you. You should keep in touch with her."

"Sister?" she said. "I don't have a sister."

Chapter Thirty-Nine

~∾

The Falls Falling

I HAD FOUND Edith, or was it Victoria? One small triumph, but at least it was something. Well, I had found Edith but I had lost Amy, whoever she was. I called the number Amy had given me to give her the news. It had connected me to her before, when she was here in town. But now it had turned into a "non-working number."

Normally I would have pursued this further, but I had someone else to find and that was my main priority. This, at least, was a success and I let that console me while I moved on to the main event—finding Julie.

Back at Clara and Sarah's home, no one was thinking about Edith Marie Pasternak, aka Victoria Diamond. They had never even heard of her. That was my own job and I had not shared that story with them. Sarah was obsessed with Bert's story. She pulled up Google Maps on her computer. "Look at this," she said. "Highway 10 goes right from Jacksonville to New Orleans. That's definitely where she was going."

I suppose that's where we were going too. Except that fate once again would stop us.

*

CLARA WAS WORKING at the hospital. I took Sarah to lunch at the West End. A crow hoarsely cooed, cawed, rattled, and clicked at us as we walked, and I recorded it. We both ordered burgers. I had a root beer. Sarah wanted a real beer. "I can pass," she said, "and I'm doing real adult work for you now. I deserve an adult beverage."

I would not hear of it. "They all know you here. They know how old you are. Order a 7UP." So she ordered the 7UP.

We were sitting at the bar, not saying much, when in walked Lorenzo. He sat next to Sarah and ordered a martini. The kid drank hard. Not a good sign.

He sipped half the thing down before he spoke. Then, addressing Sarah, not me, he said, "I've got more pictures for you guys. Back at my room." He was out of breath.

"Anything good?" she asked.

"Absolutely un-freaking-believable," he replied.

"Something new?" I asked.

"Hot off the presses. A couple hours ago."

I didn't get it, so I asked, "So you get something earthshaking and the first thing you do is run to the nearest bar and order a martini?"

"I was looking for you. This is always where I find you. You should talk."

"Well, I'm not drinking cocktails. Anyway, you're talking to her, not me."

"You guys are a team, aren't you? What's the difference?"

I allowed as to how there was none, or hardly any.

Lorenzo chugged down the rest of his drink. Sarah picked up her napkin and wiped her face. "Let's rock, Frankie."

So I, reluctantly, rocked.

We crossed the Iron Bridge and went up to Lorenzo's room. Cello Lady was playing some more Bach as we passed by her kitchen.

Lorenzo opened his laptop computer and pulled up a file.

"This is a time-lapse series I set up at the falls a week or so ago. It snaps a shot every thirty minutes. I wanted to get stuff of the water rising and falling. It's been raining, not like before, but it's rain and it comes and goes and the falls vary dramatically. It's very cool. My camera was set up just in front of the old candle company building. Unfortunately for us, it's stationary. It doesn't move around, so we get what we get. But I think you'll find this fascinating."

At first, it was just the falls falling. One shot every thirty minutes meant forty-eight shots per day, and the camera had been there about a week, so that was over three hundred consecutive shots, making it look like a choppy, slow-moving movie, with little plot but lots of sense of place.

Finally, as they say, the plot thickened. It thickened like crazy near the end.

There she was—Julie, our Nutting Girl. First you could see her off to the top of the screen, a small, lonely body standing, watching the river flow.

Then she passed right in front of the camera—bigger than life, totally turning the screen to black with her body at one point.

Then she was down on the rocks—standing, looking, moving her head around.

She was dressed all in black and her hair was tied back so you could not see its full splendor. Lorenzo's camera was far enough away that we could not see the details of her face. We could not see her move much, with one still shot at a time. There was little sense of whether she moved with an easy dancer's grace or a clunky, awkward, lost-girl shuffle.

Still, it was clear enough who this mysterious figure was that Sarah audibly gasped and put her hands over her mouth. "Oh, my God," she half-whispered.

Then Julie was gone. She was in one shot and then she wasn't. She was perched atop one of the jutting rocks, gazing downward, body weight shifted delicately toward the waters below. Then, in the next shot, not there at all. And she did not appear again.

Once more, she had disappeared into the river.

Lorenzo let it play out for us. A few more seconds of the falls falling. Followed by the girl falling. Or at least we presumed that was what was happening. Then it grew dark on screen as night fell.

"Do you know when that was taken?" I asked.

"Yeah, sure. It's all time-coded. That stuff with her was last night from about five to nine p.m. She was walking around there for like four hours."

We watched it again. And again. And again.

Chapter Forty

～

Pale Like a White Rock

T**HE NEXT AFTERNOON**, they pulled a body out of the river. Not far downstream from the dam by the Potholes. Not far from where Julie went in. Where she went in twice, apparently. But most importantly, where she went in just two nights ago, as had been captured in Lorenzo's pictures.

Details were difficult to ascertain. No one who knew anything was talking, or if they were, they didn't know anything. I first heard about it from chatter on the streets. Town was abuzz, and a thousand different versions were rattling about.

The version that sounded most likely was that a fisherman had found it—her. He saw the hair slicked back on what he thought was a rock, but upon closer inspection proved to be a human head—pale like a white rock. They were not reporting her identity, pending final confirmation and notification of next of kin. That meant fingerprints, DNA, but if in fact it was Julie, I knew nothing about her next of kin.

Sarah said Julie had no next of kin. Her mother was dead. Her father was unknown. She had no siblings or spouse or children. I had no idea who the authorities would notify, if anybody. Maybe Mooney. But I wasn't sure if anybody but

Sarah and Edith and I knew where to find him. The internet still had no reports on his whereabouts.

So we waited. I went down to the police station and talked to Loomis about the body they found, but he knew nothing. Or at least that's what he told me. He said the feds were handling this and he was completely out of the loop. He did say that no further information would be released until they found a next of kin to notify.

I believe Sarah and I were both feeling the same way—numb. There was a curious calm. There appeared to be not much doubt that she was, finally, gone—that the body they dragged out was our Nutting Girl. This realization dropped on us like a lump going down our throats, and it landed right in the solar plexus and sat there. Occasionally, Sarah would sniffle and suppress a tear. But all this had been building up and then settling back, over and over and over again. So it was as if we had lived it before. It was a horrible repeat, but its familiarity kept it from tearing us apart. As did the tiniest thread of hope that the body was not hers.

Sarah started it. "I'd love to see those pictures again," she said.

"Which ones?"

"The new ones. From two nights ago."

"Well, we know where to find Lorenzo. He's either at the West End or in his room at Cello Lady's."

He was at Cello Lady's. I think she was playing Telemann. We asked him to call up the pictures again.

He pointed to his computer, sitting on the small table. "Yeah. It's still there. It's up now. That's all I've been watching."

So we watched it once more. Then twice more. Then three times more.

On the third time around, as the very last frame played through, Sarah hollered, "Stop!"

"Lorenzo said, "Okay, yeah. I've seen it too many times too."

"No," she said, "freeze that last frame."

So he did.

"Lorenzo, can you zoom up into the right-hand corner?"

"Sure."

This was the picture right after the one where the girl was last seen. She was standing on the lip of one of the Potholes in the next to last shot. In this one, she was gone.

Lorenzo played with some controls and zoomed up to the right-hand corner. It was near the top of the rocks, near where the water rolled down over the dam, where a person could get enough footholds to walk away from the falls and onto solid ground.

There it was—blurry, out of focus, little more than a smudge, really. A figure, human, walking away from the scene. A tall figure, slumped over—whatever confidence it once had was gone. That figure had given up on pretty much everything, including life in general. It moved slowly, not out of indecision, but out of pure bone and soul weariness.

When you are partially blind, like me, you learn to identify people by cues other than their coloring—their eyes, their face, their hair. The main way you identify them is by body carriage. It's unscientific, I guess, but I've learned that each person's body carriage is unique, like DNA, like fingerprints.

There was no doubt who this figure was. It was Mooney. Mooney was there at the falls at the same time Julie dove in, or more likely was pushed.

Julie went into the river once, a month ago, and was alive when Bert picked her up. Then she went in again two nights ago, with Mooney nearby.

What the hell was going on, anyway?

Chapter Forty-One

~

Another One Gulps the H20

I HAD GONE home. It was quite late, but still I tossed some sticks for Marlowe in the yard in the dark. Dogs can see in the dark. I can't even see in the light.

There was a knock at the door. It was Chief Loomis. I let him in. Marlowe jumped on him. Marlowe was not used to getting visitors in his house. Neither was I, but at least I didn't jump on the poor guy.

After a few semi-formal greetings, Loomis sat at the kitchen table.

"She's not your gal, Frank," he said. "That floater everybody in town's been chattering about. It wasn't Miss Norcross. It wasn't that VelCro gal."

"You came out here to tell me that? My phone works. And you guys don't seem to like to tell me anything anyway."

"Well, I've got more on my mind than that. More dead people. I thought it called for a personal visit."

"I don't need a lawyer, do I?"

"I don't know, do you?"

"No."

"That's your opinion."

"And what's yours?"

"I'll tell you in a while. After we have a little talk."

"So talk."

"Why don't you sit?" he said, so I joined him at the table after first getting us both glasses of water. "Well," he went on, "first thing is your old buddy Harvey dropped dead last night. Apparent heart attack in the middle of the night. He was like ninety-four, and he was dying of cancer anyway. Led a good life. Thought you'd like to know."

I nodded, picturing the man, recalling his advice about marriage and chicken. "Michael's wife's grandfather," I said. "I liked that old dude. Damn shame. But I know that's not enough to bring you out here."

He thrummed his fingers on the table. "Yeah. There's lots more."

He had my attention. I couldn't imagine where this was going. "Yeah?"

"Yeah. I'll get to all that in a minute. But the floater ... the DNA came back on her. She was Edith Marie Pasternak. Like the Russian writer."

My Edith. My first missing girl. It took me a while to digest this.

"This is the girl they found a couple days ago, right?"

"Yeah." Loomis continued, "Yeah, Pasternak. At least she wasn't Chekov. That still reminds me of the old *Star Trek*. Or Dostoyevsky. Or Nabokov. Pasternak almost fits in around here. Sounds like one of those Polish farmers in South Deerfield."

I played dumb. "Who was she?" I asked.

"A nobody. Age twenty-one. From Los Angeles. She moved here to work on the movie. She stuck around even after things turned to crap."

"What was she doing on it?" I watched him, had begun to think he knew more than he was letting on.

"She was an actress, Frank. Not a big star but she had some lines."

"What happened to her? How did she end up in the river?"

"Those are very good questions. There was no sign of foul play. Maybe she jumped. What do you think?"

I shrugged. "How should I know?"

"I didn't ask what you know; I asked what you think."

"I think I don't know anything."

He huffed. "That's what I thought you thought."

"Then why did you come by? Nobody ever comes by here. The dog jumps on people, you know?"

"Yeah, I know. That's a pain in the ass. You should train him better. But I thought it might be enlightening to talk to you."

"Feel enlightened?" I said.

"No. Not in the slightest. Not yet, anyway."

"Okay. So now we know who that dead body is. Damn shame."

"Yeah. It's a shame."

We looked at each other awkwardly. I thought maybe he was going to get up and leave. But by now I suspected where he was heading.

"Oh, yeah," he said, "one more thing."

"I'm all ears."

"We found another floater too."

Where was he going with this? I'd thought he was going to confront me about Edith. Why was he teasing me?

"Another one bites the dust," was my clever rejoinder, but it sounded stupid even to my ears.

"Another one gulps the H20. That's how we put it down at the station."

I was wondering who the hell the second floater was. Wondering like hell. But I wasn't going to give him the satisfaction of asking.

What I did ask was, "So, why the visit, Neil?"

"Frank, since you started helping these movie folks out, people have been diving into that damn river like it's a freakin' Olympic event. I've been chief here for sixteen years and we've never had a jumper before. Now we've had two in one day. Plus that VelCro girl. What the hell is going on?"

"That's what I'm trying to figure out, Neil."

"That's not a good enough answer, Frank."

"That's all I got for you, Neil."

"Frank, I'm not here for me. I'm here for you. I've known you a long time and I don't think you're out there pushing people into the drink. But seriously, man, there are some folks involved here who kind of do think that. People with power. More power than me. They think you do know more than you're letting on, and Frank, they are this close to coming by here and arresting you. And to tell you the truth, I think you know more than you're letting on too."

"I don't know shit, Neil." But I had my suspicions.

"Oh, come on, Frank. I've known you too long. I know you too well. I remember when you were a cop yourself."

"For one day, Neil, one goddamn day."

"Only you could manage to get shot on your first day on the job. And die too, no less. You were dead, man, *dead*. No wonder you quit."

"It was more than that, Neil. Wasn't so much the getting shot and dying part that soured me on the job. It was the coming back to life part. You know what I mean?"

"No. I have no freakin' idea what you mean."

"You don't have to. Just take my word."

"Okay. I can take your word on that. These jumpers—that's another story. Frank, they've got enough to hold you for suspicion of murder."

"No way."

"Yes, way. You were stalking Pasternak."

"What?" I was amazed.

"You carry her picture around, Frank. You ask everybody about her. You harassed her out on Bridge Street and you hung out with her one day at Mocha Maya's. What are you, obsessed? That's a bad sign, buddy."

He was asking me bad questions. I was obsessed, I guess, but it wasn't over Edith Marie Pasternak. But that was cutting it pretty close. Too close for comfort.

"Her sister hired me to find her."

"She has no sister."

"So I'm told."

"This does not look good, Frank."

"So what happens now?"

"Nothing. Not yet. I just came by to warn you. Watch out, man. You are standing on very shaky ground here and there's not much I can do to help you."

"And I guess I shouldn't leave town. Weren't you going to tell me not to leave town?"

"Don't leave town, Frank."

"Don't worry. I won't. Where would I go? I never leave town. I don't travel well."

He nodded, thrummed the table some more. "I know."

"I'm not going anywhere."

That was probably a lie. I would go wherever the hell I wanted to go, possibly New Orleans. But it sounded good.

"If I were you, I'd go looking for Mooney," I told him, "He's got more to tell you than me."

"And where might we find him, do you think?"

"I have no idea," I replied too quickly.

"Yes, you do. He's right up your road. Right up that damn Hill of Tears. The old Snyder house. Or at least he was."

"Was?"

"Yeah. We pulled him out of the river this morning too. He was the second floater."

Chapter Forty-Two

∾

Busy Morning

Loomis was right. It was getting ridiculous. Too many folks were jumping, or falling, or being pushed, into the damn river. Now it was Mooney's turn.

"Shit," I said to Loomis, rising to my feet. "I'm going to miss the bastard." I meant it, despite my mixed feelings.

"No, you're not."

"No. Seriously. I will. He was a possibly insane psychopathic alcoholic, but I'm going to miss the guy. There was something about him, you know what I mean?"

"Well, yeah, I think I know what you mean. But you're not going to miss him mainly because the poor bastard isn't dead. He's still going to be around, so you won't be able to miss him. Much as you might like to. Much as we all might like to."

I wasn't sure if that made me feel better or worse. "Fill me in, Neil," I said. "You want something else—tea, coffee?"

He shook his head and lifted his glass. "Water's good. Well, this was a busy morning for us. First, a fisherman spots Pasternak floating. So, we're down there fishing her out, when what do we find but your Mr. Mooney right next door. And he's floating too. But he's got a pulse. I really wish it was the other way around, but, no, he's the one with the damn pulse and the girl's dead. So, he's at the hospital in Greenfield. He's going to survive. And that's a miracle because he looks like he was almost dead before he fell into the damn river. Or however the hell he ended up in there."

He took a long sip of water before going on, "He had blood alcohol content of like a zillion percent, which, by the way, Doc Fitzgerald says basically saved his life. Turned him into a rag doll. All kind of flexible and compliant. Nothing to resist when he bumped into rocks. But really, he missed most of the rocks anyway. So did Pasternak. Found them right near the lip of the dam. The girl drowned. Was the water that killed her, not the rocks. Mooney, though, he's a tall son of a bitch. His height kept his head above the worst of the water. He floated like a damn cork."

I sat again, gave Marlowe a few strokes. "You talk to him?"

"Me?" He raised his eyebrows. "Not me, personally. I'm lucky they tell me anything that's going on. But, yeah, they still deem me worthy of getting some reports. They talked to him three ways to Sunday, and he doesn't know anything. Or he's not *saying* anything, anyway."

"Is he under arrest?"

"For what? Being a drunken asshole? That's not against the law."

"Good thing," I said. "Or the jails would be mighty crowded."

Loomis got up from the table. "Yeah, at least we got that going for us."

Then he stood up from the table and looked me in the eye. "Frank, do you mind if I take a hair sample?"

I was taken aback. "A hair sample? For DNA? Are you serious?"

"Yeah, unfortunately I am. They were gonna come down and do it, but I said let me do it. I know the guy. And it's completely voluntary. At least at this point it is."

"What the hell. I don't care. Snip away, Neil." That's just what he was doing as I added, "You know someone's DNA can stay on you up to six weeks after you touch them."

"Yeah, I know. Just doing my job."

"Okay. Just don't take too much."

"You got a good head of hair, Frank. You can spare a little."

"Yeah, that's one thing I have in common with my dad. Well, actually there're two ways I take after that bastard—he had great hair and he drank like a fish. I've got both of those tendencies."

He laughed. Then he was done.

"Okay," he said, "I'm going to go now. I don't think you know a damn thing. I think you're as much out of the loop as me."

"I think you're right, Neil."

He left.

Christ. Edith was dead and Mooney wasn't, and the cops were this close to arresting me. For something.

I got in my car and went over to Sarah's. We drove into Greenfield to the hospital for yet another interview with Mooney.

Chapter Forty-Three

～✃～

The Most Beautiful Woman on Earth

"**G**ET ME THE hell out of here. And get me a damn drink." Those were the first words out of Mooney's mouth when he saw us.

"You don't need us for that," I replied. "This is the good ol' U S of A. We're free here. Free to do as we please, within federal, state, and local regulations, of course. You can go if you want. You're not under arrest."

He shifted a bit in his bed. "Well, I could go if I could fucking move, which I can't. Every bone in my body hurts like hell. Or it would if they didn't have me shot up with morphine or whatever the hell it is. Which feels pretty damn good, by the way. They tell me nothing's broken and it's just a matter of time before I can leave. But hell, time is something I don't have much of."

I had to laugh. "Mooney, you've got nothing but time."

"No," he said. "My time's running out. I can feel it. You're not going to have Mooney to kick around much longer."

"How Nixonian of you," Sarah said. How did she recognize the Nixon quote? Did they teach that stuff in school now? "But you seem to have enough time to sit around and drink all day."

"That's the problem, isn't it? Drinking takes a lot of time, man. But I haven't had a drink in like two days, three days, whatever it is. I'm jonesing bad here. And don't lecture me about time. My time's almost out."

"Only if you want it to be," replied Sarah.

"All I want is a drink. Morphine kills pain but I still need the drink."

"Here." Sarah reached into her bag and came out with a sealed bottle of Jameson, which she handed to Mooney. He promptly twisted it open and took a healthy chug. And then another.

He wiped his mouth and let out a deep sigh. "Whew. Now that's what I'm talking about. Thank you, sweetie."

"You're welcome. And don't call me sweetie."

"Thank you, honey."

"Oh fuck you, Mooney," she replied. "Just drink the damn whiskey and shut up."

He calmed down and smoothed out. You could almost see the physical change taking place. Ironically, this poison was bringing him back to life. Then he started talking.

"So, it was two or three nights ago. I'm sitting at home. Next thing I know, I'm lying here in the damn hospital. That's all I know. They tell me Victoria is dead. But I don't know anything about that. I don't know anything about anything. Except here I am."

"You had a blackout, Mooney."

"Yeah. It's not the first one."

"And it won't be the last."

"For a change, I think you're right, Raven."

Of course we were both stating the obvious, with a high degree of irony.

"You knew Victoria pretty damn well," Sarah said accusingly.

"Well, yeah. She was in the movie. She might even have had a couple of lines. I auditioned her. I hired her."

Sarah asked, "What else did you do to her?"

"Okay, honey, I know what you're driving at. But forget it. I didn't kill her. Why would I do that? I didn't fuck her either. I didn't know her that well. I don't fuck everybody who's in my films. Regardless of what you may hear."

"Just the stars?" This was still Sarah.

Mooney laughed and took another healthy swig.

"Oh, hell no. I'm not an elitist. I'll fuck anybody, star or not. As long as they look good."

"She looked good," Sarah said.

"Did she? I didn't notice."

"She was gorgeous, Mooney," Sarah insisted.

He blew out a puff of air. "She looked pretty ordinary to me. It was a fucking movie. It had pretty girls in it. Come on. Sue me."

Sarah continued, "I get the feeling you notice all the good-looking young girls."

"Oh hell," Mooney replied. "When you're already fucking the most beautiful woman on earth, nobody else looks good at all. Know what I mean?"

Chapter Forty- Four

Well, Hardly Ever

I TENDED TO agree with his assessment. I too thought Julie might be the most beautiful woman I had ever seen. But then I didn't live in Hollywood, where they grow them like mangos. I lived in Shelburne Falls, where someone like her was pretty damn rare.

Mooney was confirming he and Julie were lovers, which we knew anyway. If we could place any kind of credibility at all on what the sorry sonofabitch had to say. Especially in his condition.

"You know what she looked like, Raven. Who could look at another woman with her around?"

Sarah folded her arms across her chest. "How about with her not around?" she asked.

Mooney laughed at this concept, a bitter, broken sound. "What do you know about love, little girl? Have you ever been in love? I loved her more than anything in the fucking world. Yeah, she was beautiful. But, oh hell, there was so much more to her than that."

"I know," said Sarah. "I loved her too."

"Not the way I did, little girl. Not the way I did."

But Sarah wouldn't give up. "She blinds you," she went on. "I saw that too. When you're around her, it's almost a semi-religious experience. She's all you can see. But what about when she's gone? For me, she's still all I can think of. But, for you … you, you've got the damn bottle now. And I think you've got other stuff too. If you know what I mean."

Mooney stared at her, through her. "No, I don't know what you mean, little girl."

I had never heard Sarah sound so harsh. She leaned forward, relentless as an avenging angel. "I think you do, big man. And I mean that ironically, in case you're wondering. You're the furthest thing from big, you tiny sonofabitch."

Sarah's assault was starting to get to Mooney. His voice rose as he said, "You don't know much about alcoholics, do you? You don't have to tell an alcoholic he's a worthless piece of crap. We already know that. Right, Raven?"

I remained silent.

Mooney was simmering inside. His face got redder than it already was. He closed his eyes tight and bit his lip.

Sarah was unfazed. "We can stand here all day and let you lecture little ol' me on things like love and alcohol if you want," she said. "But that doesn't sound like much fun to me. Or you can actually answer my question. Remember, I'm the one who brought that bottle in here for you."

He took a gulp from it and closed his eyes, waiting for it to take effect. "Yeah. Thank you, kiddo, for that." He calmed down again and opened his eyes. "I'll gladly answer your questions. One question per bottle. That sound fair?"

"I only brought one bottle."

"So you get one question."

"I already asked it."

"Can you repeat the question?"

"Yes," she hissed. "Yes I can. I asked you to tell me about your other stuff since Julie disappeared."

"That's not a question. Put it in the form of a question. Or I won't answer it."

Now Sarah was losing her cool. I watched her hands form into fists. "What are we—on fucking *Jeopardy*? Okay—what the hell kind of other stuff have you had going on since Julie disappeared? Besides drinking, I mean?"

"Okay, since you have now put it in the form of a question, I will gladly answer."

Then he shut up.

Sarah said, "We're waiting."

He took a gulp of the Jameson. "All right, since you asked so nicely. I'm a man of my word. Sure, I was fucking that other girl. And more besides her. But only since Julie went away."

"Never before that?"

"Never."

Then he thought it over. "Well, hardly ever."

Chapter Forty-Five

~∽

The Good and the Bad

A COUPLE OF days went by. Then they came to get me. Two guys in cheap suits—one skinny, one fat. Well, not fat, exactly—husky with a gut that hung over his belt, but only a bit. An athlete gone to seed. He was the bad cop. The skinny guy was the good cop. They had the act down pretty well.

There were more of them too—three plainclothes guys. Those were the guys who grabbed me.

I was walking down Bridge Street. It was, by all appearances, a normal day. I was saying "hi" to random people, looking into shop windows. I knew pretty much everyone on the street— this was Shelburne Falls, after all. There were a few tourists I, of course, did not know. You can always spot them. They have vacant stares, walk so slowly you trip over them, and they wear cameras. They look like they want us locals to entertain them. I avoid the tourists like the freaking plague.

These guys were not tourists. The first one I noticed was chubby, very young, puffy face, pimples, and dressed in nerdy attire, complete with black-rimmed glasses. He was smoking a cigarette and leaning against the window of the newsstand.

Walking toward me was a working-class guy wearing blue

jeans, a John Deere cap, and a two-day growth of beard.

Coming up behind me was a straight-arrow type clad in a neat, businesslike, blue suit. Him I couldn't see until they grabbed me, since he was walking behind me. Had I seen him, I would have been suspicious. There are no businessmen in Shelburne Falls. Or rather, no businessmen dressed like that. What businessmen there are in Shelburne Falls dress like hippies.

As I approached the newsstand, the chubby one suddenly left his perch and was standing in front of me, blocking my path. I stopped.

The working-class guy shifted his route and he was in front of me too.

Then the businessman put his arms around my waist from behind, grabbed my hands, and half-whispered into my ear "Mister Raven? Mr. Francis Raven?"

After taking a second to absorb what was happening, I replied, "Yes."

He loosened his grip and said, "Good. Just keep walking. Follow us."

These guys were good. They were pros. The working-class guy led the way down Bridge Street with the businessman remaining behind and the nerd backing off to join him there. I was fairly certain they were going to turn into the police station, but they didn't. They kept walking down the street until they got to the new bank with the new and unoccupied offices upstairs.

Well, I thought the offices were unoccupied. They led me up the stairs, and what I saw was a bright, freshly painted, shiny, sunlit, busy office that looked like it had been functioning for a while. It had been cut up into one big room and two smaller sections, each with a desk and chairs and filing cabinets and computers. There was a woman working on the computer at one of the desks and my two new friends—Skinny Cop and Fat

Cop, Good Cop and Bad Cop—standing at the door to greet us all.

"Mr. Francis Raven?" said Skinny.

"Yes," I replied.

"I'm Agent Broadhurst and this is Agent Estes. FBI. Welcome."

They wore badges around their necks and they politely pointed them out to me.

"Nice digs," I said.

"We like it."

The three plainclothes guys who grabbed me faded away into the background, and Broadhurst and Estes—Skinny and Fat, Good and Bad—gently pushed me into the larger of the two offices, where they sat me on a surprisingly comfortable chair. Broadhurst sat behind the desk and Estes sat on it, practically in my face.

"Lovely day out there," said Broadhurst.

"Every day in Shelburne Falls is lovely," I replied.

"Yeah. Nice town you got here. I could move here when I retire."

"Everybody wants to move here."

"So," interrupted Estes, "We've got a few questions. You got a few minutes?"

"Do I need a lawyer?"

"You might."

The only lawyer I ever used was Karen Slowinski, and she was now in her eighties and more than likely retired. Possibly even dead or suffering from dementia. I hadn't seen or heard from her in years. I knew a couple of other, younger lawyers in town, but I had never needed to employ them. I decided to take my chances with these guys.

"Never mind. Let's get on with it," I said.

"What do you do for a living?" asked Estes.

"Nothing. I'm retired."

"Don't you run a movie theater?"

"Yeah. But I don't make much money from that."

"How do you pay your bills?"

"I live cheaply. My house is paid off. I never go anywhere. I don't eat much. I get a small pension from the town too. I got shot while working for them."

"That's not much income."

"I'm poor. What can I say?"

"That monster German Shepherd of yours must eat a lot, huh?"

"I feed him dead bodies."

He laughed. "Yeah. That's what we suspected. Dog eating well these days?"

"Not losing much weight."

"Yeah. Bodies all around this town."

"Yep."

"We count four of them."

"Four?" This gave me pause. I looked at him for clarification.

"Yeah—Pasternak, Norcross, Mooney. And, oh yeah— Dunleavy."

"Dunleavy? You mean Harvey?" I made a face. "You don't think I killed him, do you? He was ninety-four, for Christ's sake."

"Did you?"

"No. And Mooney's not dead."

"Not quite. Not yet. He's a body nonetheless. You been busy."

Broadhurst, playing Good Cop, said, "Come on. Help us out here. We can't help you if you don't help us. And we want to help you. We really do."

I couldn't believe this shit. "What's the FBI involved in this for, anyway? Isn't this local stuff?"

"A prominent national person like Norcross?" replied Broadhurst. "That's when we get involved. And all these others are connected to that. Somehow."

"This is ridiculous," I said.

"All we want is to ask you some questions. Then you can be on your way," said Broadhurst.

"Maybe," added Estes.

"Ask away," I said, throwing up my hands.

"Mooney and Pasternak went into the river on Monday night. Where were you Monday night?"

"I don't know. Same place I am every night—home, at a bar, at Clara's. I don't know."

"Did you buy three plane tickets to New Orleans?"

"Yeah, I did."

"Leaving town?"

"Visiting my cousin."

"Convenient."

"You don't like Mooney much, do you?"

"Not really, no. To be honest."

"Well, we want you to be honest."

"I always am."

He chuckled at this.

"You were kind of obsessed with Pasternak, weren't you? Chasing her around. Carrying her picture. You had at least one tête-à-tête with her."

"Tête-à-tête? What the hell is a tête-à-tête?"

"It's a private conversation between two people."

"Then yes."

"Okay. What was up with all that?"

"I was hired to find her."

"By whom?"

"Her sister."

"She has no sister."

"So I'm told." My sarcasm probably wasn't helping my cause, but I couldn't help myself.

"Would it surprise you to find out your DNA was on both of them?"

"No. I touched both of them recently. DNA can stick around for six weeks."

"Thank you for that information. But we know."

"You guys are good."

"We really are. How's this for good?" He leaned forward menacingly. "You meet this pretty, red-haired girl Pasternak, here for the film. You fall for her. Everyone knows you love redheads. You find out Mooney was fucking her. And you never liked Mooney to begin with. Then you start fucking her yourself. You get her pregnant. She still loves Mooney though. You can't deal with that. So you push them both into the drink."

I was shocked. I felt the blood drain from my face. "That's insane. Pregnant! Me, the father? That's so totally wrong. Do a test."

"We did. We got your DNA. It's a match with the fetus. DNA is a hundred percent accurate for paternity."

"What!"

"Yes. And we have an eyewitness who saw you push them."

That's when I called Karen. Turns out she wasn't retired or dead or senile. She wasn't working much but she was still an active member of the bar and she came right down to meet us, right after she advised me to stop talking, advice I was glad to comply with.

When she arrived, Estes slapped cuffs on me and they shuttled me down to the State police barracks on Route 2, where they were going to keep me until they could transfer me to the federal prison in Devens.

The charge—first degree murder.

Chapter Forty-Six

~⁓

Anything for a Friend

I DID NOT kill Edith Marie Pasternak, aka Victoria Fortune, nor did I get her pregnant. Nor did I ever have sex with her. I barely knew her.

I was being set up.

Karen said I was in deep shit but there were ways out. We just had to find them. And we had to find out how I was being set up, and just as importantly, by whom.

I had my suspicions. Presuming the cops were legit, which I believed they were, I could think of only one person evil enough, and powerful enough, to do that, and that person was shot up with painkillers in a hospital.

Meanwhile, I sat on a cot in a coffin-sized cell awaiting an appearance before a judge. By the time they wheeled me into Greenfield to appear before him, Karen had talked them down to manslaughter.

The judge set bail at $25,000, which Karen said was fairly standard for manslaughter, and probably what they wanted to charge me with in the first place. They took me back to my new coffin home to await my move to Devens.

I sat there for a while on that cot. I had no idea what to do.

In fact, there was nothing I could do. My fate was in the hands of others. But it was likely I was going to spend some time in jail. I didn't know anyone with $25,000 to spare who cared if I lived or died. I was wondering who was going to take care of Marlowe. He didn't get along too well with anyone but me, not even Clara or Sarah.

Then the guard came by, opened up my cell, and said, "Raven? You're outta here. Let's go."

He led me out to a DMV-like window, where a clerk gave me back the stuff they'd taken during my arrest and pointed me to the door, without a word of explanation. I walked out to a sunny day, with traffic whizzing by along Route 2.

And there he was, leaning against a red Range Rover looking like crap, like he would fall over if he wasn't leaning against the car. It was Mooney.

"Mooney, you bastard. You set me up."

"Maybe I did. Maybe I didn't."

"How did you do it, Mooney? You were in the hospital."

"They've got nothing on you. Not really."

"Sounds like they've got something. They've got an eyewitness. And they've got DNA. That's bad. I should know. I was a cop once. I know a little about the law."

"One day. One fucking day you were a cop. I made a movie about cops once. I know more about the law than you do. And here's my legal assessment. Yeah, you're probably screwed. But maybe, if you play your cards right, you can get un-screwed."

He handed me a business card. "My lawyers. They're the best. Call them. It's on me."

I looked at the card. "They're in L.A."

"Raven, you are one naïve sonofabitch. I'm powerful. I can do pretty much anything. In L.A., some lawyers are way more than lawyers, understand? They're fixers. They're doers and they're un-doers. These guys, these lawyers, they'll travel if they need to. But they won't have to. They'll get it dropped. And they'll get it dropped from L.A. Easy in, easy out. Easy come, easy go. Know what I mean?"

I wasn't sure what he meant, but I had a suspicion. "I like Karen," I said.

He laughed. "She's a hundred years old."

"I like her."

"It's your funeral. Literally."

"I'll take my chances. I don't want your help. Anyway, I thought you were in the hospital."

"I was. I checked myself out."

I didn't say anything. I waited for him to go on.

"I heard a friend of mine needed help," he continued. "I posted your bail."

"You're not my friend, Mooney, but I appreciate the bail. So thanks for that. But you set me up. And now you bail me out. And now you're offering me God knows what."

This was a guy who maybe killed two young women. Then hired me and Sarah to find one of them. This was a guy who set me up for murder, not to mention paternity, and now was offering me a way out. This was a guy who was totally unstable, untrustworthy, and fucked up. I wanted no part of him, except for a ride home.

"Let's go for a ride," he said as he got in. I got in and sat uneasily in the passenger seat.

"You okay to drive, Mooney?"

"Yeah. I'm fine. I'm great."

"Well, you look like hell. You just got out of the hospital, where they pumped you full of morphine, and you smell like booze."

Then I saw the bottle tucked between the two front seats.

"So," he said, "let's make this one short ride, okay?"

Luckily, the ride from the State police barracks to Mooney's house was less than a mile. We made it there safely in a couple of minutes, though not without a minor scare or two. When we arrived, I realized my fingers were numb from clutching the seatbelt in front of me.

Mooney staggered out of the vehicle and invited me in. I

refused. I needed to go back down the Hill of Tears to my own house.

We stood there on his paved driveway and he said, "They'll drop the charges. They've got nothing on you. That is, if you play ball."

"Fuck you, Mooney. You set me up. Now I don't know what you're doing."

"I'm trying to help a friend in trouble. Isn't that what you've spent a lot of years doing, helping your friends?"

I backed away. "Fuck you, Mooney. I'll get out of this myself. I can't take help when it comes from an evil place like your heart."

"Suit yourself. Come in for a drink."

"Give it a rest, Mooney."

He held the bottle in his hand and took a chug.

"Thank your little girl for the booze for me. She kept me supplied while I was in that damn hospital. Only thing that kept me in there."

"I will make sure to do that. But I gotta go."

"Think about it," he said.

"I'm done thinking," I said. "Thanks for bailing me out."

"No problem," he said. "Anything for a friend."

Chapter Forty-Seven

❧

Just My Imagination Running Away with Me

TIME WENT BY. I was awaiting trial, which Karen said could be a long time coming. I told her someone must have switched the DNA, because there was no way the fetus could be related to me. I wondered about the chain of evidence with the DNA sample Loomis had taken. Loomis was not used to following rigorous legal requirements and who knew how much reach Mooney's "lawyers" had.

I had not understood until then what it meant to have pockets as deep as Mooney's. Anything was possible. I think Karen believed me. She kept pushing to have the DNA retested.

Clara and Sarah believed me, of course. There was never any question. And meanwhile, no other people dove into the river. Things grew quiet again.

Sometimes you have to stop before you can go. We—Sarah and I—were going to go somewhere, possibly to New Orleans. I wasn't supposed to go anywhere, but I would go wherever I needed to go. Screw 'em. Screw 'em all. Fuck 'em. Fuck 'em all.

I was sitting and drinking coffee at Mocha Maya's, next to my theater, at a window seat where you can see everybody and everything and they can't see you because of the way the glass glares on the street side.

The music system was playing the Temptations. Or was it the Four Tops? Or was it Smokey Robinson and the Miracles? No, it was The Tempts—"Just My Imagination."

A great song. Gave me a gentle soundtrack, along with the customer buzz, to soothe my morning. It had been such a quiet morning that I had stopped to record the *seetz-tee zee-tee zee-tee zee* of a rather rare Bay Breasted Warbler while I walked across the Bridge of Flowers. The water was unbelievably smooth, reflecting the curves of the bridge base. If you closed your eyes and held your breath, you might be able to convince yourself that things were back to normal. Which they most certainly were not.

I knew this right away because I saw her again. I was sipping slowly and the coffee was bitter. I had not put in enough sugar. I like a lot of sugar.

I was watching people come and go and stop and move and live. Felicity was dressing her mannequin in front of Otis & Co. Ginny walked by as if headed somewhere important. Emily and Al pushed their baby. No one saw me there in the window, but I saw them.

And there she was again. It was her. Hair red but this time very short. She was wearing red-framed glasses. It was a warm morning, but she wore a leather jacket, flaps pulled up over her neck, and a pair of tight blue jeans. She walked hunched over, shy, sullen, silent, slow, as if she were trying to melt into the sidewalk.

It didn't really look like Julie, not superficially, but it *was* her. I was positive.

She walked directly by me, right in front of the big picture window. She stopped, put her face against the window. I was about two feet away. If it were not for the glass, I could have reached out and touched her. Grabbed her.

She could not see me. Or did not.

Then she moved on.

She wasn't going to get away. And she wasn't going to land in the drink. I left my coffee where it was, on the small square table, steaming.

I was out the door and I was right behind her. She still was not aware of my presence. I touched her shoulder. She turned around and took a glance at me and turned around again and looked like she was about to start running.

But I was right there. I grabbed her by the shoulders and held on. She turned around again and slapped me across the face and started running.

But I grabbed her again and held on this time.

She turned around again, and in a voice that was most definitely not that of our dear Nutting Girl said, "What do you want, mister?"

Not even Julie was that good an actor.

Chapter Forty-Eight

∾ᴖ

Mooney's Type

"I JUST WANT to talk," I said.

It was true. That's all I wanted. Even if she were Julie, that would be all I wanted. With her not being Julie, well that was as much as I could hope for. She looked like Julie. Sorta anyway. That was enough for me. I needed to talk to her.

"Who the hell are you?" She was trembling.

"I'm sorry. I don't mean any harm."

It's hard to lie. I can't do it. Maybe a psychopath like Mooney can pull it off, but not me. People know this when they look in my face.

So Not Nutting Girl knew it, and she said, "Jesus, you can't go around grabbing people like that."

"I know. I'm sorry."

"Okay, fine." And she started walking away.

But I was right there in her face. "Please don't go," I said. "I'd really like to talk to you."

"This is not a good time. I have to be somewhere."

Then when she saw what was in my eyes, the desperation, the sadness that she was someone other than she might possibly have been, when she saw me take in a deep breath and hold it, when she saw the tiny tear form in my good eye—well, then she no longer had somewhere important to go.

We went to Mocha Maya's, where my coffee was still hot. I bought her a cup too and we sat down.

"You scared the hell out of me," she said. "All the girls on the film have been talking about you."

I was shocked. "What? Me?"

"Yes, you. Following us around. Looking for us. Obsessed with us. Jesus, mister, what the hell is going on?"

I had the same, or similar, questions for her. "Girls on the film?"

I got my answer first. "Yeah, there's like nine of us. Or there was. Till you guys started chasing us around. One of us is dead now, for Christ's sake."

I was beyond apologizing. Who could apologize for stuff like that?

"You guys were all in the film?" is what I finally did mutter.

"Yeah. We all have small parts. Had, I should say."

"The movie's over. It's gone. You're still here?"

"There's nowhere else to go. And we all like it here."

"Nowhere else to go?"

"It's impossible to get work. We were all lucky to get this small gig. The rent was pre-paid for a while and we got a little pay up front and we enjoy this town. Or we did. We liked it a lot better before we started dying. But we're still sticking it out. At least for the summer. With all this new energy in town, we might be able to get more work. Your town's getting hot, mister." She frowned, but she was so young that the expression left no trace on her supple skin. "But not if you old dudes go chasing us and killing us or whatever. What's up with that?"

"I wasn't going to kill you. I thought you were someone else."

"Yeah, well, we all look basically alike. We're Mooney's type."

"Mooney's type?"

"Haven't you spotted it? Mooney likes us small, thin, young, warm when you get to know us, but superficially distant, complex, and talented, beautiful redheads."

I really looked at her then, trying to analyze the difference—what made her Not Julie. Eyes a bit smaller, face longer, features not as symmetrical.

"You guys aren't all redheads," I said.

"Yes we are. Or we all started out that way. Some of us had to dye our hair, change our look a little or everybody in that damn movie would look alike, but basically we're all twins. None of us are as beautiful as VelCro was, though. God, that girl was from another planet."

"I didn't notice that. I mean I noticed VelCro was beautiful, but I never noticed Mooney's type."

"Jeez, go look at his movies. That's all you'll see."

I had to admit, looking back quickly on his three previous films, that this girl had a point.

"Hitchcock was crazy about blondes," I said, "or so the stories have it."

She laughed at this. "It's Hollywood, mister. That's the way it's done. There are directors who fuck the talent. That's how we get hired. Some of us, anyway. Maybe most."

Chapter Forty-Nine

∾

The Girls' Dorm

HER NAME WAS Dierdra. There were eight of them left, and they all lived in a warehouse on Water Street. It was scheduled to be converted to several separate lofts, but for now it was just basically one huge open space with a bathroom and kitchen area. It was kind of a dump so they got it cheap. When the film crew arrived, the production company had pre-paid the rent for a while. The "girls' dorm," she called it.

I'm not sure how I pulled this off, but I talked her into inviting me over. I think I did it by being humble, apologetic, retiring, and as invisible and harmless and pathetic as I could make myself. Which was not hard to do.

It was still early morning, so they were all there sleeping on various surfaces. A couple had real beds, some had sleeping bags on air mattresses, some futons, and one girl slept on a ratty old couch. It was one unfurnished, football-field-sized open space with a section containing a refrigerator, stove, sink, and a large rectangular, rustic wooden table with nine mismatched chairs. That's where I sat with Dierdra, sipping coffee and talking in a low voice, little more than a whisper.

One by one the sleeping beauties awoke, stretching, wiping

their eyes. And they really were genuine beauties—hair all different colors and lengths, but all classically beautiful with elegant facial structures and symmetry and uniformly tiny, slim bodies. A couple still had red hair.

One might have thought there was a factory somewhere cranking them out except for the fact that they were so damn human. They had eyes and hearts and souls. That's the thing with great beauty—it comes from being human, and it halts all possibilities of lust. Well, at least for me. Might not be the case for some others, like Mooney, for instance. To me all humans deserve respect and honest, heartfelt love.

They paid me no attention. Men were probably a common sight here, though I imagined they were generally a bit younger than me.

They must have had a dress code—T-shirt and panties, though one gal wore men's boxer shorts and one wore sweatpants. There was apparently no color requirement for what little apparel they wore. I noticed all the muted, pastel colors I saw on the flowers on the bridge, and many interesting feminine patterns. One young lady was totally nude. I tried not to stare. It wasn't easy.

Soon they were all up and about and milling around. More or less fully dressed, they sat at the table, clutching cups of steaming coffee, and chatted amongst themselves. I was still invisible.

Had I been a younger man, or friskier, or in a better mood, I might have considered it heaven. As it was, I was fully conscious of the amazing pulchritude surrounding me, but I was at work and they were humans. No time for thoughts of heaven.

Besides Dierdra, they were Flavia, Petunia, Ambrosia, Gloria, Layla, Anastasia, and Vondra.

"All names that end in 'A,' " I observed.

"The 'A' Team," Dierdra laughed. "Yeah, Mooney likes names that end in 'A.' He likes the sound of 'A.' "

I looked at her questioningly.

"Oh, those aren't our real names. They are the names Mooney gave us to use professionally."

"I knew there was a Victoria who started out as an Edith. Didn't really know about the rest."

I was a little befuddled about the names. "So, what? You guys just do whatever Mooney says? What is he, a Svengali or something? What does that guy have, anyway?"

"Well, hell. He's a big director and he has some power. And he's a charming sonofabitch. He can cast a kind of spell over you, you know? People want to do what he wants. Especially women. Women love that guy. Hell, I loved him."

There was mumbled agreement around the table, and some sly laughter.

"I would have done anything for him," continued Dierdra. "Till I came to my senses."

"What brought you to your senses?"

"Well, all these dead and disappeared girls had something to do with it."

"Yeah, I guess that'll make a guy look a lot less sexy."

This drew some derisive chuckles from the gathering. "You'd be surprised," said Dierdra, who was clearly their spokesperson. "To some, that's kind of sexy too. It's dangerous. Some of us are into danger."

"That's not my style," I said.

"Mine neither," said Dierdra. "You're old and safe. Anyone can see that. That's why you're sitting here."

I looked around the table at all those gorgeous young women.

"So Mooney was fucking all of you guys?" I asked in a forthright, if rather crude, fashion.

"Was he fucking you?" said Vondra to no one in particular. At least I think it was Vondra. I couldn't be sure. They still all seemed pretty much indistinguishable to me, but I thought I recalled the butterfly clip in her shoulder-length hair when she introduced herself. "I thought I was his one and only."

"You?" said Layla, I think. Blonde hair, short. "I thought it was only me."

"No, me," Ambrosia chimed in. I'm pretty sure it was Ambrosia. Big turquoise ring. I was starting to figure out who was who.

"Me. Me," said the one I was almost positive was Petunia. Her figure was curvier than the others'.

They were pulling my leg.

"We're joking," Dierdra said, "but only barely. The guy has a way of looking you in the eye and making you feel like you're the only woman on earth. As hard as it may be to believe, there was a time when none of us knew about the others. When we all really did think we were his one and only. The bastard."

"VelCro, or Juliana if you will, was his favorite, though," Dierdra went on. "He was in love with her. He wasn't in love with us. We know that now."

"And Victoria," one of them chimed in. Flavia most likely. She had the largest eyes, though a little two round. "He loved her too."

There was more nodding and muttered agreement.

"Well," said Dierdra, "he loved her until he got his time with VelCro. Then she was history, just like the rest of us."

"At least the rest of us got it," said Flavia. "We understood the deal. Poor Victoria didn't get it."

"What does that mean?" I asked.

Flavia answered, "She didn't get it. She didn't get the fact that directors will love you and leave you that fast." She snapped her fingers. "At least he let us all stay in the film. Most don't do that. She didn't get it."

"Well, she got it in the end," said Dierdra. "She got it good. And forever."

Maybe I was starting to get it too. "She got it?" I asked, but I wasn't sure I wanted to hear the answer.

"Yeah, she got a nice swim in the river, compliments of Mr. Mooney," said Dierdra. "She couldn't let him go and she paid for it."

Sometimes I need things spelled out. "She couldn't let him go?" I repeated.

Dierdra came to my rescue. "She was pregnant with his baby. She wanted him to marry her."

Chapter Fifty

❧

The Sound of an "A"

PREGNANT BY MOONEY. Not by me, which I knew was not possible. Interesting information to have. Not that I hadn't suspected as much.

Then they started chattering at me, or at one another. It was hard to tell which. But I was tuning it out now. And sorting it out. Or trying my best to.

The girl who was fished out of the river was pregnant with Mooney's child. This was the girl we had seen in Lorenzo's time-lapse stills, the ones where we later saw Mooney hovering too. The girl we had thought was Julie was actually Victoria, also known as Edith. Some blanks were beginning to be filled in.

I gradually tuned back into the conversation there in the girls' dorm, unsure of exactly who was saying what, but slowly starting to hear it again.

"She should have had the abortion."

"She was Catholic. Can you believe that?"

"I don't know anybody over the age of twelve who's Catholic, practicing anyway."

"I thought she was Jewish."

"She was a Buddhist. She meditated."

"Everybody meditates, not just Buddhists."

"Yeah, I know. But she was a Buddhist. She told me."

"She should have just gone off and had the baby. Who cares?"

"She was like nineteen. You're nineteen. Do you want a baby?"

"No way. But I wouldn't get myself dead over it."

"Get *yourself* dead? Don't you think she had some help there?"

Someone else chimed in, "I do."

"Me too. She wouldn't jump."

The conversation continued as if I were not there.

"She's gotta take some of the blame. I wouldn't have said a word. She was stupid."

The rest of the women ganged up on whoever said this.

"*What*? Yeah, blame the victim. No one's to blame but him. Come on—"

"How is that guy not in jail, anyway?"

"He's careful. He looks like he doesn't know what the hell he's doing, but I tell you the guy's brain never stops. He's a better actor than any of us. Now he's playing the pathetic drunk and he's going to get off scot-free. From everything."

"Jeez, I hate that bastard."

"Oh, fuck you, Gloria. You were all over him the other night."

"I was not—"

"Yes you were."

"We all talk big now. And we all shut up when we see him."

"Oh, fuck him, anyway."

Everyone agreed with this coarsely expressed sentiment. There was a chorus of "fuck hims."

It was not unlike the birdsongs I so cherished. Lovely, high-pitched tweeting, some at singsong cadence and quite pleasing in an odd way. The difference was that these young women actually had something to say. I was tempted to take out my phone and record it, but I did not.

As the morning progressed, some of them got more completely dressed and wandered outside, some pulled out cellphones and began chatting on them, and a couple got online on their laptops. I was once again sitting alone at the table with Dierdra; some kind of solidarity had developed between us.

"You don't say much," she said, sipping her coffee.

"Not much room for me to get a word in edgewise, with eight teenage females."

"We're not all teenagers. Flavia's in her twenties, I think. Ambrosia is at least twenty. But we're all over eighteen. Mooney's real careful about that. He checks IDs."

"At least he's got that going for him," I said. "It's better than nothing, I guess."

"He's crazy but he's not stupid. He doesn't need that kind of trouble. He's got enough trouble as it is."

"It looks to me like he's avoiding the real trouble. Like pregnant girlfriends. And murder raps."

I finished my coffee. Dierdra shook my hand and then gave me a sweet, daughterly hug. She was a charming young woman.

"Yeah," she said, "that's Mooney. He's almost obsessive-compulsive about some things. Like redheaded girls whose names end in 'A.' He's pretty diligent about it. And over eighteen. He's careful about that. We're all legal. And actors—they pretty much have to be in the movies. He likes that. I've almost never seen him go after a real civilian, a normal girl off the streets."

"Almost never?" We were both standing now. I'd been about to leave but stopped.

She took our empty cups over to the sink. "Well, I've only ever heard about him screwing that up once. And at first he thought her name ended in 'A' too. Then he found out it didn't. But that didn't seem to faze him at all. I mean, he *really* wanted to fuck that girl. She wasn't in movies, but he didn't care. He was going to fuck her come hell or high water."

"And did he?" I asked.

She turned to look at me, leaning against the sink. "Sure. He always gets what he wants."

I didn't quite get it, though. "He thought her name ended in 'A,' but it didn't?" I asked.

"Yeah," she said. She was regarding me with curiosity, wondering why I cared. "She was another perfect little redhead like the rest of us. It didn't matter when he found out her name ended in 'H,' not 'A.' He just cared about how it sounded. As long as it sounded like an 'A,' he was satisfied."

I was afraid to ask my next question, so I didn't. I just looked at Dierdra, pleading with my eyes for her not to say what I knew she was going to say next.

"Yeah, names like that can fool you. Take my name, for instance—some Dierdras end in 'E,' but mine ends in 'A.' Yeah, he spells it out for you. Makes it official for the credits. So I was cool either way." She walked me to the door. "It was the same thing with that girl Sarah. He just had to have her, and by God, he did."

Chapter Fifty-One

~o

Almost Everything

I T WAS STILL early, and Sarah was sitting at her kitchen table, sipping tea. Clara was already at work.

I would have thought I had a lot to fill Sarah in on, but now suspected she knew a lot more than I did. And possibly a hell of a lot more than I would have wanted her to know.

She had her laptop in front of her. Immersed in something, she hardly looked up. I poured myself tea and sat down across from her.

"Where have you been?" she finally asked me, giving me a quick glance.

"Gathering data. You?"

"The same. You get anything good?"

"Maybe. You?"

"No."

Then she looked up and fixed me with a piercing stare. "Tell me what you found. From the look on your face it was pretty good."

"*Good* is not the word."

"What is the word?"

"Disturbing, maybe. Upsetting. Possibly totally hellacious."

"Tell me," she said.

"Have you seen Mooney lately?"

"Not since he got out of the hospital."

"You hate that bastard, don't you?" I said.

"That's too mild a word. I despise the fucker."

"Your feelings toward him are very strong. Always have been."

"You got that right, Frankie."

I stopped. I could not go where I needed to go. She went back into her computer, and I went back to watching the steam rise off my tea. She was, for the time being, anyway, willing to let the upsetting and disturbing details of what I had learned drop.

But I wasn't. I looked up from the steam and said, "Were you fucking him, Sarah?"

She didn't even look up. "No," she said. Then she looked up. "You gotta believe me, Frankie."

Our eyes locked. "I do," I said.

"Enough said about that?"

I thought this over. "No," I said. "We need to talk."

"So talk."

"You know about the girls' dorm?"

She did not look away. "I've been there."

"You know about Mooney's thing for redheads with names that end in 'A'?

"You mean an 'ah' sound. Yeah, I know."

"How do you know?" I was watching her for signs that she was lying, or at least fudging the truth. So far she didn't falter.

"How do you think?"

"I'm afraid of what I'm thinking."

She shook her head, patted my hand. "Don't be afraid, Frankie. Nothing happened."

"Well, something apparently happened."

She nodded, tensed. "Yeah. He came on to me real strong. He got me up there one day when the other girls were out. And he tried his damnedest to fuck me. But it didn't happen. Do you need to know any more than that?"

I wasn't sure, so I kept asking. "When was this?"

"Right before they shot that one day. When Julie was sick."

"You went up there? I can't believe you actually went up there." I felt my head start to ache and rubbed my temples.

"He was a big-time director and I was an eighteen-year-old girl."

"I thought you were smarter than that." The words emerged with a hint of a groan.

She sighed. "I did too."

"And that was it?"

"That was it until he tried again. And again. And again. He's a persistent bastard."

I thought this over. "Sarah, I'm glad you didn't fuck the sleazeball, but what's really disturbing now is that you never told me about this. We're supposed to be working together. What else haven't you told me?"

She hesitated, looked away. "Nothing. Now you know everything."

I didn't like the hesitation, the averted eyes.

"Everything?"

"Well, practically everything."

I couldn't believe what I was hearing. "*Practically* everything?"

"Yeah, almost everything."

I did not speak. I just looked at her.

"Well, I guess there was one more thing. Julie was pregnant."

Chapter Fifty-Two

~

Shattered Glass

I DIDN'T REACT to Sarah's statement. Not outwardly, anyway.

"You remember when she got sick?" Sarah asked me.

"Well, sure. How could I forget?"

"She lost it then. I was there. She miscarried."

"She had doctors all over the place."

"They weren't there all the time. I was. Nobody else knew."

"You guys took care of it yourselves?"

"Yeah, we did. She was my friend."

What a thing for two very young women to have to handle themselves, I thought.

Who was the father? I didn't think too hard on that one. I was pretty sure I knew.

But I was losing count. According to my calculations, that made two pregnant girls—that we knew of anyway—out of a total of eleven beautiful, small, slim, pale redheads. There was the original nine from the girls' dorm, plus Julie, plus Sarah. One was dead, and one was very possibly also dead.

And one drunken, sleazy director holed up in a crumbling mansion just up the hill.

I needed to talk to somebody about this. I couldn't talk to

the dead girl. I couldn't talk to the missing and possibly dead girl. So I decided to talk to the sleazy director.

I was losing count on a lot of things—dead girls, pregnant girls, missing girls, girls who ended up in the river. I was successful in keeping the count of sleazy directors, however. There was only one of them.

So I trudged up that damn Hill of Tears to Mooney's.

I found him up and about—clean-shaven, hair short and well kempt, showered, pink cheeks, chipper. His house was sparkling clean—no pizza crusts, no puke on the carpets—and he was bouncing around like he had pleasant places to bounce to. He smiled when I walked in.

Was I in the right place?

I admired my surroundings. "You cleaned up," I said.

"Not me. I hired a girl."

I looked at him. "*You* cleaned up," I clarified.

He smiled. He *smiled*. "Yeah, I did."

I was still standing by the door. He stood in the center of the room. "What's up, Mooney?"

"Me, I'm up."

"Yeah, I can see that. Why? How?"

"It was time. Or I was going to die."

"That doesn't stop a lot of people. I didn't think it was going to stop you."

He shrugged. "Me neither."

"Seriously, man, what happened?"

It was then that I saw the bottle of Jameson in his hand. He brought it to his mouth and took a big chug.

"Time to move on, Raven. I'm moving on."

"Where? How?"

"Right here. Sheer will power."

I pointed at the bottle. "You're still drinking."

"You surprise me, Raven. I thought you knew about drinkers. I'm on a toot and it's going to last a while. But it can't last if I die. I've rejoined the living so I can keep drinking."

"That's fucked up, Mooney."

He raised his eyebrows. "Would it be better if I dropped dead?"

"Maybe."

"Maybe's not good enough for me."

"It's your life, Mooney."

"You want a drink?" He held out the bottle.

"Fuck you, Mooney."

I had come to ask him about fucking redheads whose names end in 'A' and about trying to fuck Sarah. But the dude knew how to throw curveballs. What was the point of asking this guy anything at all?

"Yeah. Fuck me. Fuck you. Fuck everything. Fuck VelCro too. Forget her," he said. "She's history. She's gone."

"Easy for you to say."

This pissed him off. "Easy! Did you see what happened to me? I almost died."

"I note the 'almost,' Mooney. I hope we can someday apply that word to our dear Juliana's death."

"So do I," he replied, and I thought for a minute he was sincere.

Then I heard a crash from the bedroom. Glass shattering, followed by an "oh, shit."

A tiny, slim, gorgeous, redheaded young woman came out of the room.

"Shit, Nickie. I dropped that picture. It broke."

She looked at me. Was it Petunia, Layla, Ambrosia?

She extended a hand for me to shake.

"We haven't really met. I'm Gloria."

Chapter Fifty-Three

~∽

The Lost Verse

I SHOOK HER hand. "Frank," I said.

"I know," she replied.

Then, while I was digesting this latest development, yet another piled upon us.

Another tiny, slim, pretty redhead walked in. Not from the bedroom, but from the outside—Sarah.

"I figured I'd find you here," she said. "After I checked the West End, the Blue Rock, Mocha Maya's, and the girls' dorm, anyway."

"You didn't check my house?"

"You're never there."

This hurt. I love my house. Sarah was right, though. I was never there anymore. Poor Marlowe must feel abandoned. At least I checked in on him occasionally and took him for walks and threw sticks. But not nearly enough.

"What's up?" I asked her. Something had to be up for her to track me down like that. Something relatively big.

"This is up." She held out a postcard.

I couldn't quite see it from where I stood, so I moved closer. She handed it to me.

It was a nighttime party scene of New Orleans, streets lit up, revelers holding drinks, neon signs, a mule-drawn tourist carriage, and an orange banner curling across the top, proclaiming, "BOURBON STREET!"

It was postmarked "New Orleans, LA." The message was only these words, handwritten:

> Her flamed mane in the heather
> Did blithely take his stare
> Young Johnny was enchanted
> By the moisten of her hair
> But as he reached to touch her
> Aqua became sod
> And the sweet faint maiden
> Ascended into God

I read it aloud.

"I knew you'd be the only one who got what the hell it means," said Sarah. "So, what the hell does it mean?"

I recited it again, silently. Then once more. By memory this time. Then I put the music to it in my head and sang it aloud, the way it was supposed to be heard.

"It's a verse from a song," I said, when I had finished singing.

"Yeah. That's what I thought. Sounds like one of those dead-baby dead-dog songs. Dead-young-girl song."

"The girl in that song is not dead."

"No? Sounds like it to me."

"Believe me. I know that verse inside out."

"Okay. You're the expert here. Can you tell me what it is?"

"Yes," I said. "It's a lost verse from 'The Nutting Girl.' "

She looked at Mooney, then back at me. Mooney's expression was unreadable. Carefully schooled to reveal nothing. Gloria was staring at him, waiting for her cue.

"That's what you call Julie," Sarah said.

"Yep."

She grabbed the postcard and tapped it with her finger. "What is 'flamed mane'?"

"What else? Red hair."

" 'Moistened'? What's up with that?"

"I don't know. That's the way I wrote it. I don't know what it means."

"You wrote it?"

I nodded. She seemed to accept this without question.

" 'Aqua became sod'?"

"Water becomes earth. Fluid becomes solid. Amorphous becomes firm. Unknown becomes known. Spirit becomes flesh."

" 'And ascended unto God'? That sounds an awful lot like death."

"It's 'into' not 'unto.' There's a difference. And I didn't mean it to mean death."

She rattled the postcard at me. "You wrote this?"

"Yes I did. I wrote that damn verse. A long time ago."

"I thought that was a traditional song."

"It is. We add verses to traditional songs all the time. You know that. You've done it yourself."

"Okay. So if it doesn't mean death, what does it mean?"

"I'm not sure. Not death."

She thrust the postcard into my face. "That's Julie's handwriting, Frankie."

"I know."

Sarah's expression was quizzical. And concerned. There was some joy too … and hope. I'm sure my face looked the same. Mooney and Gloria still stood frozen in a tableau of confusion.

"When did you write that, Frankie?

"So long ago I can't remember when."

"And where?"

"A place that doesn't exist—Lavender Street."

Chapter Fifty-Four

∿

A Guy Looking for a Guitar

IT WAS HOT in New Orleans. Hot as hell.

I didn't tell Karen I was leaving. She might have tried to stop me. I wasn't supposed to leave town, but it wasn't anything the airports had checks on, so I went.

I didn't tell anybody. I was hoping for a short trip.

Clara went sightseeing. Sarah and I were there to work.

Connections led us to Ben. My cousin Tommy knew New Orleans like I knew Shelburne Falls. Tommy knew that anybody looking for a guitar in this town eventually found his way to Ben.

I wasn't looking for a guitar. I was looking for a missing girl. And for a guy who might know something about the missing girl. A guy who was looking for a guitar.

There was no air conditioning in Ben's shack. There was one rather ineffective fan trying to push dripping air from one room to the other, but I think it would have felt the same way in there if it was turned off. There were only two rooms anyway, so there was not much space to push anything into.

It smelled like wet dog, and the wet dog in question sat there panting on the porch, lying on his side as if dead. The dog was wet because he had just taken a dip in the river to cool off, a fruitless act if ever there was one.

That's where Ben had his workbench set up, on the open porch. There were guitar bodies hanging up all around him in various states of repair and disrepair, and mandolins and banjos and basses too.

He was lean and wiry and his hair was still quite dark for a guy in his seventies. His accent, for a Cajun, sounded strangely like a New Yorker's, dropping the 'R,'s and clipped and nasal. He handed Tommy what he called a "mando."

It looked immaculate and new and shiny, but it was ancient. "Lady on Toulouse found this in her attic. Peeled off the back. Warped. Redid it. Polished it up nice."

Tommy plucked it. It rang sharp and clean. He set it down. Sarah picked it up and played the opening riff from "Losing My Religion."

She smiled at me. "Your theme song, Francis."

"Didn't know you played," I said, amazed.

"You don't know much about me, Frankie. I'm in a band at school. Actually, I'm in like three bands. We've got seventeen different ones there, and I'm in three of them."

She set it back down and Ben handed the mando to Tommy.

"Don't know if that'll cover it," he said.

Tommy didn't say anything. He nodded. Guy owed him a favor, apparently.

Tommy set the mando down and Ben led us down the rotting steps from the porch to the worn path leading to the river. It was strewn with old tires and debris and tree limbs.

I looked back over my shoulder. The ancient shack was built on stilts and high up on the levee with another dozen similar homes. They might have been in the deepest bayou instead of here in an industrial neighborhood right in the city.

The wet dog followed us, limping. He could barely walk, whether from the heat or arthritis or an injury I could not tell.

We came upon a crude, eight-foot chicken-wire fence. Ben

opened up something resembling a gate held closed by a black bungee cord. We walked the few feet down to the river, and we all sat on a log except the wet dog, who found a cool mud puddle to sink down into.

"Didn't get a drop in Katrina," he said. "Around the corner at the lake was the worst place, but here … nothing. Best place to live in town. They're raising the levee two feet. No reason to do that. Now they're cutting down my trees. Wouldn't be surprised if they take my house and try to buy me off for five bucks. My lawyer's on it."

This guy looked like he couldn't afford a newspaper, let alone a lawyer. Maybe he had a million bucks stashed under the floorboards.

We sat there, watching the river flow.

"The dude you're looking for, he's coming by this afternoon, he says. Enormous white dude. Big as this goddamn house. It's an old Gibson Hummingbird I fixed up. Perfect sound. An icon—rare, mahogany, square shoulder dreadnought. Not many around. Crazy white kid's paying me $6,000 for it and I didn't have to do much to it at all."

Yep, that sounded like the guy I was looking for. A guy looking for a guitar, a poor guy who had—apparently, somehow—come into some money.

Chapter Fifty-Five

~~

Waiting for this Big White Dude

WE HUNG AROUND a long time waiting for this big white dude. Tommy and Ben started drinking home-made amber-colored hooch. A woman started to approach Sarah with some too, in a coffee cup. She looked at me and I frowned, so she walked away without delivering the cup. Quiet, small, and mousy, the woman blended in with the woodwork. I couldn't tell if she was Ben's wife, or daughter, or mother, or what. She was nearly invisible and of indeterminate age. This was clearly Ben's space, but I had the feeling she was more of a vital presence here when Ben did not have guests.

Tommy and Ben talked musician talk. Sarah picked pieces of tunes on the mando. She was good. I looked around. All the furnishings were dark, damp wood, dating back to the fifties, and considering the amount of wear, they'd been sitting in this room since then.

Frack was, if anything, bigger than the last time I had seen him.

He strolled right into Ben's shack—there were no real doors to knock on—and walked out onto the porch where we were all seated.

He was surprised to see me and Sarah.

"Mister Raven?"

"Yeah, it's me. Call me Frank. And you remember Sarah."

"Well, yeah. What the hell are you guys doing here?"

"Looking for you."

"How the hell did you find me?"

"That's what I do. I find things."

He laughed at this. "I think you just found more than you bargained for."

"More than I bargained for is exactly what I wanted to find."

The mysterious, silent woman came in and gave Frack a cloudy glass containing that same mysterious amber liquid the others were drinking. He sipped at it.

"She knew you would find us. She wanted you to. I just didn't expect it would be here."

"Funny how that works sometimes," I replied. "Sometimes you find things where you least expect it. That's what 'find' means."

Ben handed Frack the guitar. Frack clumsily made some simple chords and strummed it.

"It sounds sweet," he said. "Awesome."

"I polished it up nice," Ben said.

Frack reached into his pocket and came up with a big wad of hundred dollar bills. He peeled off sixty bills and handed them to Ben, who accepted them without counting and stuffed them into the hole of some junker wreck of a guitar. Maybe that's where all this guy's money was stashed.

Sarah picked something on the mando. Frack strummed along as well as he could. Tommy picked up a big stand-up bass from the corner. Ben was on a banjo. They sounded good, like a real band, with Frack being something of a weak link. They played for half an hour without stopping, but they changed tunes a few times.

Everyone smiled when they were done. Music makes people happy.

Frack got up to leave.

"Meet me tonight," he said.

"Where? When?" I asked.

"I'm playing tonight with Slim Stevie Slates at TJ's on Frenchmen," reported Tommy. "Anyone can tell you where it is. As good a place as any to meet up."

"That'll work," said Frack. "Ten o'clock?"

Then, as he took his new guitar and walked out of Ben's shack, he turned and said, "You'll see her tonight. She's been waiting for this."

Chapter Fifty-Six

～

The Sign of the Cross

NOBODY HAD TO tell us where TJ's on Frenchmen was. Tommy drove us there with me stuffed in the back with his gigantic stand-up bass guitar and Sarah squeezed together in the front passenger seat. They started playing at eight; we were supposed to meet Frack at ten. This was going to be a late night. We arrived at seven with Tommy to help him set up. I heard a strange chirping as we unloaded the car in the hot humid street in front of the bar. Turned out it was not a bird.

"Tree frogs," explained Tommy. "It's so damp out they're chirping like they do in the rain. Call them rain frogs then."

They were not birds, but I recorded them anyway. The sound was similar enough, and I thought that they could console me late some long sleepless night, just as my birds had been doing.

We watched Tommy and Stevie play for a while. At their break, they sipped beers and talked of various forms of water life.

"You shine a flashlight at them when it's dark," reported Stevie. "You see their beady little shrimp eyes and grab the suckers with a skimmer net."

"They stay right on the surface," added Tommy.

They continued sipping beers and talking.

At ten, Frack walked in. He was on time, and took us for a slow, hot walk through downtown streets, then residential streets. A streetcar ride was followed by more residential streets. We ate po' boys. They drank hurricanes. We watched an old man toss a ball to a dog.

And then, there it was.

"This is the place," said Frack.

The place took up an entire city block. It was surrounded by pretty, cozy-looking homes in pastel colors, some in multi-colors. Everything was green with palms and grass, all visible through the dark from the streetlights and the home lights and the starlight and the moonlight.

It was all bricked in—an eight-foot-high concrete and red brick wall all around the perimeter. On top of the wall was a three-foot black-iron railing. Except for the fact that it was considerably higher, it reminded me very much of the wall and black railing where Julie had first disappeared into the river on the day of the fateful movie shoot. Our girl seemed to have a habit of falling off high railings and into whatever lies beneath.

We walked all around the big rectangle. You could not see inside. Even in places where there once were gates, there were now bricks or wooden walls. Whatever was inside that courtyard was hidden from our view.

Then, on one side, there was a break in the wall and a real functioning gate. And a sign. The sign said we were welcome so I supposed we were, but I felt the ghosts of when I was not welcome here and hesitated.

I suppose I had been hesitating all during this entire Nutting Girl quest and adventure. Hesitating way too much. I had been chicken.

I sucked it up. "Let's go," I said.

Sarah made the sign of the cross, which surprised me. I think she had little, if any, formal Catholic training. But then I didn't know she could play "Losing My Religion" on the mando either.

I also made the sign of the cross—half out of respect and half to ward off danger.

We entered the gate of the monastery.

Chapter Fifty-Seven

～

It Looks Like You've Found Her

IT WAS COOL inside, and I don't think they even had air conditioning on. It was bare, cold stone and brick and rocks and concrete and tiles, and it was dark. It smelled of incense and disinfectant.

No one greeted us at first. The door was unlocked and we just walked in. There was a tiny entryway with a few explanatory signs we didn't bother to read, and two confessional-like grated windows—one on either side of the alcove. Both were closed tight.

There was a buzzer at one of these windows. After several minutes of just standing there, absorbing it all, Frack pushed it. We heard it buzz somewhere in the back.

We waited. No one showed up.

Frack did not push the buzzer again. No one did. We simply stood there and waited.

Then she showed up, floating in as if she had no feet. She was clad in a long, gray, simple gown that touched the floor, with a white and gray veil covering most of her face. She had an unusually pretty face, pale, some brown wisps of hair falling out of the veil, serene brown eyes, mouth flat without a smile but still somehow pleasant.

No, it wasn't "her"—it wasn't Julie. It was Sister Ofelia.

Her voice was soft. "Hello. Welcome, Mister Frack. It's nice to see you again. We don't usually entertain visitors this late at night. We're not exactly late-night folks here. But there is something very special about these late, hot nights, isn't there? And believe it or not, we can occasionally do something outside of the proverbial box here too. If this is what works for the schedules of sincere visitors, we can accommodate that."

"These are the friends I told you about," he said.

We both shook Sister Ofelia's tiny soft hand, which was nonetheless strong.

Sarah introduced herself and I said, "I'm Francis."

"Francis," she repeated. "How appropriate. We're Franciscans here."

"I know," I said. "The second order."

"You know something about us?"

"Something," I answered, "but only something."

"Well, come on in," she said.

She opened one of the doors and took us into a sitting room with a couch and three thinly stuffed chairs. We all sat down. Sister Ofelia looked out of time except for her Nike basketball shoes—white with red and orange stripes. When she sat down, you could see her feet.

Frack and Sarah sat on the couch. We were offered tea, which we politely refused. I wasn't here for tea. I was here for only one thing—Juliana Velvet Norcross, The Nutting Girl.

Sarah, bless her, took charge in her most gracious, curious-guest guise, smiling sweetly and seemingly completely enthralled with the good sister's tales.

"This is such a big space," Sarah said. "It's so cool. How many of you are here, anyway?"

"Only eight," replied Sister Ofelia. "Well, nine now."

"Wow! So much space for nine people. You have plenty of room to get lost in," Sarah said.

Sister Ofelia laughed. "Yes. I always dreamed of living in a place I could get lost in. And I found it. But one needs space to breathe and move around in for a healthy life, doesn't one?"

The good sister continued, "There used to be many more of us. Back when the monastery was in the Ninth Ward. We had upwards of thirty or forty then, but that was a while ago."

"Not that many people choose this kind of life now, I guess," Sarah said. "This can't be an easy life for anyone. It's such a commitment. I can't imagine how I would do here."

Sister Ofelia laughed. "You might be surprised, dear. If you're called here, you're called here. But that's been the case as long as I've been alive, and before that too. There are always fewer and fewer, and people keep foretelling our demise. Yet somehow, from somewhere, someone shows up. A very slow trickle, but they show up. Many of them stay. Our death has been greatly exaggerated. We will be here forever. At least I hope so. And pray so. And I believe so, God willing."

She let the silence spin out for a moment before adding, "And that's how your friend got here—Sister Sabina. She just showed up one morning, knocking on our door."

"That's pretty wild, isn't it?" asked Sarah.

"You'd be surprised. It's not unheard of. We welcome it. How one comes to us in this community is a gift from God. We talk to them first, of course. Find out why they are here, what has drawn them. Is it real? Do they have the calling? Then they go away and think it over. If they come back, they're welcome to stay for a two-week trial period. If they stay beyond that, they stay."

"It's anonymous here, right?" asked Sarah. "It must be."

"Oh, yes. They change their names and relinquish their possessions. We understand about families and people from your life who you love. No one has to give that up, but for all practical purposes, they do. This is a new life devoted to God, and all else becomes less important. We've had women here who were married. One woman has four children. We have all kinds here."

"And now you have a movie star," said Sarah.

"Do we?" asked the good sister innocently.

"You mean you don't know?"

"Sister Sabina? She was in a movie?"

"You don't know who she is?"

Sister Ofelia might have been playing dumb. Whatever she was thinking, she kept her expression neutral. "We know she's Sister Sabina and we know she was called here. That's all we need or want to know."

"Don't you read the papers? Watch the news?"

Sister Ofelia laughed again. "Well, we're not totally cloistered. We're allowed to watch television for one hour a day, but frankly no one does. We have one very old TV and I'm not even sure it still works. We don't get newspapers or magazines. Sister Breaca is the only one who goes out. She goes to the grocery, the drugstore, and runs errands for us. No one else leaves. She's the only one who uses the internet too. We need one another here. We mostly stay here and pray. That's why we're here."

Sarah recited the names: "Ofelia, Breaca, Sabina. Do all the nuns' names end in 'A'?"

"Well, actually, yes they do. It's not a requirement. It's just our little tradition. Everybody must have the name of a saint. That's required by the Church. And here everyone chooses an 'A' name. Started a long time ago when the men were here. It's all tied to a blind monk's regaining his sight. It was his preference and we just adopted it. 'A' for the women. 'O' when there were men here. I'll tell you that story if you want."

Sarah looked at me questioningly, then she said to the sister, "Wow! Are you kidding me? Blind monk? I really gotta hear that story. But I'm torn up. I want to talk about Sister Sabina too. You really don't know who she is?"

"She's Sister Sabina. That's all we need to know."

"Haven't the police been here?"

"My goodness, no. Why should the police be here?"

Sarah's eyes were wide. "Didn't they come looking for her?"

"Why should they do that?"

"Everybody in the world was looking for her."

Sister Ofelia cocked her head. I had to conclude she honestly wasn't aware of Juliana's identity. "Why were the police looking for her?"

"It wasn't just the police. It was everybody. *We* were looking for her."

"Well, it looks like you've found her then, doesn't it?"

Chapter Fifty-Eight

∾

Lavender Street

IF SHE WERE still a movie star, that would have been Juliana's cue to stroll in, hit her mark, look ravishing, say her clever, amusing lines.

But she did not, and all was still.

Sarah picked up the thread of the conversation. "You were in the Ninth Ward, you said? When was that?"

"Do you know New Orleans?" asked the sister.

"No," said Sarah. "I've never been here before. But I've heard of the Ninth Ward. That's where Hurricane Katrina wiped everything out, isn't it?"

"Yes. We were in the Lower Ninth. That's where the worst destruction was. We had been there for a hundred years, but the place was totally destroyed, wiped away like it had never been there. Even the street it was on ceased to exist. All the properties were wiped off the face of the earth and never rebuilt. It's just a bleak, brown, empty, dusty field now. Nothing is there."

She wiped away a tear before going on.

"We didn't know what would happen to us. The church could have scattered us all over the country. Or even out of the country. We all prayed a lot. We wanted to stay together.

"Then they found this place. It used to be a military academy. Isn't that ironic? We believe totally in peace and love, and this was once a place where they taught war."

"I totally get irony. Irony is everywhere," said Sarah. She was doing all the talking for us, and doing a good job.

"Yes, isn't it?" said the good sister. "Finding this place was a miracle."

"Or was it a strange and wonderful thing?" asked Sarah.

Sister Ofelia responded, "What's the difference?"

"Miracles are rare," said Sarah. "Strange and wonderful things—they happen all the time." She added, "My mom taught me that."

Sister Ofelia thought this over. "I'm sure your mother is a smart woman," she said. "But no, miracles happen all the time. They happen every day. You finding this place was a miracle. Sister Sabina finding this place was a miracle. Us finding this place was a miracle."

Sarah said, "Well, when you put it that way, I guess so. Small miracles, big miracles. They're all miracles. I guess I've never seen a big miracle. Not totally sure I've ever seen a miracle at all, actually. "

"Oh, you have, dear. I know you have. We all have."

"I don't know. What's the biggest miracle you've ever seen?"

Sister Ofelia smiled and waved her off. "Oh, honey, you can't measure miracles, or compare them. It's not a contest."

I was silent here. So was everyone else, other than a murmur or two. But me, I was particularly quiet and still.

Then Sister Ofelia went on, "But now you're leading me to that story I referred to earlier. The one you were so curious about. Once, a long time ago, when the Ninth Ward Monastery was for men and women, when there were monks and nuns, a true ecclesiastical miracle occurred. We were going to take it to the Vatican and get it certified. But they make that so hard to do."

"How so?"

"It's a complicated and drawn out process. They convene a board. They look at medical records, X-rays, CAT scans. And they vote. They actually vote on miracles. Then they turn it over to another board, and more voting. Just more than we were willing to go through. We didn't have to vote and we didn't have to turn it over to a board. We turned it over to God."

"Isn't that kind of radical? I thought you had to follow rules."

Sister Ofelia sat forward in her seat. "We didn't violate any rules. We just kept silent. We knew what we had."

Sarah nodded. "I guess that kind of makes sense. But if you didn't go to Rome with it, what did you do? I mean you had to do something, right?"

"We simply thanked God and went on with our lives. Through the grace of St. Francis, anything can happen."

"What happened?"

"A blind monk regained his sight. But that was back in a place that no longer exists—in the Ninth Ward, on Lavender Street."

Chapter Fifty-Nine

∿

Lilies and Birds

Tʜᴇɴ sʜᴇ ᴀᴘᴘᴇᴀʀᴇᴅ, not quite out of a puff of smoke, and stood there in the doorway. Her dress was the same as Sister Ofelia's—gray and white gown to the floor, a veil. No wisps of red or black or brown hair sneaking out of the veil. She must have cut her scarlet locks, or tied back her hair.

But that face, those eyes, the body carriage—it was her. It was not the ghosts of her we thought we had seen before, on the streets, on the rocks, in the river. This was really her.

She smiled. If I had thought she was beautiful before, now I saw an ethereal beauty that far surpassed that. It was the change from a lovely woman who radiated defiance to a body and soul in harmony with nature. Our Nutting Girl had grown up. She had become something else. Someone else.

She slowly looked at each of us in turn. When she got to Sarah, Sarah sniffled, gasped, and bowed her head. Then she got up, ran to Julie, and hugged her. It was a mutual hug—both girls clinging and crying, faces moist and warm and red.

"I can't believe this," Sarah said between tears.

Julie's smile got deeper and deeper. "Oh, Sarah," she finally said. "I'm so sorry."

When the hug finally broke, Sarah repeated, "Sorry?"

"I'm sorry I put you through all this."

Sarah was composed now. "Sorry? I'm thrilled! Here you are. I knew you wouldn't do anything like this without thinking. And now all I am is happy."

"Oh, Sarah. I never did anything *with* thinking before. I just flowed along. Literally."

Sister Ofelia rose to her feet. "I will leave you to yourselves now. I'm sure you have a lot to talk about. Sister Sabina will show you around. Why don't you take them out to the courtyard? It's a lovely night out."

She left. Julie sat in the chair she had vacated. "I'll show you around. This is an amazing place. But let's catch up first."

The question hung there unasked and unanswered. Maybe it did not need to be asked ... or answered.

Oh, hell, yes it did.

"Julie," I said. "What happened?"

"What happened?" she replied.

"You know. Everything. What happened to you that day?"

"What didn't happen? The whole world happened. The whole universe happened. And heaven, and hell too. And that's the right word too, Frankie—*happened*. Because I was just there. And it just happened on its own. I didn't have to *do* anything. I was there and it all took me over like a wave. Yes, like a wave. I was there. Then I was gone. Then I was back. I didn't have to *do* anything."

"Like the lilies of the field," said Sarah. "Right? I don't know the Bible really, but I know the lilies of the field. 'They toil not. Neither do they spin.' They just sit there and God takes care of them."

"Well, actually, no," replied Julie. "That's not what that means at all, is it? That's not what the lilies of the field are about at all. Is it, Francis?"

It took me a few seconds to respond.

"Well, now you're getting into serious territory," I said. "That's all part of the Sermon on the Mount. That's where Jesus really started to rock and roll. He stood up on that big hill and gave the speech of his life and then stepped down and started doing miracles right and left—curing a leper, casting out demons, calming winds and the sea, and bringing the dead to life. Dude was on a roll. All action and taking charge. Doesn't sound like those wimpy lilies of the field at all, does it?"

Julie picked up from here. "Everybody thinks that lily stuff is all about being passive and just sitting around. That's not it at all."

Then she stopped talking.

"So," Sarah said. "Are you going to enlighten us or not?"

"I hate to 'enlighten' anybody. I can't do that. I'm not enlightened. But I can tell you what I think."

"So, what do you think?"

"What I think is that it's not literal. It's symbolic and it's all metaphor."

"Whoa," I said. "Watch out where you're going. This is getting into dangerous territory."

"I've always been a dangerous girl." Then she continued, "It's all about being who you are, finding perfection, finding what's right and then staying there. It's a parable and it is not about being lazy. It's about being active rather than reactive. It's more mystical action than physical action. But it's action. Praying is action. Meditation is action. These things are not passive. It's about going where you belong and belonging where you go. It's adaptation—adaptation simply, easily, naturally and freely."

"Now you're sounding like Frankie," Sarah said. "It's almost scary."

"It's not scary. It's all real. The Bible may be allegory. But God is real. Am I right, Frankie?"

Again, I couldn't answer right away. Julie looked at me quizzically.

"Frankie?" she asked.

After a few beats, I said, "That's the sixty-four thousand dollar question, isn't it? Is there a God?"

Julie said, "Yeah, I know. Big question. Big questions all over the place. I guess you just gotta make up your mind and then run with it. That's what I did." She held out her arms to encompass her surroundings. "I learned to pray here. I never prayed before."

"Yes, you did," I said. "I've seen you dance."

She laughed. "Yeah. You told me before that was prayer and you were right. Awareness of the presence of God. That's totally what it is. I still dance here, by the way. You sang here. I dance. Same difference. God's all over the place.

"So, yeah. That's why I'm here. That's what I saw when I was sick, Frankie. I saw God. I saw God, a spirit, a force—who makes lilies and birds and people and plants and beasts and fruits and nuts, who loves them, who protects them."

I looked at this sweet young woman and I remembered the young man I once was and what I once believed.

"You can't prove any of that, Julie," I said. "You can't prove there's a God. That's the problem. Show me some proof. Can you prove God exists?"

"Proof, Frankie?" she answered. "Can you prove love exists?"

I was kind of stuck now. "No," is what I finally said.

"No," she replied. "No, you can't. Neither can I. But we know it, don't we?" This did not require an answer, so I did not give one. She continued, "That's because God is love. And love is God. And I can't prove any of it. But I know it and so do you.

"And that's about all I know."

I once knew that too.

We were all quiet for a long time.

Then I said, "Okay, I get it. But there's a lot I don't get. Why are you here? What happened? What's going to happen next? How are things going to end up? This has been such a long strange trip, and I don't think it's over. And I don't know how it got here."

Julie breathed in and smiled. "We'll walk and talk. That's where the truth comes out. Don't worry, Francis. All will be well."

Chapter Sixty

∼∽

Lots of Things

W<small>E WALKED AND</small> talked in the courtyard, lit by the moon and stars and some lights drifting out from inside. It was way hotter out there than inside.

Outside the monastery door, only a few feet in front of us, was another structure, this one rectangular and sturdy, built from cinderblocks with moss climbing up the sides and painted a dull red. Julie had to use much of her strength to open the thick brick door.

"Can you tell what this is?" she asked us as we headed in.

No one responded.

She pointed out stone and cement boxes lining most of the walls. The place was bigger than it looked from the outside. It went on and on, backwards into space. It felt like it was as long as a football field.

"These are all the nuns and monks who have died here," she said. "People aren't buried underground here. They moved each one of these from the Ninth Ward after Katrina. They got scattered all over but they eventually found each one. None of them broke open. These things are built to survive anything."

I looked them over as we walked down the aisles, half

expecting to see my name on one of them. There were all kinds of Brother This-es and Sister Thats and dates, but I was not amongst them.

I had died once but not here. Apparently there were still remnants of my existence here. But no, my miracle here was of another flavor.

We walked around the crypt and looked at each tomb. It was damp and cool and we didn't really want to leave, but there were other feelings here too—of death and of things rotting—so we did leave and Julie led us back out into the heat.

The courtyard was immense, filled with patches of both flower and vegetable gardens, fruit trees, shrubs, stone paths, fountains, and statues. It was a delightful place to stroll around and a fine place to walk and talk.

Julie looked me in the eye and got right to the point.

"It was a lovely scene, Frankie. I was happy. I was sitting on that iron railing with the river roaring under me. My best friend was sitting next to me and we were shooting a film I was excited about and you guys were dancing beautifully and it was a perfect day.

"And then, and then something clicked inside. I was happy doing what I was doing. I really was. But there was more, wasn't there? I knew there was something more and I knew I could find it. I was young, and I was smart, and I had all the money in the world, and I could do whatever I wanted. I wasn't quite sure what that was or how I would go about doing it, but I knew I was going to do it.

"Then the way I was going to do it just happened. Frack reached his hand out toward me. He got just a little too close. Just a little. He brushed me. Just barely. He touched me.

"But he's one strong dude and that's all it took. And the next thing I knew, I was in the river. It was cold and it just pushed me around. It pushed me along, but I was floating in it too. I was weightless. I was helpless. I couldn't do anything except just go where it took me. I couldn't feel anything. I didn't feel anything. I just was.

"I was adapting, Frankie. I was adapting to where I had been pulled. That's why I was smiling.

"I guess I went over the dam. I don't remember that. I really don't remember any of it. And I floated down that river a long way. 'Floated' is not the right word though. God, it was like sliding down the worst waterslide ever, one with bumps and rocks and dirt, and it went on and on and on.

"Then I stopped. Just like that. I was in a quiet pool. The waters stopped rushing. Everything stopped rushing. Everything stopped, and there I was. I was floating there. And I started to thaw out and I started to wake up and I realized I was not dead. I was still alive, Frankie. I was alive.

"I didn't know where I was, but there I was.

"And there was a little ripple in that pool and it slowly and gently moved me to the shore. I touched the shore. It was soft and green and moist.

"And I lay there touching it for a few seconds. My eyes were open this whole time and I saw a lot. I saw all kinds of stuff. Like when I was sick. Remember that, Frankie? I told you I saw stuff I needed to talk to you about? Well, there it all was again. Right there on that shore. All around me too. In that pool. In that river. Everywhere, actually.

"I pulled myself onto the bank. I was still alive. I didn't hurt. Nothing hurt. I should have had broken bones, I guess. I should have been badly hurt. Hell, I should have been dead. But I wasn't. I didn't feel great. I felt dazed and groggy and I shook my head and tried to clear my mind and figure out what had happened. I couldn't figure it out. I didn't know how much time had gone by. I didn't know where I was. And I didn't know what was going to happen or where I was going to go.

"So I didn't do anything and I didn't go anywhere. I just sat there on that bank and watched the river. And I watched it flow and flow. And then I guess I fell asleep.

"When I woke up, it was dark. And then, almost instantly, it got light. It was morning. The sun was all red in the sky and there were some clouds and it brightened up and glowed.

"And I sat there for a while. And I thought about things. Lots of things. I thought about where I should go and what I should do.

"And Frankie, I had no fucking idea. I had no idea what to do or where to go.

"So I got up and I started walking. I had dried off but I was still dressed in that costume. With the purple skirt and the orange shirt and the leggings and the red Cons and the whole thing. But it wasn't really much of a costume, was it? I might have worn something like that anyway. Hell, I could wear anything back then."

She looked down at her gray gown and smiled.

"And I walked, Frankie. I walked on and on and on. It was woods for a while and then it was back roads. I mean it was way back roads and almost nobody drove by.

"Then I started to get hungry. I wasn't tired. I was just moving and moving and I never thought about being tired and I wasn't tired. But I got hungry. I started to think about where I could get food. So I walked some more.

"Then I looked around and there I was. Back in town. Somehow I had circled back and there I was, walking along Conway Street, with the river flowing just to my right.

"So I cut through this yard to get back along the river. And I walked around. I was following the river back toward town. Then I walked by a yard and this old guy was sitting in a chair and staring out at the river. He had on one of those blue Yankees caps. And he had a big sandwich on a plate. He had a big bottle of beer too.

"So this old guy says, 'Want half a sandwich?' And I said yes and he handed it to me and I scarfed it down. Then he handed me the other half and I scarfed that down too. And he let me sip from the beer. Hell, I more than sipped it. I chugged it.

"Then he said, 'I knew you'd be back. I was waiting for you.'

"Then he said I looked like I needed to clean up. So he let me come inside and I took a long, hot bath. And he gave me clean clothes to wear. They were real old, but in good shape. Retro, you know? Cool. Belonged to his dead wife, Emma. The stuff you spend a fortune on in a vintage clothing store. If you can ever find anything as nice as that. Like old hippie clothes from forty years ago, but real nice.

"So I stayed there. He let me sleep on the bed. He slept on the couch.

"And I stayed there. It turned out I had a few bruises. Cuts on my forehead, hands, wrists. He was a kind, gentle man. He cleaned them up for me, applied some kind of salve, bandaged them. I stayed there and didn't come out for three weeks."

Chapter Sixty-One

~

Time to Go

"I DIDN'T DO anything for three weeks except sit there and think. And change my hair. Cut it, dyed it darker. That was a sign that I needed to change something about myself. Once in a while, I'd go out in the yard and watch the river flow by.

"Then I called up Frack. Frack and I had started to get to know each other at the start of the shoot. He was nice to me. All men are nice to me, Frankie, because I'm hot. I understand how that works.

"But there was something sweet and innocent about Frack, and also competent. The guy seemed to be able to actually do things.

"And he had touched me, Frankie. In more ways than one. His arm brushed me just as I fell into that river. I don't know if he caused it, but he had something to do with it. He touched me, and the next thing I knew I was gone and the whole world had changed.

"So I called him up. And he came over and we hung out for a while. We walked and we talked.

"It was his idea to come here. For some reason, he always

wanted to move to New Orleans. I've never been here, but it seemed to be as good an idea as anything.

"So I was almost ready to go. I had lots of money, Frankie. I'd been paid fifteen million dollars for this film. Pretty much all my money was in an offshore account, always has been. Me and Frack could live forever very comfortably on that. More than comfortable. Luxury."

"But I stayed there for a while. I wasn't totally ready to go yet. I had more thinking to do.

"Then one day that old dude comes up to me and says, 'It's time to go.'

"I didn't know what that meant. Him or me?

"The next day I woke up and he was still there, lying on the couch. And he wasn't moving.

"I went up to him and touched him and he didn't move. He was dead. He had died overnight.

"So I dressed in that costume from the movie again. I didn't want to steal clothes from the old dead guy.

"And I hit the road for New Orleans."

Chapter Sixty-Two

✺

Miracle Monk

"I BOUGHT FRACK some kind of cute little car. Brand new. Paid cash.

"We loaded up what little stuff we had and set off. Got as far as that truck stop in Whately, where we stopped for breakfast.

"We were sitting there in that booth and he started talking about the future and stuff like that.

"The future? Frankie, I had never thought about the future before in my life. The present was all I knew. I don't know what he had in mind. I don't think he did either. But the future? I couldn't get my head around that.

"All I had been doing for the past couple weeks had been thinking. Thinking about life, and love, and spirit and everything. But never about the future.

"And I realized I needed more time before I could run off with Frack.

"So I told him I was going to the bathroom and I got up from that booth and I walked away. I saw this guy sitting there all alone. He looked up from his paper and smiled at me. Not a sexy kind of smile. He looked kind and safe. The way you look, Frankie. I checked him out real good. The dude was okay and I knew he'd take good care of me. For a while at least.

"So I put on one of my acts and figured out I would find a way to New Orleans myself and check back in with Frack when things made more sense.

"He was a nice guy. I knew he would be. Took me to Florida. Where I did the same thing at another truck stop. This time I chose a cute family with a husband and wife and two little kids and they took me to New Orleans. They were real safe. I was looking for safe. I was leading a crazy life, filled with risk. I yearned for safety and comfort.

"So they got me here. On my first day here, I'm walking around the French Quarter. Then, sitting on a bench on Jackson Square, who do I see but Frack.

"I had bailed on him and he wasn't mad. He forgave me. He knew I was going through a lot and he just accepted all of it. He was another good guy.

"I was surrounded by good guys. There were a lot of bastards mixed in there too, but I was on a roll. Everybody was kind to me for a while now. It happens that way sometimes.

"I had given him a bunch of money and he had gotten a sweet small place somewhere in town. It was on a homey residential street and it had shade and a porch and a banana tree.

"By then, I thought I might be ready to start thinking about the future, so I stayed there.

"I walked around the neighborhoods. Just played the quiet, lost little girl. I can play anything, Frankie. You know that. I didn't have to act hard for this role, though. It was easy. Then one day, I'm walking down here. It's just a couple blocks from the house, but I had never been here before.

"And I didn't even know what it was. But the sign said 'welcome.' I figured if I was welcome, I should go in.

"So I did. And except for the time they made me stay home and think it over, I haven't left since.

"We all have jobs here. Mostly we pray, but we have jobs too. Some work in the yard, on the gardens. Some do cleaning and maintenance. Some do the bookwork. Shopping. Computer stuff. Cooking. Stuff like that.

"Me—I'm in the office. I do filing and correspondence, things like that. Part of that involves going through old files and organizing and purging stuff that isn't very important. They've got piles and piles of stuff, most of it from the old Ninth Ward place—old photos, old writings. A lot of the former monks and nuns were kind of scholarly. They wrote a lot—philosophy, history, reflections, poetry. One of them wrote songs, Frankie. He wrote new verses to old songs that they sang here. That was pretty cool, huh?

"So, I find this old file. It was actually in a box because it was too thick for a regular folder. And it was filled with writings, this guy's personal thoughts, how to live, what life is all about, what God is, what man is, what love is. And a lot of it sounded familiar, like stuff I had heard before, from someone else.

"This guy was blind. He came here blind. He wasn't born blind but he had gone blind with some kind of degenerative condition in his eyes and he was blind when he got here. He wasn't here long, though. They ended up throwing him out because they didn't like what he was writing. And what he was saying.

"The funny thing was, he stopped being blind while he was here. He regained his sight. It was a miracle. There was no medical reason for it to happen. He just woke up one day and—boom—he could see.

"And still they tossed this guy. This guy who had a miracle happen to him. Can you imagine that? They really, really must have hated what he had to say to toss a miracle monk out of here. He called himself Brother Bruno.

"Any of this sound familiar, Francis?"

"Yeah," I said, "but Brother Bruno didn't regain his sight. He regained half his sight."

"What's the difference? He could still see." That was Sarah speaking.

"It was enough to leave doubts," I replied.

"Some people expect, and accept, only perfection," said Julie.

After thinking it over for a minute, I finally replied, "They never find it, do they?"

Julie said, "But they can. They can, Francis. Because everything is perfect. Half blindness is perfect. Total blindness is perfect."

And then she surprised me a bit when she said "And Nick Mooney? That sonofabitch? That bastard. Even him ... perfect."

Chapter Sixty-Three

∿

Magic Hour

Iᴛ ᴡᴀs ᴀ low-pitched gurgling with some harsher bursts of higher-pitched squeaking mixed in. *Oka-ree, oka-ree, chek-chek.* A red-winged blackbird was perched up on the telephone line above Mooney's driveway. I recorded it.

It felt good to be home, despite the midsummer heat. The weather was pleasant compared to the sultry New Orleans steam.

Mooney didn't appear to be home. I peeked in the front window and saw no signs of life, so I opened the door and walked in. As always, it was not locked.

No one was there. I walked around a little. The place was mostly orderly and clean. Not pristine. Lived in. Looked almost like a normal house for a normal person.

Night was approaching. The sun had dipped down behind the hills, but it was not yet completely dark. Movie makers call this the "magic hour." It's supposed to be the best light for filming, the most beautiful, the most evocative, the most emotionally moving. The thickest reds, the moistest greens, the deepest, bluest rivers.

So I walked over to the river.

It was roaring. There must have been a lot of rain while I was away.

He was there. I knew he would be. He was standing on top of one of the rock ledges with the river thundering all around him on both sides, waves reaching head high, the water wetting his hair.

He looked like Moses parting the Red Sea, except unlike Moses, he didn't seem to know what he was doing. He looked lonely and helpless and pitiful.

Julie said he was perfect. He was. He was a human. All humans are perfect.

But there were some theological beliefs I no longer embraced the way Julie did. I wanted to kill him. He was evil. He had killed one young woman. He had more young women lined up and I knew he could kill any one of them if they got in his way. He had put us all through hell.

Things are what they are. That is seeing the truth. Mooney was evil.

I wanted justice. That was what my quest was all about—to restore order from chaos. Mooney was chaos.

But I could not kill him. I was no longer a monk. In fact, I had no idea what I still believed in. Every legitimate religion in the universe condemns killing. Though I had no religion left, I still knew that killing was morally wrong and I could not do it.

So, all I wanted to do was talk to him. I'm naïve. I think talking can change a person, even an evil one.

I climbed up over the rocks and jumped across a four-foot gap where the waters were rushing underfoot.

I was standing right next to him. His eyes were clear and he was clean-shaven. He held a bottle of Jameson in his hand. It was three-quarters empty and the first thing he did when I got there was take a swig and then hand it to me. I took a drink too. It tasted pretty good, I have to admit.

We could hear each other pretty well up there, even with the turbulent waters swishing all around us. We stood quite close.

"Deliver us, oh Lord, from all evils past, present, and to come, and by the intercession of all the saints, grant that we may be always free from sin," he said.

"Amen," I said.

"That's what the priest says during confession, while he blesses the Eucharist. They used to say it in Latin."

"I know."

"How do you know? You were never a priest. You were a monk."

"Yes. I was. Once. And how is it you know what the priest says?" I asked him.

"I know a lot of things."

"So do I."

"I see a lot of things," Mooney replied.

"So do I."

"Even though you're blind," he said. "Okay … half blind."

"I can still see."

His hair was wet. It looked like he was drowning.

"Who said 'only drowning men can see'?" he asked me.

"I don't know. I never heard that before."

"Somebody said it. Somebody before me."

"Do you think it's true?" I asked him.

"Might be. I've never seen more clearly or better than right now. Everything is totally clear to me, maybe for the first time in my life. Probably because I'm drowning."

I had no idea what the hell Mooney was talking about. He wasn't going to drown. I wasn't going to push him in.

He laughed, but then he changed the subject. "Where have you been? I missed you. I couldn't find you anywhere."

"What do you care?"

"I miss you. I like you."

"I was on a road trip. I found her."

For a moment he just stared at me, although I didn't see surprise on his face. "I knew if anyone could, it would be you. Didn't I say you were the best detective in Shelburne Falls? So how is she?"

"She's fine."

"Good. I'm glad. I owe you some money, don't I?"

"For what?"

"For finding her."

"No need for that."

"I'll pay. I keep my promises. And by the way, you're off the hook. They dropped the charges."

"So I heard. Karen's been keeping in touch. Somehow they lost that first DNA test. Lost it! How does that happen? Then when they tested my hair a second time. There was no match. No paternity match. No match at all of any kind. Like I said, how the hell does something like that happen?"

He lowered his voice to say, "Beats me." But I heard him.

"And seems their great eyewitness recanted. Wonder why?"

"I told you my lawyers would take care of it. No evidence whatsoever. Case closed. Charges dropped."

"Yeah. Fantastic. But how the hell does something like that happen?"

He wiped his face. He was staring off into the distance. "My lawyers are good. I told you. More than good. More than lawyers too. These guys can make DNA go away, just like they can make it show up."

"So I owe you."

He didn't seem to detect the sarcasm in my voice.

"No, you don't. That's on me. I promised."

We stood there, buffeting by gusts of wind.

"So she's alive," Mooney said. Did I hear a sob escape? "That means I didn't kill her. That should make you feel better about me."

I thought this over. "No. I guess I don't feel much better about you. Not at all."

He sneered. "You never liked me."

"I liked you fine, Mooney."

"Now you're talking about me in the past tense."

"Yeah. Why do you suppose that is?"

Now it was his turn to think. "Guess I'm on my way out."

"Are you?"

"Looks that way."

"Stick around for a while," I said. And I sat down on the ledge of wet rock.

There was room, just barely, for another person next to me, so Mooney sat down too. He handed me the bottle. I took a chug and the rushing water sprayed our faces.

"Okay," I said, "let's sort this out."

"Sort away."

"Okay. First, you show up in town with two pregnant girlfriends—Julie and Edith."

"Her name was Victoria. And I prefer to think of the other one as Juliana."

"You like the 'A' girls, don't you?"

"You too."

"Yeah. Weird, huh?"

"Not so weird. We're the same guy."

"Don't pin that on me, Mooney. I didn't do what you did."

"Didn't you?"

"No."

"I thought that's what you were all about, Raven. We're all the same."

"I'm not you, Mooney. I didn't kill her."

"Did I? She's alive, Raven. I didn't kill her either."

"You killed the other one—Victoria."

I was talking to him slowly, quietly, despite the roaring waters. Still, I knew he could hear me.

"You show up here with two pregnant girlfriends," I said. "But you had fallen in love with Julie and you were done with Victoria. And you didn't know what to do about that. So you tossed her into the river. Then Victoria died. You killed her."

"Did I?"

"Yes."

He whipped his head around and stared at me, beady eyed,

like a rat trapped in a corner. "How do you know? I mean really, Raven. Did I push her? Did she fall? Did she kill herself? Who knows what happened?"

"You were up here on the rocks with her when she went in, Mooney. We have real photographic evidence."

"Do you?" His laugh had a deranged edge. "Do you see me pushing her?"

"No. You know that. I guess only you know what really happened. What do you know, Mooney? What do you remember?"

"I don't remember anything. I had a blackout."

"You know what you did, Mooney."

"No, Raven. I really don't."

Then he reconsidered. "I knew I wanted to get rid of her," he said. "I *had* to get rid of her. And I had to set you up. But did I actually kill her? I don't know."

And now he looked near tears. "Honest to fucking God, Raven. I don't fucking know what I did."

"Think hard, Mooney."

"I don't do anything hard, Raven."

"Except drink, Mooney." I took another swig and passed the bottle to him.

We sat there together for a while, passing the bottle back and forth, and he began to come back to earth.

Finally I said, "So, the only thing I'm not sure of now is how much of this was just the universe happening randomly. Did you simply stumble upon a soul who had all these similar obsessions and decide to frame him, or did you plan it all, fake everything?"

He laughed. "What's the difference?"

"I don't know."

"No, Raven, I didn't make any of it up. It's the truth. You're just like me."

"Who was Amy? Victoria didn't have a sister."

He bowed his head in acknowledgment. "Okay, I staged that.

I'm a director, Raven, I had to stage something. That's what I do. I put on shows."

"Who was she?"

"Just another one of my gals."

"Red hair. Name ends in 'A'?"

"Yep. Portia."

"Why?"

"Just to get you digging around. To get your attention. To get you running around looking for redheaded girls whose names end in 'A.' "

"To get the police interested in me. To deflect them from being interested in you."

He slapped his thigh. "That's about it. I know how to hook you, Raven. And unhook me. And that's what I did."

"You did it. Then you undid it. You got me arrested. Then you got me un-arrested. What the hell's up with that, anyway?"

"Just a demonstration." His smile was smug.

"A demonstration of what?"

"A demonstration that I can do anything. Any fucking thing I want. I can screw you and unscrew you. And I just may screw you again."

"Again?"

"No one likes me very much, but it's still against the law to kill me. Know what I mean?"

"No one knows we're up here, Mooney. No one knows I'm here with you. I mean, if you were to die or something tonight."

"I make movies, Raven. I put on shows. You know what that means? It means I create whole universes. I make stories happen in those universes. I love stories. I come into some shit town like this and create a whole new world out of it. And I'll move on and create another one in the next little town. A better one."

"You're God, Mooney, aren't you?"

"We're all God, Raven. That's what you're all about, isn't it?"

"God is in all of us, Mooney. Even you."

Then he stood up. The wind was so strong, it even mussed his hair, which was heavy and wet from the water streaming up into it. I rose and stood next to him. I had to look up to see his eyes.

He handed the bottle to me and I drank up. It was nearly empty now.

I looked him straight in the eyes. It was like seeing my own eyes reflected back at me. We were both perched precariously on the highest and most slippery rocks in the entire falls. I could have reached out and barely touched him and he would have fallen in.

I didn't do it though.

"Things change quickly, Mooney. In a day. In a minute. In an instant. That's all it takes sometimes, to change everything."

"Like the day you woke up and could see."

"Half see. But yeah."

"On Lavender Street."

"Yeah. That's where it was."

"I know everything about you, Raven. Every damn thing. I know you're about to push me into this damn river."

"No, I'm not," I said too quickly. "I can't do that."

"Can't you?" He was wearing a devilish grin.

"No, I can't."

He paused. He was thinking.

Finally he said, "Yeah, you can't push me. You know why?"

"Well, I'm pretty sure I do. It has something to do with general morality and love for humankind. Man and God and love. Or something like that. But why don't you tell me? Clearly you've got your own theories."

"Raven, you know that's all bullshit, don't you? You can't push me because you're afraid. You're afraid to do anything. You're chicken, Raven."

I thought this over.

As I was thinking, he pushed me. *He* pushed *me*. Not sure why this surprised me, but it was the last thing I expected.

Did he, though? He touched me, but did he push me?

I didn't fall. He was drunk and run-down. He didn't have much strength, and by then it was getting dark. He couldn't see me well and he didn't hit me squarely.

But I slipped a little and then I was right there on the edge, off balance. I reached out to grab him by the arm to steady myself.

So I was there with him and holding his arm and he was squirming like a two-year-old kid throwing a tantrum and we were both slipping around on the wet rock.

Then he stopped fighting and looked at me. "We're both the same guy, Raven. We're all the same. The only difference between you and me is that you're chicken and I'm not."

"No. You kill people. I don't."

"Don't you?"

And then he started clucking under his breath. He did this *bwak-bwak-bwak* chicken cackling sound. He was doing it quietly and I could barely hear it through the growling of the river all around us. *Bwak-bwak-bwak-bwak-bwak.*

I reacted. It was blind rage. In an instant, morality meant nothing to me. I was ready to kill him. I could reach out and push him. No one would know. Mooney would be gone and the world would be better for it.

He looked at me. He looked right through me. He could see my heart and my soul. He knew who I was, better than anybody had ever known—even me.

The rage boiled over, and the killer inside a peaceful man took over.

He knew then that he had won. His eyes met mine. His eyes were meeting mine as he leaned over and was standing right on the slippery edge of the rock.

"I'm going to save your ass again, Raven. You don't have to do it. I'll do it for you. I'm already going to hell. You, Raven, you might still be able to avoid it."

That's when he jumped.

He was gone and I was alone on the rock. I didn't see him bubble under in the foam and I couldn't see him down there in the river either.

But he was gone.

Maybe for the last time, Mooney was gone.

Chapter Sixty-Four

∿

Let it Go

MOONEY HAD GONE into the river before and lived to tell the story. They had fished him out before, alive.

That didn't happen this time. Days went by. Then weeks. His cleaning woman had reported him missing. And now he was presumed dead. I had not told anyone about our final encounter. No one would have believed I had nothing to do with it after everything I had been through.

Life seemed normal, and normal was good.

I was running the theater and hanging out with Clara. Sarah was around a lot, but she was off doing stuff with her friends too. She seemed happy.

I walked Marlowe up the Hill of Tears frequently. Mooney's house remained empty. Soon grass and weeds began to take over and the place started going to seed.

One day the grass was mowed and the weeds cut and the place spruced up. Then a "For Sale" sign appeared. Two weeks later, a "Sold" banner was splashed across the sign.

I walked by every day with Marlowe. After a short while, the sign was gone and there was a gray Honda SUV parked in the driveway. Eventually, I saw a couple of young kids running around the yard, playing on bicycles.

One day, as I was making my rounds in town, I stopped in to see Loomis and asked him if he knew what was happening there.

"A young family bought the place. They're theater people. They're going to do something theatrical with the big place. Not sure what. Put on shows there maybe. Nice folks."

"What happened to Mooney?"

"Nobody knows. He could be a suspect in Pasternak's death. So they searched. Everywhere. But they came up empty. No trace. Now they're assuming he's dead. Maybe he got flushed away in the river somehow. Ya think?"

"Yeah. Maybe. Probably."

"That's my best guess too. How would that happen though? Any ideas?"

I remained silent, and Loomis went on, "Not my problem. It's up to the feds and I'm just glad to be rid of him."

"Me too."

"But they haven't fished any bodies out of the river in weeks now. And for that, I thank you. Life is back to normal again."

I didn't know what he was insinuating, but it wasn't a subject I wanted to pursue. Instead I said, "Mooney must have been around to sell the house."

"No. He never owned it."

"He told me he did."

"He lied. Surprised?"

"Nope."

"Me neither. His production company bought it from Snyder, not Mooney. He wasn't even the principal owner of that company. Most everything was in his Uncle Lyle's name and Lyle just up and sold it to these nice people. Couldn't have worked out better."

*

I HAD DINNER at Clara's that night. It was one of those rare nights that Sarah ate with us.

After dinner, Clara asked me if I wanted to go for a walk. I said no and she took off on her own. I wanted to talk to Sarah.

She was doing the dishes and she turned around to look at me, hands still dripping with suds.

"I heard from Julie," she reported.

I must have looked a little surprised.

"Yeah, I did. She emails me now. Pretty much every day."

"Oh yeah? That's good. So what's up in the Big Easy?"

"Not much. It's not like she's in New Orleans anyway. She never leaves the monastery."

"I know."

"She thinks she saw Mooney though."

"What?" I was staggered. "When?"

"Just the other day. She was walking around the courtyard one night with the moon shining. When she got to that big gate, she looked out and saw somebody she thought might be Mooney. Just walking around down the street."

"Was she sure?"

"No. Not at all. It was foggy, misty, and it could have been some other tall guy. But that's what she thought. I told her she was crazy."

"Mooney's dead," I said. "He has to be."

"Well, if he died," Sarah said, "maybe somehow it's been undone."

"Impossible," I said.

She gave me a sharp look but didn't ask for clarification. "Whatever. She thinks she saw him. But now he's gone. This time I really think it's forever. I just don't feel him around anymore. Do you?"

I shook my head.

So that was it. It was over. It was all over.

And that's what Sarah said to me. "It's over, Frankie. And we gotta let it go. You gotta let it go."

I tried. I tried like hell.

Chapter Sixty-Five

～∾

Closing the Door

In Matthew 10:28, it says "Do not be afraid of those who kill the body but cannot kill the soul."

I studied that line a lot when I was in the monastery. Maybe Julie was studying it right now in that same place.

A body can be killed but the soul lives on. Mostly I had thought of this as a positive thing—a good soul lives on even after the body is gone.

But it works the other way too. An evil body can be killed, but the evil lives on. It can be reborn into another body, or it can hover there in the ether—a haunting, dark, cancerous mist.

That night, I took Marlowe for a walk. We went into town, walked by the river, down to the falls.

There he was. He had that same black watch cap pulled down over his forehead. His hair was shaggy and longer and tied into a small ponytail and his scraggly beard was back. He looked exactly like he had that first day I ran into him on the streets, so long ago.

He was walking along the slippery rocks at the top, just where the water began spewing down over the gullies and pools.

He was slumped over. I could tell it was him by the way he held himself. And by his aura too. It reeked of him and it was scary and I pulled Marlowe to go in the other direction.

Was it him, though? It was foggy, misty, and it could have been some other tall guy.

Or it could have been nobody. It could have been just my imagination running away with me.

We took a few steps up Deerfield Street. Then I just had to look back.

But he was gone. There was no figure walking along the slippery rocks, or anyplace else.

I knew it wasn't him. Mooney was gone. He was dead. This was the dregs of the wicked sins he had perpetrated during his time here on earth. This was vile, malignant corruption being conjured up deceptively before my half-useful vision. This was the un-killed soul haunting me, as it likely would for the rest of my life.

The vision Julie had recently seen wasn't him either. She had the same tendency as I to see and sense vibrations and auras.

The evil body was dead, but we who remained among the living had a job to do and that was to avoid the spell of the evil soul that would remain in our midst forever.

We had an obligation to go on living good lives to counteract all the bad out there in the cosmos.

Marlowe and I turned around and began walking again. This time, we didn't stop and look back. We crossed the Iron Bridge and trudged back up the Hill of Tears until we were safely back in our yard.

Only then did I turn around and look back. All I saw then was the slope going back down the Hill of Tears and the tiny village sitting there peacefully at its bottom with the river winding through it like veins to a heart.

I threw some sticks for Marlowe. He chased after them happily.

I looked down the Hill of Tears one more time to be sure I did not see Mooney.

I didn't see him and we went inside and closed the door.

Fred DeVecca

photo by Susan Gesmer

FRED DeVECCA WAS born in Philadelphia and raised in Wilkes-Barre, Pennsylvania. He has a BA in English Literature from Wilkes University and attended film school at Maine Media Workshops & College in Rockport, Maine.

Fred has been a screenwriter, photographer, and freelance writer, mostly in the sports and arts & entertainment fields, for twenty-five years. His work has appeared in the *Boston Globe*, *Berkshire Eagle* (Pittsfield, MA), *Hampshire Gazette* (Northampton, MA), *Valley Advocate* (Amherst, MA), *Greenfield Recorder* (MA), *Shelburne Falls & West County Independent*, Preview Massachusetts (Northampton), *Leisure Weekly* (Keene, NH), and *Baseball Underground*. An essay on hardboiled detective fiction and a segment from his (unpublished) novel *Act of Contrition* appeared in the Scottish online mystery magazine *Noir Originals* in 2004.

He has written, produced, directed, edited, and acted in four films of his own and has worked on several more as production assistant, location scout, set decorator, grip/electric, and assistant director. From 1996 to 1998 he was a producer at TV6 Greenfield (MA) Community TV.

Fred has been a member of the Marlboro Morris Men since the mid-1980s, and since 1999, he has managed Pothole Pictures, a non-profit, community-run movie theater.

He is active on Facebook and Twitter.

Fred lives in Shelburne Falls, Massachusetts.

For more information, go to www.freddevecca.com.

Shelburne Falls, photo by Donna Seymour

Questions for Book Groups

∿∿

1. Juliana/VelCro has qualities that none of the other redheads in the story possess. How do these qualities translate into stardom?
2. Can someone be a movie star with no moral compass?
3. Could the movie in the story have succeeded if it had been made?
4. What does this story say about the nature of fame and our country's worship of Hollywood stars?
5. How does Frank Raven grow and change in the course of the story?
6. What does Frank's blindness, then semi-blindness signify?
7. By the end of the story, how did you feel about the director, Nick Mooney?
8. How is Shelburne Falls itself a character?
9. Is the "chicken" metaphor one you can relate to?
10. Mooney and Raven share some unusual qualities. Just how alike are they?

From Coffeetown Press
and Fred DeVecca

～◡

Tʜᴀɴᴋ ʏᴏᴜ ꜰᴏʀ reading *The Nutting Girl.* We are so grateful for you, our readers. If you enjoyed this book, here are some steps you can take that could help contribute to its success.

- Post a review on Amazon, BN.com, and/or GoodReads.
- Check out www.freddevecca.com and send a comment or ask to be put on Fred's mailing list.
- Spread the word on social media, especially Facebook, Twitter, and Pinterest.
- "Like" Fred's Facebook author page as well as that of Coffeetown Press.
- Follow us both on Twitter.
- Ask for this book at your local library or request it on their online portal.

Good books and authors from small presses are often overlooked. Your comments and reviews can make an enormous difference.

If you enjoyed this book, please check out our other

titles on Coffeetown Press

www.coffeetownpress.com

and its sister imprint, Camel Press

www.camelpress.com